BUTTERFLIES AND BARBED WIRES

Vanaja Banagiri was born and lives in Hyderabad. Since 1988, she has worked as a journalist there. She is married with one son. This is her first novel.

BUTTERFLIES AND BARBED WIRES

Vanaja Banagiri

RUPA

Published by
Rupa Publications India Pvt. Ltd 2006
161-B/4, Gulmohar House,
Yusuf Sarai Community Centre,
New Delhi 110049

Sales centres:
Bengaluru Chennai
Hyderabad Kolkata Mumbai

P-ISBN: 978-81-291-0882-1
E-ISBN: 978-81-291-2607-8

Third impression 2025

10 9 8 7 6 5 4 3

Printed in India

For Damodar Parthasarathy,
Thank you for encouraging me to 'go for it' and
supporting me while I did.

For Sameer Anirudh Banagiri,
Thank you for being what you are and accepting me
unconditionally the way I am.

Acknowledgements

Sita Banagiri and Rama Rao Banagiri, for teaching me that the true gift to one's self is self-actualisation

Cheenoo, for demonstrating the value of commitment; for giving a whole new meaning to 'letting go'; for being there no matter what

Magna Publications, for having had the faith in my writing abilities when I had nothing to show

The *Times of India*, for honing my writing skills

Saugata Mukherjee, for showing me the way

RK Mehra; for trust and reassurance

Rupa Books, my publisher par excellence

Janice, my editor

Hyderabad and Hyderabadis, for inspiration; for being as original as only they can be

Divine Mother, from whose womb this creation emerges

Shirdi Sai Baba and Meher Baba, my guardian angels

I do not know this city now
That I have lived in all my life.
I do not know these streets and roads
Nor these familiar men and women.
But like some forlorn spirit walk
As on the margin of the world.
Held by a slender thread betwixt
Death and the vast eternity.

—Vanaja Banagiri

Prologue

Time: Mid-morning
Day: Sunday
Date: 5 August 1978
Location: Hyderabad

Mir-alam-mandi, the famous marketplace in the old city was bustling with life. Under the hidden sun and the seeking clouds, hundreds of people—men and women, boys and girls, Hindus and Muslims—were going about the mundane business of their weekly shopping. Haggling buyers and cajoling shopkeepers, happy vendors and disgruntled customers, satisfied buyers and tired sellers. Various permutations. Different combinations. One common business. Food. Food has always been a great binding agent in the lives of Hyderabadis. On that Sunday, the Karans were to lunch with the Khans at the latter's haveli in the quaint Moazamjahi market. Living next door to each other for years had made them an integral part of one another's lives.

Karan Mama and Vimla Mami. Fifty-five and fifty. Hindus. Rehaan Khan and Shehzaadi Khan. Twenty-eight and Twenty-two. Muslims. Rehaan had practically grown up with the Karans. When he got married, they welcomed his bride the only way they knew.

Heartily. And then when Shehzaadi delivered Sameera, the haqeeqa ceremony was held at the Karans'.

From then on, for the last five years, come rain or sunshine, the Sunday lunch at the Khans' was a ritual. The menu rarely varied. Tamatar-ka-khat, kaddu-ka-dalcha, dum-ka-murgh, kheema fry with sheermal and baghara khana. For dessert, they had qubani-ka-meetha topped with fresh cream or kaddu-ki-kheer. Sometimes on special occasions, Shehzaadi served kacche-gosht-ki-biryani and mirchi-ka-salan with double-ka-meetha or shahi tukda. Ramzan and Bakrid, had, of course, a different fare.

Almost every evening during the summer months they drove to Famous Ice Creams down the street, for handmade mango ice cream.

Shehzaadi was a divine cook. But without Shama bi, her faithful maid, life would not have been as simple. 'Aap ke haath mein jaadu hai, bibi,' Karan Mama would compliment Shehzaadi, licking his fingers dry and belching noisily. Though a Kayasth, Karan Mama was a Muslim by spirit. The Kayasth and Muslim communities of Hyderabad borrowed heavily from each other—culturally and linguistically.

So, here they were, Rehaan Khan and Shehzaadi and their jigar-ka-tukda, Sameera, a bouncy two-year-old, picking up fresh meat and vegetables needed for lunch preparations. Rehaan hurried the shopkeeper to pack their pick of the day. The sky was overcast. A downpour seemed imminent. Rains in Hyderabad are as unpredictable as the herds of cattle that crossed the road. He hated driving in the rain. It was bad enough otherwise, what with congested roads and gaily walking pedestrians who could not be bothered to look before they crossed.

Walking behind him, Shehzaadi realised that their daughter had slipped out of her grasp. She looked around anxiously. People behind her were getting impatient with the amount of time they were taking. 'Hai Allah, are they buying up the whole shop or what?' Khala Bee, who lived a street away from the Khans, grumbled, displaying her khimam-stained teeth.

Shehzaadi smiled in response and moved away. She walked a little ahead. No sight of the toddler. With panic rising in her chest, she turned the corner. No luck. She turned to walk back to where she'd left her husband, hoping that Sameera was there.

That's when she heard gruff, arguing voices. A group had gathered like people normally do when others are quarrelling. With trembling fingers, she tried to make her way ahead. Chaos has a way of creeping insidiously into Mir-alam-mandi. Like it does at any place where the supply and demand equation has gone awry. Too many people, too few shops. But that was not the problem at that moment. There seemed to be more to it than what met Shehzaadi's eye.

People, sensing impending danger, had begun to run.

She simply couldn't get through them. As it was, she had a pathological distaste for crowds. Especially the rough, jostling type. So did her husband, which is why he insisted on her accompanying him, to make the whole process more bearable. 'This is the last time I'm ever going to visit this place,' she swore to herself impatiently. She turned around to see if there was any sign of Rehaan. None at all. 'Oh, hell!' she muttered under her breath.

Just then she heard piercing, gut-wrenching, screams. Before she could utter the prophetic four-letter word again, two bodies dropped with a thud to the ground a few feet in front of her. Shehzaadi watched in horror as blood gushed out of the bodies of Rehaan's paternal uncle Khan Chacha and Guptaji, their neighbour. She felt herself losing consiousness. If she had not fainted she would have witnessed the end of two more important people in her life—Karan mama and Vimla mami—who lay mute a mile away, dead to the mayhem around them. A veil of darkness engulfed her as she heard more cries of agony.

When she opened her eyes it was to the vast expanse of the sky. She was lying on what felt like a bed of pebbles poking her from underneath. She wondered where she was. Both her body and mind were numb. She turned to her side with great difficulty, only to find a stranger lying next to her. The whole sequence of events began to unravel in her mind. Startled, she sat up. She could see a sea of people around her. That's when she realised that she had been lying amidst human bodies.

Some moaning with pain. Some dying. Some still.

Everything was strangely quiet but for the steady siren of a police van. Shehzaadi could see policemen talking into their walkie-talkies as they searched for life, or the semblance of it at their feet. She also saw people being carried away on stretchers. She had always had this strange aversion for the men in khakis. For no apparent reason. But today, she was desperate to be noticed by them. She tried standing up to catch their attention. Her legs felt shaky. Luckily, the officers spotted her before her legs buckled under her own weight.

'One medam is alive here,' said one officer to the other. She struggled to stand as they helped her get to her feet. She must have walked less than ten trembling steps, when she saw a familiar figure lying face down. She recognised that head of jet-black hair. Just that morning she had told him how lucky their daughter was to have inherited it from him. She needn't look at his face, she knew instinctively, yet, she asked the cops to turn him around. She paled as she saw her husband's honey brown eyes staring sightlessly up at her. She could feel hot air buzzing in her ears. Her body went limp.

She stayed in a semi-conscious state for a fortnight in a city hospital. And would have probably continued to do so for longer, had the cops not located her father's telephone number in the handbag they had found next to her. She was then moved to Mumbai, the city her Abba lived in.

A few miles away, on the streets of Dabeerpura, a toddler wandered aimlessly, crying, 'Mummy, Mummy.' The ground around her was littered with dead bodies. The evening was overcast. The warm, sultry August air was pregnant with moisture. An eerie buzzing of a swarm of flies filled the air.

A search party from a social welfare organisation found the lost child. They couldn't get any information out of her. She had either not begun to speak or was unable to due to the shock, they decided amongst themselves.

A middle-aged policeman picked her up in his arms when the social welfare agency handed her over later that evening. 'Insaana hai ki jallad hain, masum bachi ku beghar kar diye dekho, maati mile,' he cursed as he looked into her eyes filled with sadness. The child's frightened wail brought him to tears. He had never witnessed anything so gruesome in his twenty years of service.

5 August 1978 went down in the annals of history as the day of the goriest communal carnage in the twin cities of Hyderabad and Secunderabad. What started off as a minor tiff in a marketplace had, in a matter of few hours, wiped out more than half of the old city. A curfew was clamped with shoot-at-sight orders for the next forty-five days. The city, where Hindus and Muslims had lived for generations in harmony, did not return to normalcy for years to come.

'It's the handiwork of the opposition party,' said the ruling party spokesperson. 'The reign of antisocial elements,' the opposition party countered.

However, for the survivors of the massacre, it meant just one thing—their lives would be haunted by death.

Then and forever.

Twenty-two years later...

Chapter 1

Maya—The illusion

Maya dreamt of a woman knocking at her door, calling out her name. A high-pitched voice penetrated the layers of her deep sleep, seeking her out.

She opened her eyes to a feeling of overwhelming loneliness and fear. The dream had been so real. Her body was awake but her mind was still numb. She lay on the bed looking out the window. She had forgotten to draw the curtains before she drifted off to sleep. It had rained at night. She could see droplets of water on the pane. A host of dragonflies flitted about. Watching them she felt a strange sensation of being separated from reality, lost in another world.

She turned onto her side and switched on the bedside lamp. The realisation that she was not at home but in a strange hotel room dawned on her. She got out of bed and stood by the window. She could see the Hussain Sagar. Dawn was breaking. The lake seemed serene. The shadows of the trees not yet ready to greet the approaching day. Up ahead was the marble white Birla Mandir. The view of Hyderabad was breathtaking. A landscape of water, sky and divinity. Yet, it seemed ominously quiet.

She stood there as if in a trance until daylight seeped through and birds chirped. She had a vague sense of somebody calling her but she did not know who it was or how to respond. She forced herself out of the reverie. She had decisions to make and things to do.

She thought of the words she had read somewhere, 'If a man begins with certainty, he may end in doubt; but if he be content to begin with doubt, he shall end in certainty.' And there was no dearth of doubts as far as her life was concerned. Would they lead her to the truth? Only time would tell...

Maya studied herself carefully in the mirror. She was pleased with what she saw. She was not pretty in the conventional sense but she had beautiful aquamarine eyes, full lips and a sweep of jet-black hair. Her smile was as bright as a sunrise. And her laughter, infectious. She was the kind of woman people cast second glances at. Today she was wearing a plain grey chiffon sari, which fell elegantly on her slender frame. She had decided to keep it simple and so had chosen a pair of pearl eardrops and kept her neck bare.

'Not too bad,' she said to herself aloud. 'Chin-up and get ready to take on the world.' Maya often indulged in a soliloquy whenever she was alone. She loved her solitude. Probably the result of having been an only child. Maya had no idea who her biological parents were. All she was told by Amma and Appa, when she was old enough to understand, was that she was found, lost after the '78 riots in Hyderabad. She had been too young to answer any questions. And when nobody turned up to claim her, despite repeated announcements in the media for a week, the police in consultation with the Child and Social Welfare Department, had handed her over to an adoption agency.

It was from there that the Giris had adopted her. The couple, based in Bangalore, were in their early forties and childless. They fell in love with the toddler the moment they set eyes on her. They named her Maya. And when she began to speak, she called them Amma and Appa.

'You know why we named you Maya?' Amma used to tell her when she was about five, 'Because you brought magic into our lives.' It was only when she was twenty-three, that a guru told her that her name actually meant 'illusion'. She had reached home that day ready to argue with her parents for not understanding the real meaning of her name. But her words remained unsaid for the rest of her life. The flight in which they were travelling had crashed. There were no survivors. The only parents she knew were gone.

The accident had shattered her world.

What is illusion if not magic, Appa would have probably told her.

Amma, Appa, dead. Somehow the words didn't seem to go together. How could living, moving, human beings lie so still? How could someone who had so recently existed cease to be?

She breathed deeply to make sure she was still there. Alive. She looked at her body and wondered who it belonged to. Who was she? Nothing made sense. Not anymore.

Yet, that was the truth. Satyameva Jayate. Let truth prevail, her father always told her. And when reality dawned, she couldn't tell truth from illusion.

But she knew there was no escaping it. Not when it came in the form of death.

She was frightened and helpless and if it were not for her friend Varsha, she would have sunk into depression. Varsha had taught her to look on the brighter side of things. She had made her realise how loving her parents had been and how fortunate she was to have experienced such unadulterated, unconditional love. It might have been short-lived but they had been with her when she needed them most. Shaping her personality, moulding her character and giving her the spirit to stand up for herself.

She was indeed lucky. The Giris doted on her. Appa, especially. 'You're the plum of my eye,' he would often tell her. He didn't care for apples, you see. And he was crazy about plums. 'Amazing sense of humour Appa had,' Maya thought, wiping away tears that were blurring her vision, finding it difficult to think of him in the past tense. God, she was so happy with them. Who could have asked for more loving parents?

Her life seemed to be eternally wracked by troubles. Sometimes she felt as if she was destined to live from one crisis to another. She was orphaned at two, and now at twenty-three, just as she had finished her post-graduation and was planning to look after them, her parents were gone. Leaving her behind. 'Perhaps there's a bigger picture God wants me to see,' she thought whenever she was in a more positive frame of mind.

As things turned out, her Masters in History came in handy when one of Appa's friends informed her about an Assistant Historian vacancy at the Osmania University in Hyderabad. The city where she was born. She had been adrift since her parents had passed away. Until one night, when Appa appeared in her dreams. He had told her: 'When the soul has no fixed purpose in life, it is lost. Find yours now.'

Maya's dreams had always been lucid and this one was the most lucid of them all. The morning after the dream, Appa's friend had called her about the job. It seemed to give her the purpose Appa had asked her to find. Serendipity or destiny, she wondered.

'Did my biological parents really die?' she had asked herself in the past. But it had been only out of curiosity when the Giris were alive. Somehow, she had felt she was being disloyal to them by wanting to find out about her 'real' family. Now, in a strange way, she felt liberated from that guilt. The need to find them grew stronger. She needed to know. Now that life had given her a chance to move to her birth city, there was the possibility of finding out. She was always amazed at the way her mind had blocked out all memories of her life before Amma and Appa. She couldn't remember a thing about her life before she was adopted. She had read somewhere that the human mind erased traumatic memories as a defence mechanism. Either that or she had been too young to remember.

But yes, sometimes she did dream of a particular scene—'Mummy, Mummy,' a little child called out to a young woman until she lost sight of her amidst a melee of screaming and frightened people. Maya was not sure if it was the replay of a genuine incident or something conjured up by her mind thanks to the story she had been told.

Now, she wanted to see the city she originally belonged to, the house in which she was born, the people who were her family. 'Did I...do I have a brother, sister, aunt, uncle... anybody?' she had asked herself several times in the past. Now, she may be able to find answers. Besides, what would she have done in Bangalore? Varsha had moved to Mumbai after her marriage. Most of the others she had been friends with had also moved away with their husbands or for their careers. She had no romantic interest to hold her back: invariably, the guys she fell for turned out to be either married or gay. For a while, during her college days, she dated a classmate. But things didn't work out. The urge to find her roots now was strong enough for her to stop weighing the pros and cons and move to Hyderabad.

She was giving herself a year in Hyderabad to find answers she had searched for all her life.

Here she was, ready to face the interview board at the University. That was the reason she had taken pains to dress well. She had to look good but not over-dressed. Once more she sized herself up in the mirror and was satisfied.

She went to the hotel receptionist and asked for directions. It would take about twenty minutes to reach the University, she was told. She got into the first auto-rickshaw she could find and looked out as she travelled. They drove past the Tank Bund. This was probably the only place in the country where two cities were separated by a lake. On one side was Hyderabad and on the other was Secunderabad. Both sides of the bund were lined by statues of famous Andhra personalities. In the centre of the lake was the statue of the Buddha. He seemed so unmoved by the noise around him. She had read last night in one of the brochures lying in her hotel room, that this was the only monolithic statue of Buddha in the world. Nothing about the city, however, seemed even vaguely familiar. She hadn't really ventured out shopping or sight-seeing but wherever she had been so far—the shopping malls, parks, the Chiran Palace on Banjara Hills—had not sparked a memory. You can never be sure what memory could bring back. It was capable of connecting us to places, events and people. Only the past held clues to the present. But the only key to the past lies with memory. It looked like her memory had decided to desert her when she needed it most. Just like her parents.

As far as Maya was concerned, she was a Bangalorean. That is where she had grown up and where she felt a sense of belonging. But Bangalore too was no longer what it used to be. From being the grand old garden city to the current concrete jungle, the change was more than evident all over. How could she expect Hyderabad to have remained the same? After all, isn't change the only permanence in life? 'University aagaya medam,' the auto-driver announced. She paid him and looked at the sprawling campus. A row of magnificent structures greeted her. She looked for the arts college building and found it after walking about a kilometre. The building reflected the architectural brilliance of the people who had designed it. A Persian influence was very evident. The Qutb Shahi rulers had built the most important historical structures in Hyderabad—from palaces to mosques and monuments to universities. She had learnt that the Qutub Shahi rulers were great builders and patrons of learning. The dynasty that spanned a hundred and seventy-one years in Indian history patronised Persian culture as well as the regional culture of the Deccan. The eight kings of this royal line had left an indelible impression on the land and its people.

She gaped at the imposing building in awe. Huge stained-glass windows and doorways added to its magnificence. The well-maintained lawns and avenues gave it a pleasing, modern touch. A couple of rustic seats under the trees completed the beautiful picture.

The climate was delicious. She looked up as if to seek a blessing from her parents. And there she saw it—a rainbow. Her mother, the eternal optimist, had taught her to believe in the proverbial pot of gold at the end of every rainbow. It seemed to be the harbinger of good times and good luck. She felt lucky for the first time since her parents' death.

'This is going to be fun,' she muttered under her breath. As she walked towards the entrance, she could see groups of students clustered at various places—some in animated discussion, others laughing over a funny, shared experience. All of them seemed so happy just 'hanging out.' It seemed like yesterday, when she was a student herself. She realised with a pang that she was almost twenty-five.

It seemed like a milestone but on which road, she didn't know.

With fingers crossed, she stepped into the building. After walking down a long, seemingly unending corridor, she came across a blackboard on which 'Department of History' was chalked. A peon in a white uniform collected her interview letter and asked her to be seated. She sat in the first row and wondered how she would fare. She had to make it somehow. A lot depended on this—the direction of her life, her search for her origins and most crucially, her shift to the city of her birth. Without which her quest would be futile.

Maya was normally a confident person but today she was a trifle edgy. She sat there, fidgeting with her file, waiting her turn, looking at the other candidates, tense on wondering about the outcome. She tried soothing her aching neck with her fingers. She had to do something about this annoying stiff neck. Always troubling her at these crucial times. Giving her a headache as the pain spread. Just then she was called in. She took a deep breath and geared herself up.

She needn't have worried so much though. What followed was easier than she had expected. The interview board, comprising of four senior academicians, found her to be *the* candidate they had in mind. Without much ado, she was appointed. In fact, they wanted her to start immediately. She would be provided furnished residential quarters within the University campus in a week's time.

It felt too good to be real.

She walked out with her head held high.

The sun had set.

The rainbow had kept its promise.

Shehzaadi—The Princess

Fifty kilometres away, in a sprawling Jubilee Hills bungalow, Shehzaadi was restless. She had a habit of waking up in the middle of the night and lying in bed, thinking. She tried hard but couldn't go back to sleep. The habit had become chronic now.

In the initial years of their marriage, Anwar would soothe her until she drifted back to sleep in his arms. But they had been married for more than twenty years. It wasn't fair to expect a man to now lose sleep over his wife's lack of it.

And on that night, in those waking hours, while the rest of the world slept, she panicked. It was a panic a mother experienced when she left her child unattended. She felt a strong urge to go back home and hold her daughter. And then she realised that she was at home. The one she had built with Anwar Ali Mirza. They had a son, Shahbaz, a strapping twenty-year-old. And she loved him to distraction. In fact, he was her life's sole and soul purpose.

She often felt there were deep chasms in her mind that lay hidden even from herself. Sometimes her mind behaved like a friend, coming to her aid. At others it was her enemy, pushing her to the brinks of despair. For some reason, the nights were even more terrible. It was as though the darkness that enfolded the world enveloped her mind.

When she failed to get back to sleep, she sat up. She could see her face, distorted in the television screen. It seemed bloated, her cheeks swollen and her aquiline nose, bulbous. She stared at the grotesque image. It was disturbing. How many times she had told Anwar to get rid of this TV set and get one of those flat-screen plasmas? When your mind is not at peace you tend to find fault with everything and everybody around you. She dragged her feet to her son's room. He was the cure for her troubled mind. Had always been, since his birth.

His bedroom door was slightly ajar. She stood at the doorway, noiselessly, watching his sleeping form. How tall he had grown in the last two years! There was no trace of adolescent gawkiness. He looked so majestic even in his sleep. Like a prince. With a sinking heart she remembered that in a week's time, he would be gone. To London for further studies. And her thoughts wandered to her daughter who would have been twenty-four, had she been alive. 'Sameera, my doll, wherever you are, Ammi loves you.'

Shehzaadi's friends envied her. Her world seemed so complete. A doting, successful husband and a handsome son who also seemed to be the most sensible twenty-year-old they had ever met. Soft-spoken and courteous. Sometimes Anwar would jest to his friends 'God knows how anyone born to me can have such perfect manners!' In a way, he was right. Age hadn't mellowed the brash senior Mirza one bit. He was a typical winner, like the many racehorses he owned.

Another reason for her friend's envy was her looks. Shehzaadi was tall and slim with shoulder-length auburn hair that fell in flattering steps. Her most striking feature were her large eyes—the colour, an unusual green that sometimes shone with shades of blue. Her childhood friends used to call her 'cat eyes'. At forty-five, she looked extraordinarily young. Age had not diminished either her beauty or poise. She drew gasps of admiration wherever she went. There was something regal about her. In fact, her father, had noticed the trait soon enough to name her Shehzaadi. 'You're my little princess,' he had told her all her life. And his.

However, beneath her beauty lurked a sadness that was visible only to a few close family members. Her husband Anwar, was one of them. And he knew the reason: her first husband and their daughter had died in the riots that rocked Hyderabad more than two decades ago.

In fact, when Anwar was offered a project regarding the restoration of historical monuments in Hyderabad, he was apprehensive, even as he found it interesting. But when he mentioned it to her, she encouraged him to take it. She said she would be rather glad to escape the hectic pace of life in Mumbai. What finally swung it in Hyderabad's favour was the beautiful house at Jubilee Hills that the broker had shown them. Shehzaadi had fallen in love with it instantly. It was built on a 1,500 square yard plot with a long driveway flanked by an avenue of Ashoka trees. The garden hidden behind the avenue had enormous scope for landscaping. Shehzaadi was thrilled at the prospect of having their own garden, a luxury they couldn't have dreamt of in Mumbai.

If the mention of Hyderabad evoked uncomfortable or even unpleasant memories in her, she didn't show it. She never referred to her first marriage. And Anwar did not bring it up in all their years together, scared she would get depressed. It was enough that she loved him and he her.

He still remembered their first meeting vividly. In Mumbai, at a party. She had come along with her father. He learnt later that this was her first evening out after the tragedy.

Anwar had seen her standing alone, pensive, in a corner, sipping a glass of red wine. She looked such a loner. Something about her had compelled him to move towards her, away from the crowd of women hanging on to his every word. When he was close to her, he had caught the fragrance of her thick auburn hair. The scent of her perfume was light and floral. She was so graceful and elegant. Slender but voluptuous. Mirza had had enough of emaciated women who starved themselves in the name of beauty. But what had captivated him more than her beauty were her eyes. Limpid and soulful, they seemed to have a depth of their own. And a thousand tales to tell. No one he had ever met possessed eyes like hers. And he was to remain enthralled by them for the rest of his life.

Anwar Ali Mirza had gone out with more than his share of women before he met Shehzaadi. His tall, dark, brooding looks, aristocratic family and super-successful career as an architect, had ensured him a generous amount of attention from young beauties. He was what they called 'a prized catch' in the Sunni community. But marriage was far from Anwar's mind. He was having the time of his life. That's when he had met her. She had evoked emotions that he never knew existed. It was not lust, the passion that women usually unleashed in him. It was something far deeper. He had felt this tremendous need to protect her, cherish her, and make her happy. He knew that he was in love. For the first time. At first sight. It felt strange and beautiful at the same time. There was no alternative for him but to have her. By his side. Forever. When it was time to leave, he had told her, 'If I've ever enjoyed more pleasant company, I can't remember it.'

Strangers in the night...Sinatra had crooned in the background.

Shehzaadi had raised her eyes to meet his.

The moment held between the pair that sparkled with hope and love, and the other, full of doubt and pain, was observed by her father who had watched them hopefully, his dinner untouched.

Overnight, Anwar had transformed into a one-woman man, a man with a mission—to make her his. And when Anwar decided to woo, he wooed like only a besotted lover could. As far as he was concerned, it was all or nothing—he was no good at half measures. Even Shehzaadi was unaware of how or when she had succumbed. But succumb she had. To his obvious physical charm, his need for her and his constant effort to keep her in good humour. In retrospect, she realised that the survivor in her had known that he was the much-needed balm to erase her painful past. Ultimately every action is an act of self-preservation—a human being's primary obligation towards itself. I am; therefore the world is...

Anwar was beside himself with joy.

Her acceptance of the marriage proposal had come as a huge relief to her father who was worried about her future and as a big surprise to Anwar's parents. He could have had any woman at his bidding but he had chosen to marry a widow. A woman with a tragic past. But they were happy for him. They had learnt early enough that only his happiness ensured theirs. Shehzaadi and Anwar had a simple nikaah. It was a strictly family affair though more than fifty people attended it.

Mirza had a large family. A dozen uncles and aunts and double the number of cousins, their wives and children. All of them welcomed Shehzaadi like she had always been a part of them.

Their Sunday afternoon lunches were always fun. The aroma of cooking, kebabs, koftas and biryani would waft in the air from mid-morning. They would all gather at the Mirzas' apartment at Napean Sea Road and talk nonstop even while tucking into the scrumptious spread. Somebody would start with an anecdote or a bit of nonsense and everybody would contribute, until the whole bunch would be roaring with laughter, tears rolling down their cheeks. Somewhere beneath the jesting and teasing were deep family roots. Amidst the bonding and relatively uncomplicated relationships, Shehzaadi had returned to normalcy. Well, almost. At least she thought so.

She really missed them after they moved to Hyderabad three years ago. But she loved it here. Especially their garden. Shehzaadi loved gardening and in Mumbai she had to satisfy herself with a few indoor potted plants. When they moved, much of her time was occupied doing up their house and planning the garden. The first thing she did was to uproot some of the Ashoka trees which hid the garden. In their place she planted croutons, which eventually grew into a hedge. Within a year, Shehzaadi with the help of her maali, had turned the space into an idyllic landscape: rows of zinnias, carnations, gladiolas, marigolds, chrysanthemums and roses grew on all sides of the yellow and green hedge which provided privacy when they sat in the sprawling lawn. She had also planted a row of orchids and when they were in full bloom during the winters, it was sheer visual delight.

They socialised a lot more in Hyderabad than in Mumbai. Their garden turned out to be an ideal location for barbeques and dance parties. The Mirzas' outdoor parties became famous in the city.

The social scene in Hyderabad was slightly odd. Unlike other bigger cities, Hyderabad had no celebrities as such although there were a lot of pretenders. The real billionaires and achievers rarely socialised. And those who did, felt they were the biggest celebrities that walked the earth. There was so much 'genuineness' in the well-practised pretence that their act had out-of-towners quite convinced. Added to this was the recent 'Page 3' trend that a Delhi-based journalist had introduced to the laidback town. And the Hyderabadis were lapping it up like it was the next best thing to qubani ka meetha.

In the three years there, Shehzaadi had seen them all. The moderately successful business men and their affected wives, the not-so-popular vernacular stars and starlets, their cronies, middle-aged men who strutted about like they were super studs and their 'second set-ups', journalists from the two and a half newspapers that existed, the skimpily clad and the overdressed, the ubiquitous spiritual gurus, the poseurs and the polymaths. Most of them lived from one party to another. But all said and done, they were a colourful, amusing lot.

The Mirzas had grown quite popular on the social scene. Not that it was all that difficult in the Nawabi city. People loved partying. You couldn't blame them. There was little else to do on weekends; there were no getaways, no beaches, no quaint hill-stations to disappear to. There was the lone necklace road on the Hussain Sagar but that was for the hoi polloi. So, people who considered themselves socialites clubbed, pubbed and partied—hard. Initially, Shehzaadi would invite Anwar's acquaintances and tell them to bring their friends. And then she realised that the number of people quadrupled from the figure she had estimated. Nobody had any qualms about going to a party even when they didn't know the host. Hospitable or desperate, nobody knew. Nobody cared either. These days, of course, she knew everyone—an eclectic mix of Nawabs, South Indians and Punjabis. The kind of stories that Shahbaz would tell his parents about his peers, their families and their escapades were most entertaining. The city she had left behind and the city she'd come back to had nothing in common. Thanks to the software boom, people referred to Hyderabad as Cyberabad. There was a remarkable change everywhere especially in people's attitudes.

Shehzaadi had obviously made many acquaintances. But only two of them had come close enough to being her friends. Amita and Zeba. Amita was a fashion designer, a cynical divorcee who had a teenage daughter and a sardonic sense of humour. Zeba was an architect who was married to Hamid, a doctor. The three women usually got together on weekends. For some reason, Anwar disapproved of both. Nothing in particular annoyed him but their attitudes rattled him quite a bit.

Shehzaadi, despite their affluence and life in Mumbai, had continued to remain down to earth and family-oriented. Both these women were neither. It seemed rather like they were at a loose end. Suffering from a mid-life crisis, Anwar had analysed. 'Let's have fun,' was their constant refrain. Lately, he had heard his wife using the line more often than he thought she should. And 'fun' in their parlance meant pub-hopping in clothes that would put trendy teenagers to shame, and getting sozzled. In all honesty, they did have the figures to carry off those outfits but Anwar hoped their taste in clothes would not influence his wife who had always dressed her age. And elegantly.

Of the two, Anwar considered Zeba more harmless. Amita was a flirt. She had honed the craft to perfection and went about it rather seriously. It served as an ego boost when she played the coquette with almost every man she met, irrespective of their age and marital status. And because for Hyderabadi men such excitement was rather rare, Amita had many of them eating out of her hands. But her predatory instinct told her that Anwar was not one of them and would never be. She knew how to turn herself into a picture of innocence if a man or an occasion demanded it. What she didn't know was that he saw through the act effortlessly. He had seen quite a few of her 'type' in his younger days. And he knew where to keep them. At bay. But for some reason, Shehzaadi had grown very fond of her.

Not one to impose his views, he let things be hoping his wife would outgrow her friends in the course of time. Moreover, his busy schedule and Shahbaz's impending departure left both father and son with little time to spend with her.

In July, when it was time for Shahbaz to leave for England, the Mirzas threw a lavish farewell party for him. Everybody who was anybody in Hyderabad's social milieu was invited. And all of them turned up. That night, Ali noticed his wife downing one too many, with Amita and Zeba keeping her company. It was so unlike her but then it *was* a night of celebration and he didn't feel like dampening her spirits. She seemed so happy. But something told him that her happiness was more alcohol-induced than anything else.

The day after their son's departure, he noticed she looked completely dazed. Although physically she appeared to be in good health she was looking pale, almost haggard. But then, Shahbaz leaving was not easy on him, either. And the kid was a quintessential Mama's boy. His absence had left a vacuum in her life. At least, Anwar had his work to keep his mind occupied. He had all the inclination to help Shehzaadi cope but seldom the time. And he hadn't fathomed the depth of her loneliness.

Until a month later, when on one evening he got home from work, and saw their family doctor's car in the porch. He knew instantly that something was wrong.

Babu Miya, his man Friday-cum-housekeeper informed him that memsaab had suddenly taken ill sometime ago but didn't want him to be called on his cellphone, since he would be on his way home anyway. She was still upstairs. No, he did not know what the problem was. Memsaab had appeared quite normal at lunch, which she'd had in her bedroom.

Anwar rushed upstairs and for some strange reason the doctor seemed most uncommunicative. He was extremely annoyed but managed to keep his cool and make enquiries. 'No, I can't say for a day or two whether she's completely okay,' the doctor answered handing over a prescription. 'We'll have to get these tests done.'

'But what is the matter with her?' Ali implored as the doctor moved towards the door. 'It seems like she's overdoing it,' he replied with what seemed like a look of disdain.

Anwar was moved by his wife's appearance. She looked as white as a sheet. The look he had seen in her eyes the first time he met her had returned. 'What's the matter, jaan?' he asked tenderly.

'Oh, nothing really. I just felt dizzy while having a shower. But I'll be all right. Now that you're here,' she smiled disarmingly. Although she sounded convincing, he could sense the weariness in her voice.

'Are you sure?' he asked nervously.

'Of course,' she said. Then she turned her head and glanced uneasily at the bathroom door, which was ajar. 'Could you please get Ruksana to clean the floor? I cut myself when I fell and there's blood everywhere. Don't look in.'

The sight of blood unnerved him and she knew that. He did as he was told and returned to her side. 'How did you cut yourself, sweetie and where?' he asked her.

'I just told you…I felt dizzy under the shower and cut myself on the side,' she answered shortly, before closing her eyes.

Anwar spent the rest of the evening miserable and distraught. He was deeply affected by his wife's condition. He had caught, in her eyes, a panic that he thought he had vanquished with his love and care. He was also getting increasingly worried about her drinking habits. She had taken to finishing a bottle of wine every evening and more over the weekends when she was in the company of her fun loving friends. He decided to have a heart-to-heart talk with her to find out what was on her mind. He knew there was more to it than her just missing their son. But he had to wait until she was physically fit enough to talk.

Varsha—The Storm

She was perched on a cliff of immense height looking down at a procession of several people. It was a funeral procession. She was too far away to see the corpse clearly so she began descending the cliff, at first by a broad stairway that changed into a road, which then became a narrow rocky path. She climbed down from rock to rock only to be faced by a steep precipice. She had lost sight of the procession. She was completely isolated. But now the urgency to reach out had increased to desperation. She stepped onto the edge and jumped.

Varsha awoke with a sense of having fallen into an abyss. She was relieved that it was only a dream. And she was on her bed with her husband, Somesh. She wiped the beads of perspiration on her forehead wondering what her dream meant. It seemed as though its interpretation lay just beyond her grasp. She longed to understand it. But it would take sometime before that happened.

Currently however, she was debating whether she should wake Som up. And decided against it. The last time she had narrated one of her dreams to him, he'd looked utterly bored.

It was also very important for him to get his fixed quota of sleep. A couple of tantrums when he'd had to do with less had convinced her of that.

She switched on the bedside lamp and looked at the clock. It was five-thirty. Time for her yoga session. But somehow she didn't feel up to it. It had been another one of those nights; another awkward conversation with Som. She had, for the zillionth time, tried to convince him that now was the right time for a baby. 'I do love kids, honey,' he'd told her, nonchalant, bored, 'As long they're somebody else's.' She had told him how much she longed for a child. Their child. 'It will bring us closer, Som,' she said, 'Can't you see we're drifting apart?' And then she realised that he had already stopped listening to her. He had a way of shutting her out. Just like that. And she hadn't succeeded in crossing the impenetrable wall between them. Not in five years of marriage.

In fact marriage had done strange things to their relationship. In the early days of their courtship, a married life with him held promise and excitement. But five years later she felt she was drowning in his apathy. Som was not a bad person or even mean. Sometimes, she felt that *that* would have been easier to deal with. At least she would have known what to expect. But Som's indifference was killing her. He would retreat into his shell and come out only when he felt the need to. That fitted his zodiac description—Som was a Cancerian. But he displayed no love or even interest for family and relationships and that was supposed to be the most distinct characteristic of a Cancerian, at least according to Linda Goodman! Varsha was yet to meet a human being as self-absorbed as Som. Even her mother, whom she regarded as highly individualistic, paled in comparison.

She wondered what made him so emotionally aloof. So devoid of any passion. He had become so grave, so serious—the epitome of dullness. All her attempts at getting him interested in sharing and doing things together were met so coldly that it sent a shiver down her spine. Their relationship was so superficial now that she wondered how it could have all gone so dreadfully wrong. It was even worse because she couldn't even put a finger on what exactly the problem was.

All she knew was that they were becoming more distant each passing day and she didn't know what to do about it. It was as though all the warmth she had hoped for them to share was flowing out of their lives; evaporating, vanishing into nothingness. Their future together looked so bleak, so devoid of love, that she was desperate to have a baby to salvage whatever was left. She felt that having a baby would be the antidote to his disinterest, and their relationship's lack of direction and purpose.

After all, this was the man she had defied her mother for. Revati Rao, the dynamic MP, was aghast when her twenty-year-old daughter had announced her decision to get married. She could not fathom that the reason for her hasty decision was her own sham of a marriage to Varsha's father. Her daughter had rebelled against everything her parents stood for.

Ranga Rao belonged to one of the wealthiest families in Bangalore. Rao's only two interests in life was wine and women. Strictly in that order. His one-afternoon-stands ('Nights are for the wife', she had heard him telling his cronies, when she was a toddler) with women of all ages, were legendary, the stuff Bangalore's soiree conversations were made of. His male friends envied him for it. Varsha loathed him. Revati was indifferent.

When Varsha was an adolescent, she thought the only time her parents had probably made love or rather had sex, was when she had been the result. Enough to put you off it for life. Mom and dad, for most children, meant their whole world. In her case, they inhabited completely different worlds although they did have one thing in common—their dislike for staying home. As far as she could remember, they loathed domesticity. Revati was almost always out travelling to her constituency, attending a party meeting or the parliament sessions. And whenever she looked at her dad, a terrible nausea rose in her chest brought on by a sense of shame that he had made her. Flesh, blood and bone.

Varsha was brought up by a series of ayahs. She often wondered why her parents even stayed together under the same roof.

Earlier, when she was about sixteen, Varsha had decided that she would get married as soon as she was a graduate. Only then would she be able to lead a normal life. She would have a husband. A home. A family. And they would have children. They would give their children everything that she had been deprived. A warm home. Loving parents.

She had met Som the next year. He was her mom's friend's son. They had a lot in common. Similar backgrounds. The same values. Or so it seemed.

The first time they were alone in her house, they had kissed. She remembered it all so vividly. It was a bright, warm afternoon, a rich smell of earth in the air. It was magical. That was the first time a man had touched her. She could feel their breath mingling as they came up for air. She didn't want the kiss to end. She was prepared to not resist him if he had shown a desire for closer intimacy. But he made no effort to draw her to him. Instead, he whispered in her ear, 'Let's wait till we get married. I want the first time to be special for us.' 'Is that a proposal?' she had asked and caught him off guard. He had said, 'Yes. You won't marry anyone but me. You won't, will you? Promise me you won't. She had replied, 'No, I won't. I promise.' 'You won't marry me or you won't break the promise?' he asked, wanting clarity. 'I won't break the promise,' she had whispered.

Though she longed to experience physical pleasure, she felt a surge of warmth that he did not want to hurry things. Here was a young man who had both the opportunity and a willing partner but he resisted. Because he believed in something. He had values. He had convictions. Above all, he loved her.

The uniqueness of the experience appealed to her immensely. He was so refreshingly different. She had heard stories from her girlfriends that all a guy wanted was to 'get into a girl's pants'. Even the way he proposed was so unusual. There was no solitaire, no customary going down on the knees, but there was respect, there was bonding. She felt very special.

She thought of her father who had no values, no morals and no respect for the woman he was married to. It was at that precise moment that she decided she was in love with him. And she would go to any lengths to be with him.

'Good morning baby,' Som's voice broke her reverie. She was about to respond when she heard him calling out to the servant for his morning cuppa. 'I should've known by now that my responding to him or otherwise hardly makes any difference,' she thought bitterly. She wondered if he even noticed her these days. He had not made love to her for ages. Was she getting fat, too unattractive? To make conversation she said, 'Could you pass me the colour supplement please?' He did not look up. 'I'm reading it.'

'No, you're not. What you're reading is the main paper.'

Quietly, he pulled out the magazine section and tossed it onto the table next to her. As if she didn't count at all.

'Thank you,' she said with mock politeness.

'You're welcome,' he said evenly, still reading, ending the conversation she had tried to begin.

This had been their routine for the past three years—at least. She would wake up earlier than him. He would wake up an hour later. They would read the day's newspaper over cups of tea in silence that was more dead than shared. Silence, she had read in many books, was more powerful than words. But in their case, it was deafening, almost scary in its frequency and depth. She used to switch on music earlier but he would insist on turning it off. And once he finished scouring through the newspapers he would toss them on the sofa and vanish into the loo for an hour. He would emerge bathed and dressed, peck her customarily on the cheek, wave goodbye and drive away. She would eat her breakfast alone—he never did—get ready and leave as well. She would get back home much later than most of her colleagues but always earlier than him. Sometimes, they planned on dining out but he would never make it. Worse still, he wouldn't even call. She would wait for him endlessly and then call his office only to be told that he was out. Then she would try his cellphone, which he would pick up after several attempts, and tell her that he was stuck in a meeting. For the last year, she had stopped suggesting they go out because it only added to her agony. It didn't matter to him at all, she was sure. If it did he would at least have mentioned it sometimes. But he didn't. She could be invisible and even that wouldn't be noticed by him.

She had noticed in all their years together that the one thing Som loathed was change. There were many constants in his life. Including his job as the Finance Manager of a public sector company. When he complained often to her about how his job sucked, how he was stuck in a rut and how every change he wanted to make was a Herculean task, she suggested that he set up his own consultation firm. After all, he was a brilliant accountant who had turned around the losses the company was making in a mere five years. He could be his own boss. Their life would change for the better, she told him. 'But what's wrong with our life now?' he asked her. Seemingly, nothing. To an onlooker it was perfect. They were both young and had high-profile careers. They never even argued! Som was neither an alcoholic or a womaniser. He had no vices, so to speak. Why then, did she feel this all-encompassing web of discontent tangling her up inside? She probably needed to get her head examined, she decided. After all, the companion to routine was security, right? Exactly. There was nothing wrong with her life. If there was something askew, it was her attitude. Definitely. In fact, she had so much freedom and nobody to question her despite being married that she should actually be ecstatic. Som never asked her where she went, what she did, who she went out with, nothing at all. There were no questions asked, no answers expected. She had heard from so many of her friends how they had trouble coping with curious, possessive husbands who wanted to know everything. 'Come on, am I not entitled to any privacy?' her friend Sujata had said in indignation when her husband had enquired with the office receptionist where exactly she had gone.

At the other end of the spectrum was her, Varsha, the wife of Somesh Kumar, who had the advantage of straddling two worlds. Sailing in two boats at the same time, so to speak. Being a married woman and a free bird, a wife and an independent woman. She should count her blessings instead of wishing that they had one life and not two—His & Hers. Like two cloak rooms. 'Oh hell. I think I'm going batty,' she said to herself. And if she went mad and landed up at the asylum, would Som come to visit her, would he even care? There, she was falling into the same pattern again. Thinking senseless thoughts. 'What I need to do now is develop other interests apart from work and obsessing over Som,' she decided. At the same time, she wondered why a couple needed to get married in the first place if they were to lead two different lives, develop different interests and spend time doing different things. What men and women did to each other in the name of marriage was nothing short of lunacy.

~

Chapter 2

RELIEF. THAT'S WHAT MAYA FELT AS SHE WALKED OUT OF THE University campus. Relief at having found a job, of now being able to stand on her own feet and of finally recognising her calling. A sigh escaped her lips inadvertently. She knew her journey had just begun, with neither the route nor the destination in sight. Yet she was uplifted by the optimism that things would fall into place and that they would take definite shape. And she was ready for the outcome. What it would be hardly mattered. What did make a difference was that she was trying. She didn't want to look back at fifty or sixty and wonder what it would have been like if she had searched for her family. She wanted no 'ifs'. No more probabilities. She knew how important, how vital in every way, this job was for her. She had to seize the breaks that life gave her. One lost chance sometimes, meant no more to come.

She needed to move out of her hotel room. She was tired of the place. For the first time since her stay in Hyderabad, she longed for a home. A place she could call her own. Where she could put her feet up without a care in the world. Like she used to, not so long ago. When her parents were alive. How she missed them! How she missed their home built by a strong, loving woman and a wonderful, devoted man. A home that would remain irreplaceable though some semblance of it was what she needed now.

The following month passed in a whirl. After her parents died, she felt as though time stood still. Now that she'd moved to Hyderabad, it flew. It was all a matter of perception, she thought. Days are all the same. 24 hours. 1,440 minutes. 86,400 seconds. Time doesn't fly. People do. Like she was, at the moment. But she wasn't complaining. In fact, she was more than glad to have her days filled with various activities. There was a certain comfort in waking up and knowing what she would be doing in the following hours. Especially for someone like her who had always had everything charted out by her meticulous mother and father. Yesterday, when she moved into her new residential quarters, she realised how much she had imbibed those qualities from them. Amma's words were ringing in her ears while she was going about setting up the place. 'There is a place for everything and everything has to be in its place.' By the end of the day, she had almost everything under control. Most of it was already done. All she needed to do was shuffle the furniture around according to her taste. Once she settled down, she decided, she would refurbish the place with new upholstery, some terracotta pots and other bric-a-brac. But for now, this would do. The next morning when she woke up, she almost felt 'at home.' The best part was that she was actually looking forward to the day.

When she reached the academic department that she was now quite familiar with, she felt eager and light-hearted. She still had a week to go before completing her orientation. She already had a deep respect for Professor Mohommed Abdul Hai, Head of the History Department who she reported to every morning. The middle-aged professor was a gentle, cultured Hyderabadi with dark hair that was graying at the temples and a face that was pleasant without being remarkable in any way. Well-groomed and neatly dressed, he was equally liked by his peers as well as his students. She wondered how a nice guy like him was still unmarried. The other staff members had nicknamed him 'chronic bachelor'. Like it was a disease or something. Somebody at the campus had told her that he was gay. Nobody knew for sure though. Why on earth, she wondered, did people have to speculate about sexual orientation when somebody preferred to stay single? As though marriage was the ultimate goal in life. God! What conditioning! As far as she was concerned, it hardly mattered. Each to his own. Besides, she enjoyed the company of gay men, presuming he was one of course. They were so much more fun to be with. And cheerful. That's probably why they were called 'gay' in the first place. She liked men who were in touch with their feminine side. She felt it made them more sensitive than so-called 'straight' men.

Mohommed Abdul Hai was fun to work with. He was witty, clever, a lighthearted man despite being a serious academician. She rarely saw him in a sombre mood. The students loved and looked forward to his lectures. Apparently, his classes were the least bunked and that was a record on campus.

When she entered her room, she found him lounging in the visitor's chair tilting it so it rested on two legs instead of four. He was wearing a checked shirt in shades of grey and black with a pair of dark trousers and black suspenders. She had noticed that he always wore suspenders. And somehow they made him look distinguished. Apparently they were his trademark. Sometimes he wore a tie but not today. She had been told by somebody, she couldn't remember who, that he belonged to an old, wealthy Hyderabadi family and that academics was in his blood. His grandmother, apparently, had been the first graduate from the Hyderabad University.

Hai was a stickler for time. No matter how punctual she was, he always seemed to arrive earlier than her. 'Good morning, sir,' she greeted him and said, 'One of these days I'm going to outdo you.'

'Good morning, Maya,' he replied informally, 'The biggest compliment to a teacher is when his students outdo him.'

'I meant reaching office earlier than you.'

'Oh, that! Not going to happen, young lady, but no harm in trying. Aaj tak koi mai ka laal nahi paida hua jo humse punctuality me muqabla kar sakey. I'm kidding. I'm feeling rather melodramatic today. Caught an Amitabh Bachchan movie last night on telly. He always has that effect on me.'

'Lekin sir, aapka saamna is baar laal se nahin, laali se ho raha hai,' she said wondering what the feminine equivalent to 'laal' in Hindi was.

He laughed wholeheartedly and then said, 'Okay, let's get down to some serious work.' He went on to tell her that several historical monuments were languishing in Hyderabad about which, even the mulkis, were unaware. Hai's idea was to generate enough material on these monuments so they could educate students and also rouse the government to their historical importance and the dire need for their preservation. 'The government has been talking for ages about its intention to preserve the rich cultural heritage of our city but it's more hot air than anything else. Finally we have a chief minister who is taking it seriously. But even his attention has been limited to those structures that generate revenue. That's why the focus is on landmarks like the Charminar, the Golconda, the Salar Jung museum and the tombs. But I guess at least he's made a start. Now, as the university's history department, I think we have a major role to play in taking this to the attention of the authorities. This will be Osmania University's contribution to the city. That's the main reason why we appointed you. An "assistant historian" was unheard of on campus. I convinced the Vice Chancellor that we needed to create this post for the purpose of research. In that sense, you're spear-heading our effort. That's why I want you to take this up immediately. You and I need to justify your presence at the campus,' he spoke passionately, breathless from his long speech. She noticed he had a habit of dangling his spectacles in his right hand whenever he had to make a point.

'That sounds very interesting,' she replied earnestly, 'What is the project called?'

'Heartless in Hyderabad.'

'Like the movie *Sleepless in Seattle*. Doesn't it sound a wee bit corny, sir?'

'Wee bit? It's downright ridiculous. I was kidding. I like your diplomacy though. Very impressive!'

She laughed,'Thank you!'

'How about "Forgotten Memoirs".'

'Isn't "memoirs" autobiographical in nature, sir?'

'Yes. The monuments speak for themselves. The narrative will be ours but the language theirs.'

'Sounds interesting if not slightly complicated to me. Besides, do you think the governement babus will understand the word "memoirs" or even be able to pronounce it?'

'Hmmm...you have a point. Let's make it "memories" then. What do you say? I think it conveys the meaning and the intent.'

'Yes, I guess it does,' she answered quietly.

'That's settled then,' he thumped the table and stood up. 'Let's chalk out a schedule for you first thing tomorrow morning. You should be in a position to start next week. Your orientation will come to an end by then, right?' looking at her from above his spectacles.

'Yes.'

'Good, see you later then.'

Her eyes lingered on his back as he left the room. In the short time she was there, she had grown to admire the senior professor's talent and ability, in the classroom and out of it. Occasionally he sidetracked serious lectures with bits of interesting trivia and anecdotes but his history classes were popular mainly because he made them so informal. She was fortunate to be working with somebody like him. She was lucky to be here, at the university, doing what she was doing. As a student, she had been confused about her future. With no burning ambition to do something in particular, she had sailed along with no clue about what she wanted to do with her Masters in History. But now, it felt like coming home. The sense of belonging seemed to expand her horizons. She felt she was destined to be here. The atmosphere at the university filled her with an eagerness to learn and explore, to put theory into practice. She hadn't lost sight of her ultimate goal, her job just made the process so much more enjoyable. But to begin with, she needed to find her bearings in the new city.

She turned her attention to her day's programme. Before she had reached half-way through the schedule she heard someone enter the room. Raising her eyes, she found Sumathi standing in front of her asking, 'Ready?' Sumathi was in her mid-thirties, five feet nothing. She had a dusky complexion, kind brown eyes, a mass of curly hair and a merry laugh. She was from Vizag, a beach town in Andhra Pradesh, but her parents had moved to Hyderabad when she was ten. 'That makes me a total Hyderabadi at heart if not a true blue one,' Sumathi had told her. 'Ok, if you're through admiring me, shall we?' Sumathi jested. 'Yeah, I'm ready,' Maya replied with a smile. 'Let's go to my room. I'll familiarise you with the procedures that are followed here. For all the hype of being a paperless office, we thrive on memos and inter-office emails. Even if you need a stapler, you need to put it up to personnel. You'll learn as we go along. And then, I'll take you to all the other departments and introduce you to the professors. That should take care of the first half of the day. Listen, why don't we share my lunch. I've got this amazing fish curry that only my mother can make. I'm sure you'll love it.'

'I'm sure I would have, if I were non-vegetarian. But, thanks, that's very thoughtful of you,' Maya replied.

'You're a vegetarian? Oh, how boring! You don't look like one,' Sumathi quipped.

Maya constantly heard that comment and it puzzled her. How on earth was a vegetarian supposed to look? Like a rabbit? she wondered, but kept it to herself not wanting to offend Sumathi who was trying to be amiable. So far, she had found most people on campus very friendly. She mentioned it to Sumathi. 'Wait till you meet, Mrs Beddell, the English lecturer, Madam Prim and Propah. Don't ever eat with your fingers if you want to be friends with her. She'll refuse to even acknowledge you. She's the typical churi-kaanta type. That's okay yaar, I mean, do what you want but why judge others by your standards? Actually come to think of it, she's the perfect English lecturer. Nose in the air, stiff-upper lip. God! What airs man! I swear...' Sumathi dived into a monologue dripping in honesty. Maya knew she was going to like Sumathi. She preferred people to speak what they thought. So unlike her. She could only open up in front of certain people. So far only her parents and Varsha.

For the rest of the day, Maya followed Sumathi like a lamb. It was evident that Sumathi was fond of Maya and had taken her under her wing. Before she realised it, it was time to go home. Home. The word had so many connotations for her. She was happy she had her own place now, one that she could call home.

She gathered up her things and started walking back to her quarters. Down the corridor admiring the Ellora paintings adorning the walls, she bumped into Professor Hai. 'I'm extremely sorry. Did I step on your foot?' he asked.

She replied apologetically 'No, it was my fault. I wasn't looking.'

'Well, I never do either! Heading home? Care to join me for chai at the canteen?' he asked.

Without waiting for her reply, he walked off towards the canteen. This had always been her problem. She let everybody else lead. Amma often told her when she was a teenager to be more assertive. And she wanted to as well but when the time came, she never was. Always drifting along, towing somebody else's line. 'When will I ever discover myself,' she sighed. Did she even know who she was?

'Penny for your thoughts,' Hai teased.

'Nothing, nothing at all,' she replied.

'So, how are you liking it here? You're from Bangalore, right?'

'Yes, I am.'

'So, how do you like our city? As much as you thought you would?'

'Actually more. Honestly, I didn't know what to make of it at first. But now, I really love it here.'

'Good, good. I'm glad. So what made you take this job away from home? Did you want to get away from your parents' memories?' he continued gently.

She nodded. Luckily, he had answered his own question. Else she wouldn't have known what to say. Any which way you looked at it, she was here because of her parents. Dead or alive. Sounded more like a call for a fugitive. The craziness of language!

'Strangely enough,' the professor said, keeping up the dialogue, 'the people we love the most are also the ones we run away from when they're gone.'

The canteen-wallah saluted the professor as they settled down. He raised his hand in response and said, 'I often wonder why we seek the company of people who are like us in many ways. Is it because we're self-obsessed and need to see ourselves in others too or do we understand people who are similar to us more and therefore like to be in their company?' Maya wondered what prompted his train of thought. She didn't voice her query though. 'You know, there's a reason behind my question. And it's you,' he resumed. She looked at him bewildered. 'To be more precise, it has to do with my fondness of you. It's barely been a month since you've been here. But I already feel I know you. I feel the need to look out for you. Do you know why?' he paused for a while and then answered, 'There's something about you that reminds me of myself when I was your age. Alone but not lonely. Independent and self-reliant. More perhaps by chance than choice. Am I right? And, it appears to me that you're seeking something. I could, of course be totally off the mark.' This was the first time he had spoken so seriously. She didn't know what to say or whether to say anything at all. When in doubt, keep quiet, Appa had told her many a times. She decided to follow his advice. In any case, the professor didn't seem like he was expecting a reply. He seemed to be simply voicing his thoughts, rather like talking to himself. 'Someday, when you have the time and I, the inclination, I shall tell you my story,' and broke the seriousness with a smile. 'His story by a history professor,' he laughed aloud and stood up to leave. 'So, what are you planning to do once you get home? You're welcome to come over to my place and chat when ever you'd like to. That's a carte blanche for you. And remember, it's not everybody I make that offer to. Ciao!' With that he walked to his car, feeling his shirt pocket for the keys. She didn't even know where he lived. That's when it occurred to her that he was probably expecting her to reciprocate the gesture. Actually, she wouldn't mind having him over. But now, it was too late. He was gone. 'Never mind,' she told herself, ' Some other day.' Like the shloka Appa had translated from the Upanishads 'That which is not to happen, does not happen, but that which is to happen, does, even without effort.' And then he had told her, 'Never ever sweat over anything. Remember that this applies to even the simplest of situations in life. For everything there's a predetermined time and place. Even for something that might seem unimportant to you.' Would she ever get over his loss? If she did succeed in finding her biological parents, would she ever feel the same intensity for them? Then, again she reminded herself of the shloka. She felt more at peace.

She reached home, showered, changed into her night clothes, cooked a quick, simple meal of huggi—a typical kannadiga dish made of rice and lentils eaten with tangy tamarind sauce—and ate heartily. Then she lit the stove, heated some water and poured it into a filter heaped with coffee powder. She had brought it with her from Bangalore. She had grown up on filter coffee—a huge mug of it first thing in the morning. Now she didn't have Amma to make her some before she left the house. She knew how irritable she got without her caffeine 'fix' so she went through the entire process before she turned in. All she needed to do in the morning was add hot milk to the decoction. She went into the bedroom and crashed. Within seconds, she was dead to the world, her bedtime prayer—the Hanuman Chalisa—still on her lips.

She woke up needing to use the loo. She didn't even have to look at the clock. She knew it was five-thirty in the morning. Her body-clock had worked with absolute precision from as early as she could remember. Once through washing up, she made herself a huge mug of coffee. She pressed the warm mug against her cheek relishing its warmth. Taking the first sip she said to herself aloud, 'This is life.'

She suddenly realised that she had, in fact, gotten quite used to life on her own. 'Good for you, girl,' she patted herself on the back. The pleasant November weather outside was so inviting that she decided to go for a short warm-up run in the garden. So she changed into her tracksuit, put on her Nikes—a birthday present from her dad—and ventured out. The morning was indeed lovely. Calm and pleasantly cool. A few clouds floated in the sky. Like scattered cotton balls. The moon, still silently visible. How could that serene, radiant thing be said to turn people loony, she wondered.

There were other people out too whom she hadn't gotten to know yet but they smiled when her eyes met theirs; each flexing their limbs, walking, jogging. She decided to do this often. She always got excited at the prospect of a new day, new acquaintances, fresh attempts and chances, and a bit of mystery. As she was revelling in the morning tranquility, huge drops of rain started falling without warning. Just as people were debating on whether they should head back, the rain stopped. 'That's strange,' she said aloud, 'isn't it supposed to be winter?' 'Well, Ma'am, that's Hyderabad for you,' she heard a deep voice say behind her. She turned back. 'Hi, I'm Madhav. I teach chemistry. You seem to be new around here,' he said, extending his hand. She placed hers in his as he said, 'Initially, the weather was baffling for me too. But after five years, I know now that anything is possible in this city at any time of the year, in any season. You have heavy rain in winter and scorching heat during the monsoons. To quote a cliché, expect the unexpected. But barring these natural disasters, the city is amazing. It grows on you.' Voices have nothing to do with their bearers. Madhav was an ordinary looking man unlike his sexy voice, probably in his mid-30s, with deep set eyes, a podgy nose and a bushy moustache that covered half his upper lip. He was not very tall and slightly on the plump side. Something about him told her that he was a genial, harmless guy. They got talking and she learnt that he was divorced and the father of a little girl. He also only had weekly visitation rights. 'My ex-wife found her colleague more interesting than me,' he told her in a tone that betrayed no emotion, 'To be honest I agree with her. So, when she told me that she had fallen for this guy at her office and that she would be happier with him, I appreciated her honesty and let her go. I miss my daughter terribly but I know Rama's a good mother. So…' he didn't complete the sentence. She found it strange that he should divulge such personal information to her so soon. They had just met! Was it something about her or was he like this with everybody? She realised it was the latter for later in the day Sumathi had a good laugh over the whole thing. 'For some reason Madhav has this pressing need to tell everybody about his ex-wife,' she said nonchalantly, 'either he's lonely as hell or he thinks that everybody's interested in him. Haven't been able to figure out which. Honestly, I haven't even tried. You don't either. Some men are just not worth the effort. And this one is as interesting as a math lecture to a literature student.'

'Poor fellow,' Maya said aloud.

'You can say that again!' concluded Sumathi gathering her books.

Earlier that morning Professor Hai and she had worked out the schedule for the 'Forgotten Memories' project. The entire exercise gave her such an adrenalin rush that she couldn't wait for the week to pass. Is my desire to find my roots lessening, she asked herself. She knew the answer. Not one bit.

Chapter 3

PROFESSOR HAI DROVE LEISURELY. HE FELT NO URGE TO GO home. In fact, he didn't really want to go anywhere. He brooded over the events of the past few days and wondered if he had done the right thing by extending an invitation to Maya. He had lost the habit of socialising with people, making friends and cultivating protégés. For the life of him he couldn't figure out what had made him say all those things to her. He hadn't the faintest idea he was going to until the words were actually said. And yet he wasn't sorry because it seemed right. Somehow.

He had developed a soft corner for her in a short while. At work, Maya had settled in quickly. He had expected, in fact he was ready, to train her and be patient with her inexperience, but surprisingly, she had taken to her work easily and quickly. Several times, he noticed that she sat with her nose buried in a pile of books, even after working hours. He was impressed. He also saw that she had a habit of taking notes when he spoke. And when she was doing her research. She had a sharp, observant eye for detail. Besides that, she was extremely meticulous. One afternoon, he had asked to see her work-diary and was amazed that she had a schedule drawn out everyday. Everything was listed: her work for the day, a detailed guide to the filing system, a run-down on the day's events, what she had learnt, how she planned to use the information. Her habits reminded him of himself when he was new at his job. She held promise. He hadn't seen many people, especially in the last few years, who had shown such keen interest in their work. She was not in the least perturbed when he had explained to her that this project was a first for the university. In fact, she seemed to love the challenge. Good, good, he nodded. He was so lost thinking that he didn't realise he had passed his house. Since it was a one-way road, he had to drive a mile to turn back.

Hai lived at Banjara Hills, Road 12. Road 12 was home to many old Hyderabadi families. He remembered how the area used to be when he was growing up. Wilderness. The back of beyond. The Banjara Hills area was full of lakes, rocks and untamed shrubs. You could actually spot peacocks and on rare occasions, panthers too. Wild boars, of course, roamed freely. But now, it was the poshest area to live in. Next only to Jubilee Hills when it came to snob value. His parents, especially his mother, had been traditionally wealthy. His dad had studied in Oxford and met his mum there. Both of them had fallen so deeply in love that they got married soon after they returned to India. In fact they called him their 'love child'. But that was much before the term acquired different connotations.

After his mother passed away a few years ago, his father had decided to migrate to England where his brother lived. Hai had then experienced, what he jokingly referred to, a reversal of the empty-nest syndrome. He loved home but hated walking into it at the end of the day when he knew there would be nobody waiting for him. His mother had told him several times to get married before he was 'over the hill.' But what use was marriage, if he hadn't found a partner he felt comfortable with in every way; intellectually, physically. 'You're a Mama's boy,' his dad had admonished him countless times before finally giving up, 'you're not going to find a woman who lives up to your expectations. Chiraag leke dhoondne se bhi nahi.' Hai knew it was true. But there was not much he could do about it. Initially, he tried going out with women his friends set him up with, all of them pretty and well-bred, but he would end up comparing them to the image of this perfect woman that he had in his head. He wondered why it was so difficult to find someone simple. Like his mother, who had no airs and pretences. Someone who also made him laugh. He'd never felt the need to pick up the phone and call a woman the second time. He knew people speculated about his sexual orientation because he had only male friends but that didn't bother him. He had no intentions of being caught in a relationship that couldn't offer him what he was looking for. Hai had seen enough couples trapped in loveless marriages that resembled war zones. If people gossiped, let them. They would have gossiped anyway, whether he was single or unhappily married.

Now, after a long long time, he felt a stirring, for a woman almost half his age, that was definitely not platonic. A mixture of guilt and exhilaration overwhelmed him. What was he doing, at this age, letting such feelings crop up? These things never worked out. He was not going to let his feelings show. He must be out of his mind to even think on those lines. What was the matter with him? Was he turning into a desperate middle-aged man? A mid-life crisis perhaps. The thought was unpleasant but that didn't stop him from wondering why, instead of revulsion, he felt lighthearted joy. Why did he have this feeling that something important in his life had just begun? She tugged at his heart in a manner that he had always wanted and dreaded at the same time. Surely he was not contemplating making a move...even if she was willing, which was most unlikely! But he felt so sure that she was somebody he had been looking for. Her simplicity was so refreshing. Hai sighed and drove into the empty porch.

Chapter 4

SHEHZAADI SAT AT THE DINING TABLE, NIBBLING HER FOOD. They were at the table, Anwar and her, having breakfast. A sumptuous spread of khichdi, kheema, til-ki-chatni, pickles, papad and dahi was laid on the table. Ali watched her surreptitiously. He had asked Khansama, their cook par excellence, to specifically cook khichdi, which was Shehzaadi's favourite, so she would eat well. The previous evening's incident was still fresh in his mind but he wasn't sure if he should broach the subject. After looking at her disinterest in food, he decided to postpone it. 'How are you feeling, jaan?' he asked, tenderly, 'How's your cut? I thought you loved khichdi.' 'Yes,' she replied weakly, 'Normally, I do. But I guess, I have no appetite.' 'Tell you, what,' he said, making an effort to sound enthusiastic, 'Let's go out for dinner tonight. You're probably bored of eating at home. Let's check out the new restaurant at Banjara Hills. My secretary, Stella, was telling me that they serve some fabulous fusion cuisine. The change will do you good and give me a chance to hold hands with my wife. What say you?' 'Okay, fine,' she replied with what sounded to him like disinterest. What could be the matter with her? Missing Shahbaz was one thing but not even wanting to talk about it was something else. Unless, of course, there was something else he couldn't see or wasn't aware of. Now, however, was not the right time to worry about it. He had a meeting with the Chief Minister to attend to. 'Okay, then, jaan, we have a date in the evening,' he told her cheerfully, 'I need to rush now. You take care.' After touching her forehead lightly with his lips, he headed to his car. He noticed that she hadn't followed him to the main door to wave to him the way she normally did. He sighed deeply and turned his attention to the day ahead.

The meeting was crucial. Anwar was submitting his report on what needed to be done, on a priority basis, in the restoration project in addition to the funds required for the first phase. He had devised a clear plan for three structures in the old city—Purani Haveli, Chow Mohalla and the King Kothi palace. This was the first time he was meeting the CM about whom he'd read a lot besides hearing about his efficiency from Muralidhar, the Director of The Archeological Survey of Hyderabad who had entrusted him with the project. 'You better be quick,' the director had warned, 'And make sure your presentation is either on power-point or is a multimedia one because that should impress our CM. He's extremely computer savvy so thanks to him, every minister in his cabinet has gone on a computer crash course and each one now owns a lap-top.'

Anwar had seen this when he had visited the Andhra Pradesh Tourism office. It was equipped with Pentium IVs, a touch-screen kiosk that gave a brief history of Hyderabad greeted visitors at the entrance. And then he was efficiently guided by a smart receptionist through the department who took him on a virtual tour of each monument—its location, how to get there, the duration of the journey from his house and how much it would cost if he chose to go on a guided tour. It was extremely convenient for tourists and Anwar was highly impressed. So he had spared no effort to ensure his presentation was catchy, interesting and well-researched. He had worked on it for the last two weeks, driving his advertising agency up the wall with his late night phone calls and perfectionist's incessant demand for detail. One of the reasons he could not spend enough time with his wife. But, he had resolved to make up for it, once he settled into his job.

Tonight, at the dinner, he would gift her with a Basra pearl set that he had planned to buy from Laxman Das, a famous old Hyderabadi jeweller. He had seen it sometime back and was spellbound by its beauty. 'A befitting gift for my princess,' he'd decided. He concentrated on the road as he drove unhurriedly. The CM's house was in the next street and whenever he felt an important project needed his undivided attention; he summoned the meeting at his house. 'That's the first indication that he's taking us seriously,' Muralidhar had told him while the pressure mounted, 'All the more reason for you to make an impression. And remember you don't get second chances with first impressions.' He was ushered into the lounge after his credentials were checked and was received by Radhakrishna, the CM's Personal Assistant, who shook hands with him and said, 'Pleasure meeting you Mr Mirza. The CM's allotted you precisely twenty minutes. So I suggest you get to the point and don't waste time.'

The CM looked much younger in real life than in photographs and on screen. After exchanging pleasantries, they got down to business. The CM was an attentive man, he paid great attention to the slick presentation and asked all the right questions after. 'Looks perfect to me,' he said and stood up as if to mark the end of the meeting, 'I'm meeting with the Director and Minister of Tourism. We'll get back to you in a week. Nice meeting you, Mr Mirza. Apparently you're from Hyderabad.' Anwar nodded and explained that his ancestors had worked for the Nizams as advisors. 'Interesting,' the CM commented, 'Please tell Mr Muralidhar that I'm happy with his choice.' With that he shook hands with Anwar and left the room. Radhakrishna followed him to see him off. When he noticed Anwar looking at his watch, he laughed and said, 'I told you no, Mr Mirza, precisely twenty minutes. Nothing more, nothing less.' 'That's true,' said Anwar, 'Do you think a week will be enough time for him to sanction the funds, Mr Radhakrishna?' 'What did I just tell you, Mr Mirza? If sir says one week, one week it will be. Just you watch,' he said emphatically, 'By the way, you can call me RK.'

Anwar breezed through the rest of the day happy with the outcome of the meeting. Muralidhar was pleased too. A couple of lengthy meetings later, Anwar was startled to see that it was getting dark. He remembered the dinner date with Shehzaadi and looked at his watch. It was already seven p.m. 'Shucks,' he cursed himself, 'I should have called her earlier.' He decided to go home directly. But before that he had to pick up her gift.

It wasn't all that late he consoled himself. He would reach home in about forty-five minutes if the traffic was smooth, which it should be, since rush hour ended an hour ago. As he walked out of office, he tried their landline number from his cellphone but failed to get through. Then he tried her mobile, it was switched off. He knew that she kept it off when she was home. He got into his car and sped. Anwar loved being behind the wheel. He loved driving. He was a fast driver but not reckless—an art he had perfected.

Traffic in Hyderabad was chaotic. A couple of years ago a Japanese team had visited the city to study the traffic scenario. At the end of their month's research they filed their report which consisted of a single line—'A divine hand protects the lives of people on the roads of Hyderabad.' Now, the divine hand seemed to have lost patience—there were accidents happening frequently on almost every road. When they had just moved in, Shahbaz gave them a scare—his car had suffered a head-on collision with a van that was coming in the wrong direction. He had escaped with only a scratch on his arm but Shehzaadi was terrified when she came to know of it. Their son's car had been battered beyond recognition. Looking at the wreckage, Anwar believed that there was, indeed, a divine hand. Not all people involved in such an accident were so lucky.

He was glad to find the entire stretch of road to the jewellery store clear. He spent precisely fifteen minutes there and dashed back home. 'That was lucky,' he thought with relief.

He parked in the porch since they would be going out again anyway and walked in whistling light-heartedly. He was looking forward to dinner. He had made a booking at the restaurant. They had been to Dum Pukht and both of them had loved the kakori kebabs there. But that was a long time ago, no less than three months. Fusion cuisine should be a good choice. Shehzaadi loved continental food. After dinner, he decided, he would take her for a long drive along the lake and have a heart-to-heart with her.

He was greeted by Babu Miya, in the living room, duster in hand. 'Babu Miya, when Memsaab doesn't like you dusting after sunset, why do you do it? If she catches you now, you've had it. Bhaago!' he ordered him. 'Saab,' he replied, baring his nicotine-stained teeth, 'Memsaab's gone out with Amita madam and Zeba madam. That's why I'm doing dusting.'

'Gone out? When?'

'Half an hour ago, Saab.'

'Okay. Well, get me a cup of tea.'

Anwar slid into the grey leather sofa in the living-room, suddenly drained. How could she do this, he thought. Had she forgotten? But she always called him when she made last-minute plans to go out with her friends. He sipped his tea and his lips recoiled at the heat, adding to his annoyance. He tried her cellphone and hung up as soon as he heard the familiar music that preceded the 'not reachable' message. He found these 'out of range', 'switched off' messages most irritating. Now, his exasperation at his wife's unexplained disappearance reached its height. But she had looked so tired that morning. And, he remembered, she hadn't answered his question about her injury.

'Babu Miya,' he called out.

'Ji Saab.'

'How was Memsaab feeling? I mean, was she alright?'

'Ji Saab, didn't you speak to her during the day, Saab?'

'No,' he said, almost apologetically, 'I was busy in a meeting.'

'Saab, Memsaab told me she would have her dinner outside and come back late in the night.'

From Babu Miya's expression, Anwar could see that he wanted to say more. But he didn't encourage him. He was tired now and wanted to be alone. But first, as Babu Miya was now saying, he had better eat.

He followed Babu Miya to the dining-table, waited while the table was being laid, grabbed a quick bite and walked into the bedroom. He was angry and disappointed at the same time. Angry that she didn't feel the need to speak to him before she left and disappointment for not having been able to spend an evening with her. He didn't even feel like a drink. Not that he was a regular drinker. He preferred liqueur—Cognac, Kahlua, Bailey's, Amaretto. He changed into his nightclothes and stood in the balcony. They had a wonderful view of the rock formations from there.

Unfortunately, the quality of the rocks made them excellent construction material because of which many incredible boulder sites had been blasted. Anwar remembered as a kid, Hyderabad was surrounded by these beautiful, grand formations. In the last decade they had been blown into smithereens or sliced into halves of a pathetic giant potato.

Several times, he had stood here with his wife admiring the view, exchanging bits of gossip about his day, holding her hand. But that was before she had met her 'friends'. That was when she had always been there for him. And, he thought regretfully, when he was not too busy to spend time with her. That seemed so long ago. Or was it? He wondered whether he was holding her back, begrudging her her happiness. Probably, she had waited for him to call all day. He should have. Now, he didn't even know where she was. But, he decided, he would not make an issue of it when she returned. After all, she had waited for him several times in the past. He had a feeling she was out at a pub with Amita and Zeba. Was she enjoying herself so much that she didn't even remember to call?

Shehzaadi was sitting on a bar stool next to Zeba at a swanky Begumpet pub watching Amita do her alluring act with a hunk who was the lead singer of a band. She was wearing a low-neck, strappy top on a skirt with thigh-high slits and everytime she bent forward to listen to what the guy was saying, everybody treated themselves to a generous view of her ample bosom. Such adoration was tonic to her soul. She revelled in it.

She had modelled during her college days, she told Shehzaadi once. Even today, she had the figure of a twenty-five-year-old. A perfect 36-24-36. It wasn't like she was blessed with it—she slogged to keep her figure the way it was. The enthusiasm with which she did her crunches and push-ups bordered on fanatic. Her personal trainer had many a celebrity client but Amita outshone them all. Apart from the drooling men and envious women, even her trainer gaped at her in awe. Fitness was a religion as far as Amita was concerned. What was the use of working so hard if she had to hide it behind a salwar kameez, no matter how trendy they had become of late? Amita believed that Indian clothes, except the sari, were matronly and meant strictly for fat women who needed to camouflage shapeless bodies. The icing on the cake was her fabulous height. 'Look at her crossing and uncrossing her legs for no particular reason,' Zeba whispered into Shehzaadi's ear. 'To show off her shapely legs. That's good enough reason. Why do you think she wore that skirt?' she whispered back.

Shehzaadi thought of Anwar and felt a twinge of guilt for not calling him before she left. But then, Amita would have none of it. 'Did he bother to call you even once during the day to reconfirm your dinner plans? So stop your devoted wife act and get a life, woman.' She had dragged her out without giving her any time to protest. She was dressed and waiting for Anwar when they had waltzed in and stormed out with her in tow. Not that she wasn't having a good time but at least she should have left a note. She didn't approve of leaving messages with the domestic help because she felt it would create an impression that Saab and Memsaab didn't communicate. 'What're you thinking?' Zeba gesticulated. 'Nothing,' she shook her head. A few more bloody marys, screw drivers and a couple of tequila shots later, they decided to leave. In any case, the pub would shut at twelve. That was the rule in Hyderabad and the police were pretty strict about it. A couple of pubs that had decided to take it easy, when the law was enforced, had incurred the wrath of the officers and had to close their shutters. That was a lesson to all other pubs and now they played by the rules.

Even as they were getting off their bar stools, the lights came on and the music was switched off, an indication that the bar had closed. The music was replaced by animated chatter. Amita seemed pretty high. On men or booze, nobody knew. 'Let's dump her first,' Zeba told Shehzaadi, 'And then I'll drop you.' Shehzaadi agreed. Amita was grinning foolishly from ear to ear. Shehzaadi regretted the fact that she couldn't drive. She had always had a chauffeur and had never learnt. Usually, it didn't bother her but sometimes, like tonight, she felt dependant and incapable. None of them spoke on the way back. The silence was sometimes broken by Amita's bursts into song, Shakira's *Underneath your clothes*, that was played at the pub.

By the time, Shehzaadi reached home it was almost one. Anwar had left their bedroom door ajar. She tiptoed in and saw him fast asleep. Walking into the bathroom carefully, she removed her make-up, rinsed her mouth with mouthwash—she was feeling too lazy to brush—changed and got into the bed. In the glow of the night-lamp, she looked at Anwar's face and felt a surge of warmth for him. She snuggled up to him waking him in the process. 'I'm sorry. Didn't realise there was no network reception at the pub?' she whispered. 'Never mind,' he said, warming up to the snuggle, 'As long as you had a good time.' Her breath smelt strange. He was quite familiar with the wine and mouthwash smell, so tonight she probably had something else to drink. 'I had a blast,' she said, closing her eyes, 'you should have been there to see Amita in action.' He didn't have the heart to tell her that he was not remotely interested in doing that. And despite his sleepy state, Anwar felt a tight sensation in his chest like something stuck against his rib cage. A sinking feeling came over him—his heart seemed to burn and melt away.

~

Chapter 5

When Zeba reached home, she discovered that Hamid had not yet returned. He had called in the evening to tell her that he would go to the club directly from his clinic. Though, they had a membership in almost every club in town, Hamid preferred the Nawab's Club, the one that old-time Hyderabadis frequented. The food there was divine but Zeba preferred the Hyderabad Club. She believed that since membership there was extremely exclusive, it had more class.

Somctimes, Zeba thought, there would be more meaning in their lives if they had children. But what was the use in thinking about the impossible? When she had failed to conceive even after two years of unprotected sex, they visited a doctor who had tested them both. The verdict—Hamid had a low sperm count. She was eager to give other methods a try but Hamid didn't approve. Fortunately, she was so busy with her work that she didn't miss not having kids except when she got back home. Within her, she felt empty, she needed people around her all the time to fill the gap. Yet she felt lonely at the end of the day. So she was always looking for more people to keep her company, to make her feel less lonely. That was why she went out every evening. When she returned she was pleasantly high on alcohol and the hollowness didn't bother her all that much. Ever since she had met Shehzaadi, some of the vacuum had got filled.

Zeba picked her friends with care. She was extremely choosy about who she was seen with. It was important for her, with the press photographers following her wherever she went, snapping whatever she did. She admired the natural, elegant poise of her new friend. Something, she didn't have. She knew that it came with the kind of upbringing that she lacked.

If people considered her a fair-weather friend, well so be it. What did they know of what it had taken for her to reach where she was at the moment. She had grown up in a middle-class religious family in which all that mattered was how many times a day they prayed. When Zeba had compared herself with wealthy people, she always received the same reply, 'Beta, you must be happy with all that Allah has bestowed on us. Look at all the starving people. Don't compare yourself with people who have more than you.' This advice didn't go down well with Zeba. If Allah was All powerful, All merciful, He would understand her ambition and grant her all that her heart desired. And now He had.

She had started out as an apprentice with a renowned firm when she completed her graduation in architecture from JNTU and her talent hadn't gone unnoticed. Or unrewarded. Her bosses, an aged childless couple, were impressed with her dedication and commitment. She played a major part in the rise of their firm. When they retired, they handed it over to her, retaining a fifty percent share. Zeba was ecstatic. She had arrived. Her success catapulted her into Hyderabadi high society. That's where she had met Hamid, who was not so much successful as traditionally wealthy. There were no major sparks between them but Hamid was smitten by this young, pretty, successful woman. When he proposed, she saw the chance to belong to a world she had always yearned for.

Once she had reached where she wanted, Zeba shunned everything and everyone that reminded her of her impoverished background. Her parents had accepted her behaviour, concealing their disappointment with a resigned 'all up to God' attitude. But her only brother, Shaukath, abhorred the fact that his sister had disowned them in the most heartless manner. It was nothing short of sacrilege, he felt. She had never once invited her family home. He had attempted to visit her once, earlier, but Zeba made it clear that his low-brow clothes and manners embarrassed her. She never disguised the fact that she was ashamed of him. Shaukath had understood, in no uncertain terms, that as far as his sister was concerned, he no longer existed.

Zeba however, saw nothing wrong with her attitude. She hated people—even if they happened to be her own blood—who did nothing to rise above their mediocre existence. For her, being ordinary was nothing short of a crime. If she, despite her government school background, could succeed, what excuse did her brother have? She believed that if she continued to associate with such 'losers', her good luck would desert her. Her extreme caution with picking friends sprung from there. She had no say where her family was concerned but at least she had the freedom to choose her friends. And she exercised it with a great deal of care.

After a lot of experimenting and sieving, she had finally struck a friendship with Amita and Shehzaadi. Both of them had the class that supposedly comes only from being born into old, distinguished families. Sometimes she wondered if she exuded a nouveau-riche aura when she was with them. Zeba was proud to be seen in their company. She loved it even more when trigger-happy reporters desperate for gossip clicked pictures of them together. Pictures that illustrated stories on Page Three of various newspapers. The Zeba-Amita-Shehzaadi trio, for her, spelt pride and wealth. She was with the two most celebrated socialites in town and that was not an achievement to be scoffed at.

However, she didn't tell a soul—including her so-called best friends—about her secret. Whenever somebody asked her about her background, she painted a picture that closely resembled her wealthy friends'.

~

Chapter 6

AFTER A BUSY, FULFILLING DAY AT WORK, VARSHA EXPERIENCED a great sense of satisfaction. She knew she was good at her job. And so did her clients. The fact that her agency had just bagged a prestigious account had proved that hers was one of the most creative brains in the advertising industry. Varsha loved writing, developing and creating ad campaigns. And whenever others, especially her clients, appreciated what she did, her sense of satisfaction turned into delight. In this industry there was no yardstick to measure if work was well received by the audience. Doubts often prevail about the end product, living in hope that it was not all a waste of time and energy. Even if the client is impressed, the real test lies in the target audiences' response. Today, her art director and she had set up an exercise. After the client had approved of their presentation, they gathered together a few people at random—prospective buyers of the product—and showed them the commercial. The response was terrific. More positive than she had ever expected.

Her happiness was replaced by gloom when she reached her apartment and found it still locked. Did Som ever use his spare key, she wondered. Yeah, sure, he needed it at midnight because that's when he returned home. She too believed in hard work but Som was taking it to the other extreme. She was determined, however, not to let him, his presence or rather his absence, dampen her mood this evening. She and her creative team had arranged to meet later at a nightclub to celebrate their success. After a long time, she was actually looking forward to an evening out.

She walked in and turned the CD player on without putting on the lights. Chris Isaac's *Wicked Game* came on. She removed her shoes, slid onto the comfortable sofa, pulled her feet up and closed her eyes, surrendering herself to the soft melody. She didn't know when the tears started flowing. She knew why—it had finally sunk in that she had lost what she used to share with Som; he was never there for her, to share either success or failure. Wiping her eyes, she thought, 'We'll get through this somehow. There's got to be more to life.' And she was going to find it. No matter what. She uncoiled her legs from the sofa slowly and placed them on the ground, it suddenly seemed colder than usual.

She needed a shower badly. She stared at herself in the bathroom mirror and realised she needed to lose weight. It was alarming how lethargy and indulgence took their toll silently, without you having noticed. Combine that with disinterest and its a sure-shot formula of turning into an 'aunty' for all the neighbourhood teenagers. There was a time she had sworn that she would never let 'fat' happen to her. Especially after having seen her grossly overweight mother. She detested the sight of loose flesh hanging on the arms or the back. Luckily, it wasn't that bad, yet. But if she didn't do something drastic about her lifestyle, she knew that weight would be another issue to deal with.

Varsha felt much better after a hot shower. She chose a black skirt with slits on the sides up to her knees and a white top and teamed it up with a red stole. Tripti, the art director, had decided that all of them should have some white in their outfits because the lights at the nightclub made white stand out. 'Good fun,' she thought as she waited downstairs for Tripti to pick her up.

Thirty minutes later, they were at the entrance of a nightclub, giggling like teenagers. When they walked in, they found the others already sipping their drinks and moving to the music. 'Couldn't you wait for us, you swine?' said Tripti, lightly punching Prakash, their graphic designer, in the stomach. 'Oh please,' he protested holding the hand that delivered the punch, 'This is not office okay. Just chill.' They headed to the bar and ordered their drinks. Tripti was having her usual vodka-tonic while Varsha surveyed the menu and settled for a Blue Lagoon, a Vodka-based cocktail with blue curacao and limejuice. She tapped her fingers lightly on the counter while she waited for her drink to arrive. It wasn't too crowded being midweek, there was just enough space for them not to jostle. Everybody—the young and the not quite so young—seemed to be making merry. Varsha felt light-headed as she sipped her drink. The rest of them were on the floor dancing to loud, foot-stomping music and they were having a great time. That's what mattered. Actually, that's all that ever matters, thought Varsha. Having a good time. Tripti called her from the dance-floor to join them and she signalled 'later'. After finishing her drink, she felt confident enough to walk over. Everybody cheered and clapped when she started swaying to the music. Varsha closed her eyes and moved to the rhythm. Suddenly she tripped and found herself steadied by a stranger. He walked her to a chair close by and the both of them settled down. 'Would you like another drink?' he asked. 'Yeah, I'll get one,' she replied, standing up. He pushed her gently into the chair and said, 'Allow me, I'm going for a refill anyway.' He returned a while later and handing her her drink, he introduced himself. His name was Rajeev, he was twenty-two and worked night-shifts at a call centre. Tonight he had an 'off'. He was younger to her by three years; Varsha mentally calculated and said aloud, 'Oh, you're a bachcha.' 'Yes, auntyji,' he guffawed and she wasn't sure if he was joking. They chatted with ease and when he found that both of them lived in Chembur, he offered to drop her back. That suited her fine. In fact, it made things easier; Tripti wouldn't have to spend an extra thirty minutes driving. She walked to the dance floor and whispered to Tripti that she would find her own way back home. Tripti nodded and Varsha returned to her table and drink. She said to Rajeev, 'Have you noticed how one's spirit goes up as the spirit goes down.' He replied, 'As long as it's all in good spirit, who the fuck cares.' Yes indeed, she agreed and before long, they decided to leave.

On the drive back home, Varsha observed that Rajeev was quite good-looking. But like her ayah used to say, 'Even an ass looks good when he has youth on his side.' Rajeev had more than just youth, he also had a cool dress sense. He was dressed in a short white kurta paired with faded jeans. She admired his profile as he drove and her eyes wandered over his fit, lean body. She felt a faint stirring of desire, as if it was waking up from deep slumber. In no time, it had raised its ugly head. When he stopped the car on a remote street and kissed her, it didn't feel ugly at all. In fact, it was delicious. When his hand cupped her breast, she realised that she had forgotten what it felt like to be touched. Their tongues intertwined and she didn't know how or when he raised her skirt and stripped off her panty. When he penetrated her, they moved in perfect rhythm, bringing her to a climax, shudders of delight shaking her entire being. Only when he started the car, did she remember to tidy herself. They didn't exchange a word as he drove her home. She had told him earlier where she lived and he knew the apartment block. He had a cousin who lived nearby.

When she unlocked the door and walked into the bedroom she found Som fast asleep. She hurried into the bathroom for a quick shower. Standing under the running water, the entirety of the situation started sinking in. When the seriousness of what she had done hit her, she was jolted. She had committed adultery. Obviously, her body had a mind of its own. But it felt so good. To have sex without a care in the world. To touch and to be touched. To allow yourself to be drowned in waves of pleasure. To surrender to animalistic passion. In the next moment, a sense of shame pervaded her. She felt sickeningly guilty. Now, she had lost all right to be judgmental about her father. Once or several times. What did it matter? She had done exactly what she had stood against her entire life. Where had her values vanished? What was she thinking in the car? Well that was just it, she wasn't thinking. But the experience had awakened something she had forgotten she was capable of feeling. And despite the guilt, she still recalled the pleasure. Reminding her of the act she now so desperately wished to forget.

She walked back to her bed in a daze. She didn't know when sleep embraced her in all its warmth. She dreamt of Som making passionate love to her and felt waves of pleasure hitting her, drowning her. She woke for a fraction of a second and drifted back to sleep. This time—a dreamless one. Relaxed. Relieved. Rested.

Varsha woke up the next morning refreshed. Rejuvenated. As if a burden had been lifted off her shoulders. When she turned on her side and looked at Som however, the memories of the previous night came flooding back. Everything seemed like a dream. There had been something so erotic about doing it with her clothes on. The searching and touching. She never knew that she was capable of making love without being in love. She barely even knew the guy! Yet, the abandonment was exhilarating. Yes, it was sheer release that made her feel so refreshed. She lolled around in bed and got up reluctantly when she looked at the time. Varsha knew what the next couple of hours would be like—the both of them doing their own thing.

She found him knotting his tie when she came out of the bathroom. 'Listen, Som. There's something I need to tell you. We need to talk,' she said in a voice that didn't sound like hers. 'What?' he asked. She repeated herself, hating the uncomfortable scene. It made her seem like a complaining wife. He gave her a tolerant smile, which she resented and said, 'Not now, honey. I'm already late, will wind up early tonight. Got to run now.' And with that, he was off.

What on earth did she want to tell him now? Was she going to confess? She couldn't even imagine his response. Would he feel betrayed? And if he did, would he ask her for a divorce? God, it all felt so strange. So alien. How could she, of all people, who believed in staying committed, have strayed? She thought about her father. But her parents never had a healthy marriage in the first place. That's when it hit her that there was something drastically wrong with her marriage as well. It was not just about an errant woman and a neglectful husband. It went much deeper than that. They had drifted so far apart—physically and emotionally—that an extramarital affair was only natural. She wondered if Som had his needs met elsewhere too. Perhaps, that explained his preoccupation. Even if it happened to be true, Som wasn't the kind to confide in her. Whatever the outcome would be, she was prepared to face it. But it was time that they spoke to each other and sorted it out. Or not.

When she left home, she did not feel like driving and so decided to take the nine-thirty local. She put her car keys safely into the smallest zip of her bag and started walking, watching a couple of street urchins run ahead of her, happily and freely. Despite their poverty they looked like they had not a care in the world. Varsha sighed and walked faster. Before she actually got down to speaking her heart out to Som, she had a lot to deal with on her own. Should she tell him about last night? Once again she was clueless about her uncharacteristic behaviour. And the funniest thing was, she felt nothing about the man in question. Her partner in crime. It wasn't like she had felt particularly drawn to Rajeev when she saw him the first time. Strange. And now, she wasn't longing to meet him or any such thing. Lost in thoughts, she almost ran into a passing car. Whew! That was close, she gasped.

Later during the day, she received a call from her boss in Italy, Agnivesh, who owned the agency, telling her to expect his arrival soon in Mumbai. Agnivesh had started a small advertising agency, Sixth Sense, back in the 80s. He had moved to Italy after falling in love with Sylvia, an Italian, whose only condition to marrying him was that he move to her country. He had thus entrusted the agency to Varsha and moved to Florence a few years ago.

As things turned out, the agency had grown with an annual turnover of twenty-five crores since then. Agnivesh was proud of Varsha and made no attempt to hide it. She had discovered how casual a boss he was on the day of her interview itself. He was going through her CV when she entered the room. Gesturing for her to take a seat he said, 'Hey Varsha means rain, right? You know we're gonna have loads of fun. Me fire, you rain,' he guffawed and then continued, 'didn't you get it?' For a second she wondered if that was a pass. But that, as she discovered later, was the way he spoke to everybody. Yet, in his own way, he was a hard taskmaster. 'The bottom-line, my dear, always the bottom-line,' he would remind her though she didn't consider it her area of expertise. She had learnt the ropes of advertising from him and though her strength lay in creativity, she had succeeded in running the agency much better than he ever had. It would be good to see him. To show him how she had nurtured his baby. She wasn't sure, though, if she was in the right frame of mind at the moment. But 'duty comes first' like her mom would say whenever her daughter clung to her sari refusing to let her leave the house every morning. Varsha sighed as she left her room to inform the others of Agnivesh's arrival.

On her way back home after a long day of planning and discussing, she was once again confronted with her morning's dilemma—whether to tell her husband about her one-night stand. Oh god, how profane the expression sounded. But it was just that. In every sense of the word. She still couldn't come to terms with it. It had lasted all of fifteen minutes. And for that, should she be foolish enough to risk losing her marriage. But what kind of marriage was it? What had she got out of it?

'Hey, how come you're on the train today,' Anita, her neighbour, interrupted her thoughts. And they got talking. In the next forty-five minutes Anita spent forty talking about her husband and her two children. But beneath the cheerful chatter, Varsha sensed a deep dissatisfaction. When they parted, both women were relieved. One, for having found a listener and the other, for having been one.

'Wow,' Varsha thought as she inserted the key to unlock her door, 'women have an amazing knack of disguising sacrifices. Even to our own selves.' Out of choice or none. God alone knew and if He were a he, He probably wouldn't.

She switched on the lights and as usual, turned the CD player on. Elton John's soothing voice wafted through the room. She kept the bathroom door open so she could listen to music while she showered. 'Two hearts living, in two separate worlds,' she hummed as the warm water ran down her body. Varsha spent at least half an hour every evening in the tub and another fifteen minutes under the shower. She had little else to do. Music, shower, TV and dinner, not necessarily in the same order. But more or less. Day after day. Evening after evening. So she was jolted when she heard the music turned off abruptly. She heard Som's voice over the phone, and, heaving a sigh of relief, she slipped into her robe and got out, her hair dripping. Som was still on his mobile. For the rest of the evening she would have to mute the music or the TV depending on what was on when his cellphone rang while she had to turn a deaf ear to him yelling at some poor bloke over the phone. Come to think of it, despite cribbing that he never spent time at home, Varsha had gotten used to her space. Today, she decided to stand up against the intrusion. 'You can't turn off the music the moment you step in,' she protested, 'And if you have to keep talking on your phone, what's the point in coming home early?' 'Oh please, Varsha,' he said in a voice that was both impatient and irritated, 'Don't annoy me. I've had a long day at work.' As though *she* was at the club playing cards. But she decided to keep quiet, remembering her agenda for the night. She had better keep him in a good mood if she wanted him to listen to her. She felt like a dentist putting her patient at ease before extracting a tooth. But there was a difference. The dentist had it easier.

Varsha was a naturally optimistic person. Despite the depression she sometimes felt, her spirit usually remained unshaken. Besides she was a strong believer in communication. She felt that the lack of it was what had gone wrong in their marriage. She would put it right.

Or at least try. For starters she began with, 'What would you like for dinner?'

'What are you having?' he asked, loosening his tie.

'I'm rustling up some pasta with tomatoes and olives for myself. But I can make something else for you, if you like.'

'Hmm... sounds okay to me. Would you mind adding some chicken to it?'

'Not at all. In fact, that's a great idea.'

Som walked into the bath while she got busy with dinner. When she was younger, she had an image in her mind of a husband who would be more of a friend, laughing with her, sharing her chores and generally having fun together. But Som rarely ever walked into the kitchen except when he wanted something that wasn't on the table. Even that happened only when he was home in the evenings. Which was rare.

In about thirty minutes both were out of the kitchen and the shower respectively. Varsha poured wine into fluted glasses, a gift from Maya on her wedding day, and placed them on the centre table. She sank into the sofa and stretched, yawning, a little nervous. Som emerged in his nightclothes and occupied the chair to her right. It creaked as he sat. Varsha switched on the music system to lighten the mood. Normally, there was noise outside, cars passing by, people out for their evening walk, but today was unusually silent. 'So, how was your day?' she enquired. 'Oh, the usual,' he said, sipping the wine. 'There he goes again,' she thought, 'his one-line responses.' But she couldn't afford to let pride or his preoccupation come in the way now. She was determined to get it off her chest and get it over with. 'Som, I need to tell you something. A confession, actually.' He arched his eyebrows and knotted them in quick succession. After a moment he gestured, asking her to go on. He quietly sipped his wine. 'Last night...I was unfaithful. Don't ask me how...I don't know how it happened. There's not much I've figured out. Honestly I don't know what to think even now...but if you want to know why, I think I have the answer,' she blurted in one breath. Som bent his head looking lost. This was getting more difficult than she thought. Why can't he say something? Anything. Five minutes passed in deepening silence and Varsha felt she could slice through it with a knife. And then all of a sudden he spoke, his head still bent. 'Okay, now that you've said it, I've done it too. So that makes two of us.' Something in the way he said that struck her like a whiplash. For a minute, she sat stunned and pale, her lips parted. Then it sunk in. 'So what are you suggesting, huh?' she asked, 'That we call it quits and pretend nothing happened. Or that we have an open marriage and continue sharing our bed while we sleep with others.'

'Yeah. Something like that.'

An overwhelming shock assaulted her senses, her head spun but she managed to get a grip on herself and say, 'Have you ever wondered why you or I did this?'

He said nothing and stared at her coldly.

'Tell me Som, please. I need to know what's going on in your head,' she pleaded.

'Well, what do you think?' he questioned back as was his usual strategy.

'I seriously think we've drifted apart. And we need to act now if we want to save our marriage.'

'I think we've reached a point of no return,' and he said it with such finality that it almost sounded like a judge's verdict.

'When did you realise this?' she asked, tears pouring down her cheeks.

'Just now when you told me that you had strayed.'

'What?? It was okay when you did it. But now that I've confided in you, you're shifting the blame on to me. And what if I hadn't told you? Like you chose not to tell.'

'Listen Varsha, this is the reason I'm afraid to talk to you. You keep dissecting, analysing everything. I really don't know how to react when you do that. It really annoys me. You're too bloody serious about everything. Just relax, okay. We can continue with our lives the way we have been doing, if you want to.'

'And what about you? If you could have it your way, what w you prefer?'

He shrugged indifferently. 'One way or another make difference to me.'

'What do you mean?'

'It's up to you what you make of it. Just don't get after me all these questions.'

By then Varsha was hysterical and Som did not attempt comfort her. Nor did he say anything. She curled up on the sofa l she couldn't bear the weight of her body anymore and sobb uncontrollably. Much as she tried, she simply couldn't stop cryi Finally she exhausted herself. She didn't even realise that he had le Leaving her behind to deal with the pieces that not so long ago w their marriage. She was lying on the sofa in the dark, when So returned and walked into the bedroom without glancing at her.

Varsha was shattered. She would have been better off withou making the confession. Or attempting to have the conversation. A this time she fretted about their lack of things to talk about, yet tha conversation was the final straw for their marriage. She knew it had reached a dead end. There was no way out.

She had noticed that he was always preoccupied. But she had put that down to the way he was. Sometimes his work. But now she understood that he didn't love her. Where could she have gone wrong? Was she too serious? Isn't that what he'd said? And even if he felt that way, why hadn't he told her. It did not justify him being unfaithful to her. She had been so carefree last night. Was that what had attracted Rajeev to her? Despite the fact that she was much older. So that was what men wanted. A lighthearted, no strings-attached fling.

But she couldn't figure out Som's indifference. Had she not initiated tonight's conversation, he would probably not have told her what he felt. Ever. And they would have lived like countless other married couples. Sharing their home without caring for each other.

She couldn't understand how anybody could lead such an existence. Or is that how all men were? She had seen two in her life. Her father and now, her husband. Perhaps they were all the same.

She couldn't believe that she had committed herself to a man who would eventually turn their marriage into one which her parents had. Exactly what she had always run away from. And in that realisation, she felt a sudden surge of sympathy for her mother. How long had it taken for her to see through her father? Now she understood her mother's compulsive need to work. Still, it was difficult for her to come to terms with the fact that Som didn't care for her. And that she had chosen him. Thank God, she hadn't had his child. And she had only him to thank. Thank you Som for big mercies!

Chapter 7

A MONTH LATER, VARSHA MOVED OUT OF THEIR APARTMENT into a flat on the ground floor of a building that she found closer to her office. She emailed Agnivesh saying that she needed official accommodation, something he had offered her when she joined. Now, she was within walking distance of her work place. This flat was hers alone. When Varsha informed Som that she was moving out, he had told her that 'it was her decision.' And like always she didn't understand what he meant. But now she was beyond caring. All she wanted was to get out of a place that was becoming more oppressive with every passing day. She moved in haste that weekend, with her things bundled up in a tempo. All the same she felt odd leaving. She had lived in Chembur ever since first arriving in the city. Chembur had meant home. Part of her was relieved, yet she felt like crying. She wondered what women who had no choice did in a situation like this. And what about those who had a choice and didn't exercise it? Like her mother. But she supposed *that* was a decision too.

After she moved, Varsha's days went by in a daze. She woke up, ate, worked and the cycle continued. Office seemed more a respite than an occupation. An escape from herself and her morbid thoughts. For a while, Tripti tried asking her about what happened but when Varsha didn't open up, she stopped. These days, like Tripti, her other colleagues too left her alone.

Sometimes she felt that her life had ended with her marriage. She thought of Som often and wondered whether he was happy. Did he miss her? But she knew that he didn't care. He hadn't bothered to call even once to find out how she was doing. If she was still alive. As far as he was concerned, it was as though she didn't exist. And that hurt. Like hell. She called him once. At his house, which was once their home. She heard the phone ring and it felt so strange. That night, she cried herself to sleep after downing more than one tranquiliser. When she awoke, the pillow was wet. She was alone. It was midnight. The rest of the night she spent listening to music. Music had always played a big part in her life. It made her happy and soothed her when she was sad. Even as a child, she would hum tunes she heard on the radio. Sometimes a tune would stick in her head. Like it had possessed her. To get rid of it she had to latch onto another tune. Music always cured her of depression, unfailingly. But of late, even music seemed to have lost its magic.

Why do people you love the most also happen to be the people who hurt you? By loving them you gave them a license to hurt you. It wasn't fair. Everything around her seemed so unreal, as if she was looking at the world through frosted glass. She was also suspicious of the people she spoke to. When somebody asked 'So what are you up to these days?' it sounded like 'You poor thing, living all alone.' She flinched when they remarked, 'You must be relatively free now, why don't you drop in?' She never bothered to reply and didn't venture out either. Sometimes she enjoyed this total disassociation with life. At other times she felt it was all quite pathetic. Nothing was as it seemed. Nobody meant what they said.

Mumbai was supposed to be a city where no one had time for others. But in her case, everybody who knew her had come to know about the split. Despite having lived here for five years, Varsha could neither understand Mumbai nor come to terms with it. Her mother had told her when she was moving to the city, 'You're going to either love it or hate it but you can't be indifferent to it.' It was true, in many ways. The city had more life and lights than Bangalore. More poverty and slums. More people and many more things to do. Everything in excess. Moderation seemed to have no meaning in Mumbai. The crowd at her office was an example, they travelled, worked, drank, partied, excessively. They were so exhausted by the time they got to bed that they couldn't sleep. When she was new to the city, after a few exhilarating days Varsha was a wreck. Not like she wasn't having fun but most of the time she swung between awe and contempt. She preferred Bangalore. It was home.

She hadn't broken the news yet to her mother. She didn't even know how she would react.

What Varsha didn't know was that Som had called Revati Rao the same evening she had moved out. 'Mummy, it's my responsibility to let you know that Varsha and I are no longer together. She left this morning to live on her own.'

When Varsha did finally call after a month, Revati Rao had almost forgotten about the whole thing. 'Mom, I need to tell you something,' Varsha said. Revati wondered what it could be but suddenly the conversation she'd had with Som flashed into her mind. She knew what it was from the tiredness in her voice. 'Don't tell me what Som told me is true,' she asked in disbelief. So he had already told her. And her mom hadn't even bothered to call. But that was too much to expect. Ms Revati Rao, the dynamic MP-turned-minister, to have time for something as inane as a failed marriage. Even if it happened to be her daughter's. Varsha hung up after muttering something incoherent. Som had considered it final enough to let her mother know and she hadn't bothered to find out how Varsha was coping. But after the mockery they had made of their marriage, nothing really mattered, especially relationships. If it did, it would only to Maya. Her best friend. Their friendship was the first casualty of her marriage. They had tried to stay in touch through emails but even those had become sporadic. She picked up the phone to call her and decided against it. Poor thing had been through her own hell. She had no business to add her share to it. But she knew at some point she would have to confide in her. On an impulse, she decided to visit Hyderabad, stay over at her place and speak to her personally. There was no better alternative to a face-to-face.

Varsha called Agnivesh to get the specifics of his visit. No, he wasn't arriving all that soon, in fact he would only land in January. That gave her two whole months. So she told him that she needed a break and that she was taking a holiday. Pronto. He was cool with it saying that she deserved it after having worked so hard. Next, she met with Tripti to brief her about the agency's schedule for the coming fortnight that she planned to be away. And then she called Maya to check if it was okay with her. 'Okay? You moron. That's great news, it'll be amazing to see you again,' Maya spoke with unconcealed excitement, 'I had almost given up on you, didn't think I'd hear from you ever again.' 'Don't say that,' Varsha pleaded, 'There's a lot going on in my life. And I need you.' 'What's wrong?' said Maya, sounding concerned. 'We'll talk when I get there. Will you come to the airport to pick me up?' Maya took down the details of her flight assuring her that she would be there.

After Varsha hung up she wondered...was there a lot going on in her life like she had told Maya? Whatever was going on, had ended. Now, there was nothing at all.

All the way on the flight to Hyderabad, Varsha could hardly sit still and contain her excitement. There was something about shared childhoods, a certain comfort that came with growing up together that nothing else could compare with. Maya and her knew most things about each other. Their tests and triumphs, each one's little quirks. It would be fun to see her after so long.

An hour and a half later she landed at Hyderabad. Entering the airport, she saw Maya waving at her. She stood at the conveyor belt to collect her luggage thinking, wow! She looked so lovely and fresh. 'You're looking great,' Varsha screamed much to the amusement of everyone else. Most of them turned to look at Varsha's object of admiration. Maya was so embarrassed. Varsha, she thought, hasn't changed at all. Except that she looked plumper. And much too pale. Like the colour had drained off her cheeks. But then Mumbai had a strange way with people. Some bloomed. Some withered. Now that she was here, they would have a blast. And Maya would make sure some colour came back to her face. Like Varsha often said, Maya was the mother hen of the two. Looking out for her friend. Varsha, on her part, had provided her the much-needed support when her parents had died. And Maya could never forget that.

They hugged for so long that it seemed almost suffocating to onlookers but they were soaking in the warmth and comfort of each other's presence. 'So good to see you' both of them said at the same time and giggled. In the half-hour cab ride, Varsha asked questions. How did she like her new job? Had she settled down properly? What was it like living alone? And Maya answered. Then Varsha stopped. There was a sudden silence. Conversations with Varsha, Maya had experienced in the past, were like getting on an escalator. You could never get off half-way. And the end was always abrupt. That hadn't changed even now. She told her that. Varsha laughed and held her hand tightly.

Maya knew instinctively that something was not right. But there was enough time to find out. To share. To listen. To understand. Right now it was enough to just hold hands.

The next morning Varsha awoke to find her friend all dressed and ready to leave. 'Where you going?' she enquired, still groggy. She had had a good night's sleep after what seemed like ages. She never realised when she was living with Som, how accustomed she had become to sharing her bed. In the last three weeks of living alone, the toughest parts were the nights. She had forgotten how it was to have the entire bed to herself. That's when Tripti had suggested downing a tranquiliser to soothe her nerves. Last night was the first time she hadn't realised when she dozed off. They were talking until midnight before sleep lulled their conversation.

'To work, sweetie,' Maya smiled as she replied.

'Don't tell me I've come all this way to spend time with myself. That's exactly what I was doing in Mumbai in any case.'

'Why, where was Som?'

'Well, that's not quite the problem now. The problem is, in the next fortnight how much time are you going to spend with me? You should have told me when I called you that you were going to be busy.'

'Listen stupid, don't get upset. You have to understand this is my first job. I've just about completed my orientation. Hang on for a day. Tomorrow, I promise I'll take you with me wherever I go.'

'Like I want to follow you. Maya has a little lamb, little lamb... please count me out.'

'Listen to me. I'm going to be touring Hyderabad, exploring and understanding its history. Can you imagine what fun that'll be?'

'You mean, Charminar, Golconda and stuff?'

'Yes, that too.'

'Hmm...that sounds pretty cool actually.'

'See, I told you, you impatient woman.'

'But, that's tomorrow. What about today? Now?'

'What you do is chill. Just relax today. Put your feet up. I picked up some great Suzanne Vega CDs. Check her out. She's damn good. In any case, by the time you wake up and have a bath, I'll be back for lunch. I've made your favourite bisibele today. For now, there's some bread in the kitchen. Pop it into the toaster if you get hungry. Okay, now I have to go. My boss is a stickler for time and I'm already ten minutes behind schedule.' With that she gave her friend a kiss on the cheek and rushed out.

Varsha sat on the bed staring blankly at the dressing-table mirror in front her. The silence was so refreshing. Unlike the ever-present noise in Mumbai. The city never slept! After a while of doing absolutely nothing and with no schedule to keep, Varsha got out of bed and walked into the living-room. Maya had done it up quite well. Simple but elegant. The furniture was all cane and wicker including the bed, the diwan, the side-lamps and even the dustbins. The upholstery was in beige and maroon pochampally fabric, with curtains to match. She walked back into the bedroom, put on the CD Maya had recommended, and went into the bathroom. It was quite airy and spacious. She let the water run for a while in the tub and then plugged it. In about five minutes it was filled with warm, inviting water. She threw in some bath salts she found on the ledge, dipped her hand in and stirred, letting the bubbles form. She slipped into the tub, stretched herself and closed her eyes. When was the last time she had actually enjoyed a bath like this? She couldn't remember. She wondered why humans closed their eyes when they found a sensation pleasurable. Like when they pray, kiss or make love. Was it to shut off all the other senses to make the pleasure more intense? Or last longer. Her eyes still closed, she listened to the music that was coming from the bedroom. Maya was right. The singer did have an amazing voice. She soaked in the warmth of the water, it was comforting, almost maternal. Finally when the water turned quite tepid she reluctantly got out of the tub. Her skin was tingling, like it had come alive after a long spell of numbness. She towelled herself dry and reached for a bottle of body-lotion placed in front of the mirror. She helped herself to a generous dose and spread it evenly, rubbing it in until it disappeared. When she reached her breasts and massaged them gently, an uncontrollable desire overtook her. For the next five minutes she was blind to everything else except her fingers that sought and found her softest spot instinctively, arousing herself until it gushed and turned soft again. What relief! Her thoughts turned to that one night as she washed her hands mechanically. God! It had aroused passions in her that had been dormant for years. She was never like this before. She hadn't ever brought herself to a climax, even as a teenager. Now, at twenty-six, she had discovered that she could provide such pleasure to herself. What had happened to her? Whatever it was, it had a lot to do with that one-night stand. With Som, sex was predictable, almost boring. To add to that she had never been good at undressing. She was convinced, for some reason, that she was better off with her clothes on. She needed a lot of reassurance, which Som never displayed or had patience for. So it was one of those lights off, hands-on quickies. None of their sessions had lasted more than five, seven minutes, she was sure. Sometimes when the music was on, their mating ended before a song did. But she had been okay with it. She had never found anything wrong with the fact that she rarely, if she ever did, climaxed when they made love. In the last one year, of course, it had become more of a chore than anything else. Some nights, when she had felt that they *ought* to do it, she dressed in his favourite black lacy lingerie and walked around suggestively. She had felt stupid after doing it a few times when he hadn't bothered to raise his eyes up from the TV to look at her. After she abandoned that effort, nothing remotely sexual had transpired between the two of them. But then, he had said it, hadn't he, that her seriousness put him off. So what were his other sexual experiences with 'non-serious' women like? Smouldering? Passionate? Somehow she couldn't picture Som even enjoying sex, least of all being passionate. She remembered that he remained silent all through. Maybe he was turned on by women on top. Her imagination turned graphic and she chided herself, 'Whatever!' Why was she beginning to think on those lines again? NO, she had to put an end to obsessing over him and get on with life. Anything she thought somehow led to him. And *that* was driving her crazy.

She was still in her bathrobe, drying her hair, when she heard the doorbell ring. Maya walked in when she opened the door and said, 'And here I was guilty and all for having left you alone. Look at you, madam, busy indulging in the Cleopatra act.'

'Oh, I pampered myself with a long bath,' Varsha replied, 'After ages, you know.'

'Good, good, I'm so glad you weren't bored,' said Maya, wondering, after a second, when she had picked up the 'good, good' phrase from Professor Hai.

'Listen child, I'm starving.'

'Why, didn't you have breakfast?'

'No, I was too busy having a bath.'

'I don't believe that.'

'Okay, I grabbed your neighbour and made mad, passionate love to him and now I'm ravenous. Satisfied?'

'How can I be the one satisfied when it was you who rolled about in bed? In any case, my neighbour is Madhav, a podgy divorcee who's not your type. Also, he lives a kilometre away.'

They helped themselves to delicious bisibele huli anna, piping hot from the microwave oven and attacked it with a vengeance.

'You know what Maya, the guy you're gonna marry is one lucky bastard. You cook amazingly and you're a wonderful listener, what more would a man want? Even though I'm no authority to speak on the subject. I have no clue what a man wants.'

'Why, Som keeps you guessing, does he? By the way, I've been meaning to ask you, how is he?'

'Who knows? And who cares?'

'Hey,' quizzed Maya, taking the plate from Varsha and putting it away in the sink, 'What's the matter?'

'Long story, darling.'

Maya wrapped her arms around Varsha, held her for a second, and said, 'Listen, Varsha, I knew there was something wrong. We'll talk about it when I get back, okay. Now, just put your feet up and relax. I'll see you in the evening and we're going to talk.'

Varsha instantly felt better.

When Maya left, Varsha shut the door behind her and went back to Suzanne Vega. She put her feet up, literally, like Maya had recommended, in the little verandah behind the house. The sun shone in a clear blue sky. The weather was beautiful. She could see the Flame of the Forest and the red and white bougainvillea in full bloom in the distance. Maya was lucky to have found a job that offered her such a nice place to live in. She hadn't been into the university yet but from what she could see the buildings were old-fashioned, high-roofed, architectural delights. But here, it seemed so quiet, so far removed from the hustle and bustle of a busy student campus. She was glad she had taken this break. It was doing her a lot of good. The rest, lack of schedule and the knowledge that at the end of the day she had someone she could relate to, talk to, confide in. Tonight, she would pour her heart out to Maya. And she knew that it would unburden her to a great extent. She could have tolerated anything from Som but his silence. If he had only told her what he felt, she would have understood.

Varsha remembered winning a debate in college, speaking against 'The eloquence of silence'. The root cause of all problems in the world, at a macro and micro level, she had argued, was a lack of communication. Nothing could be achieved if people remained quiet and kept their feelings to themselves! Everything was possible if only we could learn to communicate our thoughts and feelings to people who matter. But in the end, it was a conversation between Som and her that had dealt the final blow. She smiled sardonically at life's ironies. Now just the thought of having someone to converse with was comforting enough for her.

~

Chapter 8

When her son-in-law called to inform her that Varsha had left home, Revati Rao hadn't probed. It sounded like they were having a tiff. And which marriage didn't have problems, she rationalised. That's what made it exciting—the quarrels, the making up, the agony, the ecstasy, the highs and the lows. It proved that there was life in the relationship. Unlike hers. It had been ages since she and her husband had communicated except during public appearances.

Revati Rao was disappointed when her daughter married so young. In the dreams she had for her daughter's life, she had seen marriage as a long way off. She was sure that Varsha had a bright future ahead given her talents and intelligence and was disappointed when Varsha failed to display any burning ambitions. But perhaps if she truly thought about it she had only visualised that future in terms of a political career. Her mother had always seen her as her political heir. But she had not been aware of it until now. What a deeply buried, unrealistic dream. How unfair to expect another individual to tow your line. But in the case of your child—how tempting.

But somewhere deep within her she was also happy that her daughter found what she never did. Love. But then hers had been an arranged marriage. Her daughter was in love. So it didn't rattle her too much when Som called to give her the news. Nor had she bothered to share it with her husband. These days she couldn't even bear to breathe the same air as he did but her political career gave her no such privileges. She had to put on an act no matter what.

But now after listening to Varsha, she realised that the situation was pretty serious. She wanted to speak to her, tell her that she always had her mother's support no matter what but Varsha had ended the call abruptly. When she called her back, there was no response. She tried her office the next day and Tripti had informed her that Varsha was on leave for a fortnight. She hadn't told anybody where she was headed. Revati Rao was worried. Where could she have gone? Back to Som? No, if she knew her daughter well enough, when Varsha made up her mind, she really made up her mind. The trouble was—she didn't know if she knew her daughter at all.

Even as a child, Varsha had always evoked feelings of guilt in her. As she grew up, she displayed so much resentment towards her parents that Revati could never muster up enough courage to talk to her. What could she say anyway? That her mother and father didn't respect each other? That her mother abhorred having sex with her father and therefore didn't care if he found pleasure outside? That her mother felt trapped in a marriage that had no exit? Or that she had been in love with a spineless man before marriage who couldn't defy his parents? What could she have told her? And how? Revati was not very comfortable demonstrating affection. Nor was she confident that she could convey her feelings to her daughter. She was a good orator in public. In fact, she had risen rapidly in her political career because of her excellent oratory skills. However, when it came to expressing her emotions she always found herself speechless. She had expressed her love, her fears, her insecurities, only once in life and that man had abandoned and betrayed her.

Perhaps, if Varsha had stayed home longer she would have spoken to her daughter, woman-to-woman, in the course of time. But she had been in a hurry to get married. And that had removed all hope of making her daughter a confidante. And now, it was too late. Or was it? Probably not. Now that her daughter had experienced marriage and its complexities, perhaps she would be more receptive to her mother's side of the story. She may even empathise with it. There was hope, after all. But where had she disappeared and where could she find her?

She kept thinking into the wee hours of the morning when she remembered Maya. Yes, there was one person Varsha turned to in times of need. The two had been inseparable before Varsha's marriage. Maya had called her a month or so ago to inform her about her new job at Osmania University. But she hadn't asked her for her contact number. Nor had Maya volunteered to give it. But it wasn't all that difficult a task to track her down. All she needed to do was tell her PA and it would be done in no time. Yes, she decided, that was a good idea and her only choice.

The next morning Revati Rao called Devraj, her PA. 'I need the information by tonight, Devraj, it's really important that you find her number as soon as possible,' she ordered. She trusted him to do the needful. He was pretty efficient compared to the others in her secretariat. Most of them had started out by not taking her seriously because she was a woman. Revati Rao had shown them how wrong they were to think that. She lamented the fact that there were very few women in politics. If every educated, intelligent person considered politics only as the last resort for a scoundrel, what would become of the country? She had wanted her daughter to consider politics as a career option but Varsha had decided to carve out her own niche, leaving her mother proud yet rather disappointed. But then disappointments were a way of life for her and to let them linger for longer than necessary would be accepting the defeat of her strong will. And she wasn't willing to let her daughter's choice affect her anymore. Now, the scene had changed. She wouldn't let Varsha wilt with a lack of direction if her marriage had failed. What would be the use of her status, her position, of her as a mother, if she couldn't be there for her daughter when things were going wrong? This was the time for her to prove that she cared. Perhaps someday Varsha would understand what her life had been all about. And that, she hoped, would happen soon.

Devraj managed to track Maya down in less than half a day. Revati Rao stared at the piece of paper that had her number on it. She resisted dialling right away. First, she had to think of what to say to her daughter. And if she called and Varsha wasn't there, what would she tell Maya? How should she begin the conversation? Would her concern sound unconvincing? She went over what she should say...what she shouldn't get into was a battle of wills. And she must make it clear that she was there for her. She knew it wasn't going to be easy but she had to begin somewhere.

She picked up the phone and dialled quickly, as though she may change her mind. It started ringing and she held the receiver to her ear for at least five minutes. There was no answer. But she waited patiently.

Varsha awoke with a jolt when she heard the phone ringing. It took a while to orient herself and run inside. She picked the phone up, dropping it from the little wooden table it was placed on. She grabbed hold of the instrument, balancing the receiver between her right ear and shoulder. Before she could say hello, the line disconnected with an abrupt click. God! How frustrating! After all she had gone through! She knew it was a long-distance call from its single ring. Who could it be? Probably somebody from Bangalore for Maya. Cursing the caller for not hanging on for another second, she headed towards the basin to splash her face with some cold water. Her appetite for food, sex and sleep seemed to have risen in a day of being away from Mumbai, she thought. Just as she turned on the tap, the phone began ringing again. She closed it in a hurry and grabbed the receiver screaming an angry 'Hello' into the mouthpiece. On the other end, Revati Rao was dumbfounded for a second when she heard her daughter's voice. She regained composure and said gently, though nervously, 'Varsha?'

Varsha was shocked. The call had come out of the blue and her mother's voice had never sounded like that before. 'Mom? How did you know I was here?' she asked, perplexed.

'I've been looking for you all over the place after you hung up the day before yesterday. Where have you been?'

'Oh, it didn't occur to me to inform you. It's not like you and I are in the habit of telling each other about our movements and whereabouts. I've travelled countless times without your knowledge and so have you. So, what's the matter mom?'

'What do you mean what's the matter? *I* should be asking you that. I've been worried after what you told me and you're asking me what the matter is!'

'Oh mom, don't try this new strategy now. Since when have you begun thinking about me? Don't tell me you've been ousted from your ministerial berth or something? Why this sudden show of concern, pray, tell me,' she said sounding bitter, much as she wanted not to.

'Varsha, I know it may not have seemed this way...' Revati paused, not knowing how to go on, as usual finding it difficult to say what she felt, 'but it's not true that I don't care for you. Who else do I have in the world?'

'You tell me, mom, why you didn't feel the need to even call me when Som informed you so dutifully about our split?'

'Well, to be honest, I thought it was just one of those tiffs married couples have. I didn't think it was anything major.'

'Uh-huh. And when was the last time Som or I confided in you about any matter between us?'

'Never.'

'How could you even think that one of us would call you over a minor lover's quarrel?'

'I'm sorry, Varsha. That's true. I didn't think about that honestly. I know you're hurt. But the truth is, this time, like all the other times in the past, you've misunderstood me.'

'Oh mom, come off it. I've never understood you in the first place. So where's the question of misunderstanding you?'

'Will you give me one chance, just one more chance, please?' Revati pleaded.

Something in her mother's voice calmed Varsha down. 'What do you want me to do, mama?' she asked, less harshly. Revati was ecstatic—her daughter had called her 'mama' the way she used to when she was a child. When her love was unadulterated by adult complexities.

That was good enough for a beginning. Enthused, she said, 'Why don't you come home, Varsha? It would be so nice to have you back. This time, I promise, I'll make it up to you.'

Varsha found it strange, her mother pleading like a child. 'Let me see how things go, mama,' she responded, 'I'll try. But I can't tell you when. Right now, Maya and I are catching up on each other's lives and it hasn't even been a day since I've been here. I'll call you when I get back to Mumbai, okay.'

'As you wish, my baby,' Revati said before hanging up, 'But remember, I'm always there for you.'

Revati Rao felt an enormous sense of relief as she hung up. It hadn't been as difficult as she thought it would be. In fact, saying that she cared and showing that she did took a great deal of effort but it was worth it.

Varsha placed the phone back in its cradle and stood there like she was rooted to the ground. Her mind was blank. Numb.

Later in the evening after she had narrated her tale between tears and sobs, she told Maya about her mother's phone call. 'I don't know what to make of it. Seriously,' she said. Maya listened to her attentively. Maya always did.

She said, 'There's no need to make anything out of it. Just understand that your mother cares for you. Listen to me; every relationship goes through its own stages before hurting or comforting the people who are involved in it.'

'Just what do you mean by that? Your philosophy always leaves me feeling profane. And Som thinks I'm the serious one. He should have met you before he met me. I would have paled in comparison.'

'You know what, Varsha, from the time you finished telling me about Som, this is the *nth* time you're mentioning him. What is it with you? Let him go. Unless you do that, you won't move on. You can't. Talking endlessly about situations you can't change is pointless. And I think you're going overboard. Stop now unless you want it to become an obsession.'

'I know. I'll try. To be honest, I'm doing far better than last month. You should have seen me then. You know what I've understood from this disaster?'

'What?'

'Every man wants these glossy, glamourous women with no problems. Easy-going and fun. An entertaining companion with no demands on his time or attention. Everything's perfect until you start asking for more than what he condescends to give you.'

'God, you sound so cynical.'

'On the contrary, I've just turned practical. Realistic.'

'Not all men are like that, I'm sure.'

'How would you know?'

'Well, you can't generalise. I've seen my father. And you haven't forgotten Gautam, I hope, my first boyfriend. I wouldn't have broken up with him if he hadn't wanted to get married. And even then he understood. I broke his heart yet he respected my feelings. And if you think I didn't hurt, you're mistaken. It doesn't matter if you've rejected or you're rejected. The pain is the same. Sometimes, more for the person who has done the rejecting. There was no mud-slinging or name-calling. We parted like friends who knew the other was right.'

'Oh, one romantic liaison with an uncomplicated fella doesn't qualify you to speak on the man clan.'

'Yeah, right. Just a while ago you were saying "how would you know" and now you're disqualifying me totally. Lemme make one thing clear, I'm not speaking for or against men. I'm just saying that you can't make such sweeping statements about anybody. Even if certain characteristics may be similar, characters aren't. Anyway, I don't think Som treated you like a plaything. He wouldn't have married you, if he did so.'

'I didn't say Som treated me like a plaything. He didn't ever treat me like anything! I didn't even exist for him. Forget it babe, why are we getting into this? It'll lead us nowhere. And he's not worth it. Someday you'll understand what I'm saying. Until then, you stick to your point of view and I'll stick to mine. And thanks for arguing with me...I'd forgotten what it was like to talk. Can you believe that? In the last three years, I haven't had a conversation except in office.'

Maya's heart went out to her friend. She moved closer and held her. What vague expectations people have, Maya thought, to realise that you want something and on finding it, to see that that was not what you wanted. Oh how complicated! Varsha was the same. And probably Som hadn't changed either. What had changed was their relationship and how it served them. It had served them well, then. It no longer served their purpose, now. So simple. So transparent. Why do people fail to see it? If only Varsha realised that both of them had simply stopped defining each other. That their relationship no longer provided them the fulfilment they needed now. Only a relationship that helps someone realise himself or herself works. Because, for a person, nothing comes before the self.

If only Varsha would stop being so cynical. Why do people feel this need to portray the other in an uncomplimentary light when something they share no longer works? Perhaps they mourn the loss, maybe it was disappointment for not having found what they were looking for. But do they even know what they're looking for? That one night she had shared with a stranger only made her aware of herself. Conscious of her desires, leading to their realisation. Finally, everything boils down to that one term. Desires, needs, emotions, ecstasy ... every word and experience leads to just that—self-realisation.

Varsha rested her head on her friend's shoulder and closed her eyes.'Maya, if only you knew how badly hurt I was...how much effort it took to survive a day.'

The next morning Varsha joined Maya for her jog in the garden. Madhav was there already, warming up. Maya introduced them and Madhav said, 'Oh, so you guys have been friends since you were kids, huh? How wonderful. I had a best friend too when I was in school. His name was Rajesh. I wonder where he is now. I still remember everything about him. His dad got transferred and I never saw him again.' Maya had always noticed the animation with which people spoke of their past, their youth or their childhood. But Madhav was different. He lived in his past. For every person you spoke about, he had one of his own. For every experience you narrated, he had several equivalents. 'So are you married?' he asked Varsha. She was taken aback and couldn't figure out how anybody could get so personal in their first meeting. It takes all kinds, she thought and replied 'Technically, yes.'

'You sound like I used to when my wife fell in love with her colleague,' he said and went on to narrate his sob story. Maya had moved away since she had an idea of what would ensue but from the expression on her face, Varsha seemed to be quite taken in. She was adding her own cynical two-bits. Towards the end of the exercise session, Maya felt like she was the newcomer. Nevertheless, she was happy that her friend was distracted from her misery. Albeit temporarily. Madhav accompanied them back to Maya's quarters and invited himself for coffee. At such times, Maya and Varsha would have normally burst out laughing but the seriousness with which he spoke kept them silent.

'How come?' Maya enquired, 'Do you have time? Won't you be late for work?'

'No. Is that a hint?' Madhav asked trying to sound amusing while following them into the house.

'No I mean it. Because I will be, if I don't leave in thirty minutes. That's just about enough to bathe, pray and eat...for me at least.'

'No. Well, I don't pray and my first hour is free today.'

'Oh okay, make yourself comfortable. Varsha, please look after our guest. While you're at it, make me a cup too, sweetie, please. I gotta rush now.'

'So how long have you been divorced?' What the heck, Varsha thought, if he can take the liberty of asking her, why shouldn't she?

'It's been three years, six months and fifteen days.'

'Wow, talk about precision. Is your memory always that good?'

'No. Not really. To be honest, I don't remember what I had for dinner last night but somehow all the memories of my marriage and the end of it have stuck on.'

'I know what you mean. What went wrong?'

'I don't know…I'm still trying to figure it out. Everything was fine. At least that's what I thought. I was happy or rather blissfully unaware. Rama and I have a lovely daughter. And then one day, out of the blue, she tells me that it's over. And that she's in love with her colleague.'

At that point Maya walked out of the bedroom, fresh and fragrant, and said goodbye, grinning broadly at Varsha.

'Come on Maya. Have some coffee,' Madhav offered, as though she was the guest. Maya found it rather funny. Varsha asked, 'So what's the POA ma'am?'

Maya spoke in between taking hurried gulps of hot coffee, 'Listen, I'll come by at about twelve. You better be through with your bath by then, Cleopatra. We'll have lunch outside and head to the old city. Professor Hai will be joining us. Okay, I'm off now.'

'Yes, your majesty. Will do,' replied Varsha.

'I like the way you girls talk,' said Madhav, 'you know I suddenly realised now that Rama had no women friends. I wonder why.'

'You mean you had never noticed it in all those years of marriage!'

'No.'

'Don't you find that strange?'

'No, but now that you're mentioning it, yes, it does.'

There it was. The indifference. For all that interest he was showing in her, a stranger, he hadn't even noticed that his wife hadn't had female friends. Wow! Good for Rama that she found her soulmate elsewhere. What was it about marriage that made men behave the way they did? Deciding to treat it like an academic study, she probed further.

'Did you love each other?'

'I loved her. I don't know about her actually. I presume she did. Why else did she have my child?'

Momentary lust, for instance, she thought. Lust could happen anywhere, anytime. Sometimes even with your spouse! Pregnancy then happened by chance.

Aloud, she said, 'You actually believe children all over the world are born out of love! And women bearing their partner's children do it because of love. Come on, you can do better than that.'

'No. Believe me, she gave me no indication that she wasn't in love with me. Why else would she have married me?'

'Let's not assume here. Did she ever tell you that she loved you?'

'No. Come to think of it, only once or twice.'

'And you?'

'What about me?'

'Did you tell her that you loved her?'

'No, umm... yeah. I guess I did.'

'You mean, you don't remember!'

'No. Well, I did, several times before we got married.'

'I'm talking of after marriage,' she persisted.

'No. I mean yes. On the day she delivered our daughter I told her I loved her. But honestly speaking, why do women want men to say everything. Why can't they understand that love's not just about saying "I love you". It's much more than just that.'

' Like...'

'Like putting up with moods, tantrums, insecurities, illnesses and what not?'

'I agree, but life is so mundane in its very nature that both partners have to make an effort to show each other how much they care. And what better way than putting it into words? Besides, what's in a marriage if there is no conversation and laughter? At least that's how I feel.'

'No. I guess you're right. In retrospect I do feel that I should have been more open about my feelings. But by the time I realised it, it was much too late. Rama had already gotten involved elsewhere. When I saw them together once, I realised how happy she was. Her husband... god...I still find it difficult to say that, is a very confident person. When people are comfortable with themselves, they're comfortable with others. It comes naturally to them. Rama is also a very open person. There's no hide and seek with her. When she got involved with this guy, she told me straight away. There were times when she used to cry and ask me, "Madhav, what should I do now? I really love him but I feel guilty that I betrayed you." At least when she confided in me, I should have asked her to give our marriage one more chance. But my ego didn't let me. Also, somehow I was happy that she had found happiness even if I wasn't part of the picture.'

Varsha listened. Wonder why Maya said he was a boring guy, she thought. He's not as shallow as he seems. Take the time to scratch the surface and you may see a person's true colours. In fact, he talked much more than Som ever did.

After a brief introspective pause, he continued, 'No. You know, Varsha, for all the jokes men crack about their freedom when their wives are out, they have no inkling what to do with their time when they're alone. Initially, when Rama left me, I felt so lost. I didn't even want to go home. I didn't think it would be so difficult.'

'Women respond to loneliness similarly, Madhav. If you look around you, you'll notice that most of us are terrified of loneliness. I know of women who stay in a marriage with violent men, alcoholics, drug addicts, only because they can't bear to think of living by themselves. They're scared to be alone. And I'm not talking of financially dependent women who have no choice. I'm talking of professionals who are perfectly capable of taking care of themselves. Loneliness is perhaps the only aspect of life, men and women respond similarly to.'

'Women, I think, are better equipped to deal with life. Look at Maya. She seems perfectly happy being on her own. And look at me. I'm always looking for someone to keep me company. Even now, when I can get back home and do my own thing, here I am, talking to a woman I have met only a few hours ago.'

'I guess Maya's is a different case. She's never been in a long-term relationship. A person who's married or has had a long-term relationship responds differently to being alone. And it's not only about sex, in fact, it's not about sex at all. Married couples are not exactly making passionate love every night. You and I know that for a fact. And yet, they stay in the relationship because they don't even want to think of life outside it. Tell me about yourself. Were you like this when you were with Rama? I mean did you like talking to her.'

'No, not really. Only now because I miss a hearty chat, I've realised the value of it. And when I find someone like you who's remotely interested in what I'm saying I latch on to them at the risk of being called a pile on. There were times when I used to feel terribly sorry for myself. But now, I'm more or less okay with it when people pretend to be busy just to shrug me off.'

Varsha felt sorry for the man in front of her. To change the subject she said, 'Don't you think you're getting late for your lecture?'

'No. See, that's exactly what I was telling you. You're already bored of my company.'

'Of course not. I just looked at the time and realised we've spent more than half an hour talking. Also, I need to get ready or that devil will strangle me.'

'Okay, bye then. See you sometime.'

'It was nice talking to you. I mean it,' she said following him to the door.

In the evening, she asked Maya, 'That Madhav fellow is funny, you know. Almost every sentence of his begins with a "No".'

Maya agreed and said laughing, 'You know what we've nicknamed him? Abominable No Man.'

Varsha laughed, 'But he's not so abominable, you know, poor chap is just over-eager.'

'Don't know about that. But the way he says no to everything is a bloody pain in the you know where.'

'He's got a nice voice though.'

'I wish he had learnt how not to say no!'

'You bet.'

Chapter 9

THERE ARE SOME PLACES AND SITUATIONS THAT MAKE YOU experience a sense of déjà vu. You feel you've been there and done that before. Anything you say or do, you feel as though you've already said and done. You seem to have wandered there many a times before. There's nothing much you can do in such places and situations except experience it. Take it in. Even if you rack your brains, you know it's futile, because you know, you've never been there. Never done what you were doing.

Maya was overwhelmed with nostalgia as they were driving down the old city. But she wasn't sure that she had never been there. Nor was she sure if she had. Professor Hai was behind the wheel explaining to them the history and geography of the roads and landmarks as they drove past them. Maya was sitting next to him. Varsha was in the back seat.

Hai gave them a brief history of the city—Quli Qutub Shah had seized the reins of power from the Bahamani Kingdom in 1512 and established the fortress city of Golconda. The inadequacy of water, and frequent epidemics of plague and cholera forced Mohammed, the fifth Quli Qutub Shahi ruler, to venture out to establish the new city with the Charminar at its centre and with four great roads fanning out in four directions. Hyderabad's fame, strategic location and Golconda's legendary wealth attracted Aurangazeb who captured

Golconda after a long siege in 1687. After this defeat the importance of Hyderabad declined and the city fell into partial ruin.

As the Mughal Empire decayed and began to disintegrate, Asaf Jah-I proclaimed himself the Nizam and established independent rule of the Deccan. Hyderabad once again became a major capital city, ruled by successive Nizams of the Asaf Jah dynasty until the state was merged into the Indian Union in 1948.

As they explored the city, Maya realised that the bustling four hundred-year-old metropolis possessed a special charm. Despite the evident growth and cosmopolitan influences, Hyderabad had, in a strange way, retained its old-world feel. Yes, there was apathy, there was neglect, sometimes there was utter disregard towards retaining the various heritage sites on the part of its people and the authorities. Yet, the city had withstood the indifference and bounced back with amazing vitality. Nowhere was it more evident than in the magnificent ancient glass and chrome Persian edifices. Their first destination was the Salar Jung museum situated at Dar-us-salam, a densely populated area, one of the oldest in town. The closer they approached it, the denser the pedestrian crowd was getting. Bicycles, cycle rickshaws, mopeds and scooters were almost toppling over each other as the red traffic light turned green. There were very few cars on the road unlike the other parts of the city. Lining the roads were gimcrack buildings that made you wonder if they had ever seen better days, second-hand bookstalls, tyre shops, road-side vendors, shoe-polish boys, everything looked gloomy and messy despite the buzzing activity and atmosphere. Varsha and Maya exchanged views on how far removed everything seemed in comparison with the developing city they had left behind. 'Though you find people moving around in all directions, the city itself seems static. Almost at a stand-still. Don't you think?' Varsha said.

'Yeah,' replied Maya, 'And look at the people. Though they seem to be busy, they don't appear to be doing anything. I guess, it's their body language. Have you noticed?' Prof Hai laughed saying, 'As they say, you haven't seen nothing yet. My dear ladies, the best is yet to come. This is the real Hyderabad. This is where you get the true essence of the city. Not at the University or at Banjara and Jubilee Hills. Those areas are beautiful but they have nothing to do with real Hyderabadi culture. Hyderabadi culture is fashionable there. But, for the people living here, it's a way of life.'

As they turned the corner of the road leading to the museum, the change was sudden. The noise of traffic faded and the street looked like a stage-set. Deserted. Dramatic. For a second, it seemed like they had loitered into a theatre waiting for the curtains to go up. For the play to begin. Once they walked inside, it was indeed, straight out of another world. A splendid one at that. There was a treasure trove of thousands of antiques and objets d'art belonging to Nawab Salar Jung III. They gasped in awe when they entered the Jade Hall that had artifacts belonging to the times of Aurangazeb, Tipu Sultan and the Asaf Jahs. Luckily for them, the Nizams' personal collection of jewellery was also on display. By the time they got to the end, both women were tired, more with excitement than physical exertion. Prof Hai marvelled at their keen interest. He noticed that Varsha spoke non-stop, commenting on the objects on display while it was Maya who observed. The last time he had visited the museum was years ago with his parents and his mother had displayed the same knack for observation. Maya soaked in everything, speaking only when needed. He sighed deeply, prompting Maya to look at him. 'Any problem sir?' she asked. 'No, none at all,' he replied quietly and continued, 'So, what kind of food would you ladies like to eat?'

'Very Hyderabadi. Biryani, perhaps,' volunteered Varsha.

'Actually, there is much more to Hyderabadi food than just biryani. For some reason, only that dish has become famous. Okay, I'll give you two options. The first is that we head towards Charminar and eat at Nayaab, a very old Hyderabadi eating-joint that serves typical chowki lunch. The other option is to go back to Abids.'

'Let's go to Nayaab. What do you say, Maya?' Varsha enquired.

'Fine.'

'But don't expect posh surroundings there,' Hai warned.

'Oh, come on Professor, unless we throw caution to the winds, we can't experience life. Right Maya?' Varsha looked at her and noticed that she was looking a little off-colour. 'Hey, what's the matter with you girl? You look distracted.'

'No, no, I'm fine. Just assimilating everything.'

Varsha believed her but Hai didn't. There was definitely something that was disturbing her, he thought and wondered what it could be.

They reached Madina, the area that was named after a hundred-year-old restaurant, close to the Charminar, and looked for parking space. It was one hell of a task but Prof Hai finally managed to convince a shopkeeper to let him park outside his shop. They walked into the quaint eating-joint that looked deceptively small. Once inside they discovered a huge spacious dining hall with a separate section for families. There were mostly men feasting on rich, delicious looking dishes at various tables. Obviously, women in the old city didn't believe in lunching out. That's what Varsha said aloud. 'They don't need to go outside to eat this kind of food. The food they cook at home is far more delicious than what is served here. But, this place is the most authentic, as far as I know,' responded Prof Hai.

After looking through the menu, he suggested they ask for the waiter's advice. The waiter did it most willingly, reeling out names of dishes that were appreciated by tourists and the names of the day's specialties. The Professor ordered kheema-do-pyaza and ande-ka-khageena with sheermal. Varsha settled for haleem and checked with him if he would share a mutton biryani with her. 'No, I won't be able to handle anything so heavy, why don't you share it with Maya,' he suggested. 'Maya is a vegetarian,' informed Varsha. That was news to the Professor. 'Oh, I didn't know that. You should have told me... I suggest you have plain rice with mirchi-ka-salan or baghara baingan and kaddu-ka-dalcha.'

'Whatever you say. These are names that I've only heard or read about. As long as there's no meat in it, it's fine,' said Maya.

They placed their orders and Hai asked Maya, 'Are you a strict vegetarian? Or are eggs okay with you?' Varsha replied on her behalf, 'Oh no, she can't stand the smell. She's what you call a pucca Brahmin.' 'So was my mother,' he said aloud and was asked to narrate his parents' love story. 'She was a vegetarian all her life but she cooked amazing non-vegetarian food, especially anything Hyderabadi. My paternal grandmother had taught her everything she knew. Very often my daadi jaan used to say that her bomman daughter-in-law had turned out to be a far better cook than her other Muslim daughters-in-law. Unke haath me jaadu tha...' he said. Something about the way he said the sentence stirred Maya. But she didn't know why. She was feeling unusually sombre that afternoon. She put it down to all the excitement of the day. Out of curiosity, she asked Hai, 'When was the last communal riot in Hyderabad?'

'Hmmm...it used to be an annual event at one point in time. But that was a long time ago. Twenty years. The most ghastly one that almost wiped out everyone in the old city was in 1978. There never was one like that before and hopefully never again. We lost several of our relatives in that riot. Families were wiped out. Nobody was spared. We couldn't even identify the bodies of our own relatives. So you can imagine. The city is yet to recover from that. Though new people have inhabited the old houses, they're still haunted by the ghosts of their memories.'

Maya listened in rapt attention without missing a word and wondered if Hai would have known her parents. Even if he did, how would she know? She didn't know their names. She didn't even know her real name. She was chasing shadows. But she could think of no other way to reach the people she wanted to find.

Hai liked the way she was interested in everything. He was also intrigued by the sense that she was searching for something. Yes, there was definitely something that she had come in search of to this city. Somehow, he was not convinced that it had been a career move at all. He could be wrong, he said to himself. But he knew that so far his intuition had not failed him. With most people. And how could he be wrong about someone he felt so strongly about? Just being around her and having her around was making him feel so alive. That there was more to life. My god! She had the most incredible eyes he had ever seen. Anybody who looked into them could drown in their depths, he thought looking at her. He had never known, until he met her, that eyes could change colours in different light. Sometimes they looked green, at times blue, a hypnotic mixture. What was she thinking? He caught Varsha watching him stare at her friend. And he averted his gaze, clearing his throat self-consciously.

Varsha looked away but she had caught the undisguised adoration in his eyes for Maya. She looked at her friend who seemed so caught up in her own thoughts that Varsha was sure she hadn't noticed the Prof. A fleeting doubt crossed Varsha's mind but she brushed it off as far-fetched. She had grown fond of the senior Prof though they had met just a few hours ago. Life's so strange, she thought. There are people who you barely know and yet you feel comfortable in their presence. And then there are people whom you spend lifetimes with in search of that comfort. She stopped herself before she slipped into the familiar pattern of thought that invariably led her to think of the one person she was running away from.

Content with their meal, the trio headed to the car. And then decided that they would walk the stretch to Charminar as it was close by. It would be too much of an effort to find a place to park given the crowd surrounding the beautiful monument. Despite the fact that it was just a kilometre away, it took them half an hour to reach their destination. It was so crowded and chaotic in the area. A couple of times, both the women would have fallen if Hai had not steadied them with his arm. And when it was his turn to topple, they laughed uncontrollably. With his humour intact, Hai quipped, 'Will somebody rescue a fallen man?' Both of them extended their hands but Hai took Varsha's. Despite confusion reigning all around them, Hai was clear in his mind why he did that.

The architectural jewel of Hyderabad, the Charminar, stands on four arches known as the Char Kamans. Apparently, Sultan Quli

Qutb Shah had knelt at the crossroad and prayed to the gods when a terrible pestilence had swept his kingdom. After it subsided, he built a structure at the same spot as thanksgiving to the gods. Often referred to as the Arc de triumph of the East, the Charminar comprises four graceful minarets with its central structure soaring to a height of a hundred and eighty feet. They stood admiring the structure as the professor gave them the historic details. The four minarets from that angle looked like they were touching the sky. At the entrance, they noticed a small Lakshmi temple. Quli Qutb Shah had dreamt of Goddess Lakshmi and had built a temple for her. Obviously, the Muslim rulers were not as fundamentalist as they were perceived to be. They went up to the first floor of the clock tower and the view of the city was breathtaking. As they climbed further up Maya said, 'Have you noticed how people have this amazing capacity to turn the awe-inspiring into the awful?' pointing to the inscriptions of people's names on the walls. Both Hai and Varsha agreed with her. After admiring the structure, praising the builder and criticising the destructive attitude of some of the visitors, the three walked back to the car. 'That's enough excitement for the day,' Hai remarked and the two women agreed. 'But if you want to explore Lad Bazaar in the midst of which we're standing right now, I have no hassles. I'll wait in the car while you ladies shop. You don't find bangles like the ones here, anywhere in the world. Go ahead, it's not everyday that we get to come here. Anyway, in a couple of days, the Ramzan month will start. Then you can forget about coming here for a month till Eid.' They debated for a while and decided that they may as well, as the lure of shopping was too hard to resist despite the weariness they felt. 'We need that little bit of exercise after we hogged the way we did,' said Maya. 'Look who's talking? Compared to me you have a bird's appetite,' teased Varsha.

The scene they were faced with upon entering Chudi Bazaar left them completely awestruck. There were about five hundred shops flanking either side of the Charminar, with over two thousand craftsmen weaving their magical bangles. Though not too fond of jewellery, Maya couldn't help but gasp when she set her eyes on the dazzling Hyderabadi lac bangles. The shopkeepers, in addition to being excellent salesmen, knew how to gain the attention of their customers. Apparently, this common Hyderabadi ornament had people from all over the world flocking to buy them. They looked like they were worth a million but cost next to nothing. When she adorned her wrists with a long row of bangles that caught her fancy, Varsha said, 'Babe, just noticed how pretty your hands are. Now, don't take them off. You can wear them with almost anything.'

Even before they had recovered from their experience with the bangle shops, they entered Pather Gatti, the adjacent lane. The entire street comprised row upon row of shops selling pearls. Everywhere they looked they were greeted with the sight of luminescent teardrops. Wonders in white, pink and even black. Maya had always read about Hyderabadi pearls but had never really paid attention to how they came to Hyderabad. Echoing her thoughts, Varsha asked, 'Do you have any idea why Hyderabad is famous for pearls. The city is neither on the sea-coast nor anywhere near it. Strange isn't it?' One salesman who knew a prospective buyer when he saw one, and who didn't have to strain his ears to eavesdrop given the volume of her voice, didn't let the chance pass him by. 'Madam, please come in and sit down. I'll explain.' As they made themselves comfortable on the white gaddas after removing their shoes at the entrance, the paan-stained teeth salesman offered them velvet bolsters to lean on and summoned a young boy, 'Arre chotu, thanda laa re.' They protested and he said, 'No problem if you don't buy madam. Hyderabadis are not into business. For us, guests are like God. Is this your first visit to our city, madam?' he enquired while displaying strings of pearls in red velvet boxes. 'Why, don't we look like we belong to Hyderabad,' Varsha shot back smiling. 'Arre madam, what are you saying? You must be from Bombay. Correct or wrong?'

'Well, I'm from Mumbai. This madam is from Bangalore. Where are you from?' Varsha responded. Maya admired the ease with which her friend bonded with anybody she wanted to. In the next half hour he enlightened them on how pearls came to be associated with the city, interspersed with bits of information about himself (Myself Abdul Karim, tenth pass in English medium), his owner (Allah bless our Seth. Next to God, we are loyal to our employers madam), his wife (fair, reads namaz all five times, now-a-days-becoming-fat) and six children (two sons, four daughters, Allah has been very meherbaan madam). Apparently, when Hyderabad was a princely state, it was one of the richest cities in the world. The royal patronage nourished the burgeoning growth of arts, crafts and cuisine. Their rich lifestyle beckoned many a craftsman from distant parts of the world, especially the Arabian Gulf where rare original pearls are still found in abundance. Hence, Hyderabad became famous country-wide for these precious stones.

Abdul Karim was fishing out several different ornaments. The satlada and panchlada haar—seven and five stringed necklaces interspersed with emeralds and onyx gems. They had never seen anything like this before in their entire lives. 'We think we've seen everything there is to see but there's so much beauty we haven't yet appreciated' philosophised Varsha. Maya simply nodded but Abdul Karim continued, 'That is what is life, madam.' Both the girls exchanged amused glances trying hard to stifle their laughter.

They gaped at the unlimited variety of chokers, earrings and pendants. Besides the traditional designs there were some trendy contemporary designs as well.

Contrary to his altruistic claims, Abdul Karim succeeded in emptying their wallets. He lured them further with 'credit cards also okay,' but before Varsha could succumb to that hazardous one-liner, Maya dragged her out. Varsha was thrilled with her purchases. 'You don't get stuff like this in Mumbai, you know,' she said. Maya retorted, 'I don't know about that but what I do know is that you're behaving like you've lived all your life in that city. Amazing how people change.' Varsha pooh poohed.

'Poor thing that salesman. I wonder how he feeds his family on his meagre income,' Maya sympathised. Varsha laughed so loudly that a couple of people passing by turned around to look where that came from. 'Idiot, it's we who are poor now. He must be several thousands richer. I have a strong feeling he's the owner of the shop.'

'Really?'

'I think so. Didn't you notice how the rest of the staff were behaving with him? You're so gullible babe. But today's most gullible man-of-the-day award must go to Professor Saab. Poor man, he didn't know what he was in for when he encouraged us to go shopping. He must be cursing us.'

'Oops, I totally forgot about him.'

'You ingrate!'

They were both feeling heady and light-hearted. Shopping was indeed cathartic, they conceded. They giggled like schoolgirls while balancing their innumerable shopping bags. Hai looked at them from a distance and sighed, which, he knew, would have evoked a reaction from Maya if she were around him at that moment. She was around, he thought, and yet so far away.

Chapter 10

SHEHZAADI WOKE UP WITH AN AWFUL HEADACHE. SHE complained to Anwar. 'That's called a hangover, my dear, in case you didn't know,' he said. 'Don't you get a hangover only when you get drunk or something? I hardly had a drink or two,' she whimpered. 'Depends on what you drank,' he said.

'One bloody mary and a few tequila shots.'

'That explains it. You're not used to drinking vodka and tequila is very strong, it hits you like a bolt from the blue.'

'Oh...what do I do now?'

'Lie down. I'll get you some black coffee. That should make you feel better.'

'Thanks.'

'No problem,' he planted a kiss on her cheek and got out of bed.

He asked Babu Miya to organise a pot of black coffee and hung around. He sat on a dining room chair and picked up the day's newspaper. Though his eyes were glancing through the articles, his mind was telling him that this was the time to tell her to go easy on the drinking. The occasion and her discomfort were good enough reasons for him to broach the subject. He took the tray from Babu Miya's hands despite his protests and walked into the bedroom.

He propped a couple of pillows behind her and asked her to sit up. 'Listen darling,' he said softly, 'I think you should go easy now. You're not used to drinking everyday. Why are you switching drinks? You've always drunk wine. If nothing else at least try not to mix your drinks.'

'Yeah, I know. You're right. In any case, Ramzan is around the corner. I'm going to stop.'

Anwar couldn't believe it had been as easy as that. Yes, he thought, the month of Ramzan was due to begin. And he knew how devoutly Shehzaadi had always kept her roza. Divine intervention or what, he thought, and muttered an Alhamdulillah. Whistling an old Hindi film tune, he walked into the loo. Shehzaadi fell into a restless sleep with the tune ringing in her ears.

When she woke up, she was feeling much better. The coffee had done a lot of good and now she was starving. She called out to Babu Miya while brushing her teeth, asking him to serve her lunch. Her stomach was growling and she had no energy to take a bath. She looked at herself in the mirror...in the next moment, she found herself thinking of Sameera who had inherited the colour of her eyes. Everything else she had inherited from her father. 'If she had lived, she would have turned out to be an unusual beauty,' she sighed. She loved her son but the bond she had had with her daughter was hard to explain. Sameera could have been herself when she was young...

The magic of first love, a first born can never be repeated. The first maternal tug at your heart-strings remained strong forever. After all, the first born makes you a mother. She was ecstatic the day Shahbaz had learnt to utter the word 'Ammi' but it was Sameera, who had made her feel that way first.

And it was Rehaan who had awakened her heart to the longing of love. It was he who had introduced her to the pleasures that her body was capable of enjoying, who touched her like a man would touch the one he loved.

No matter how many men a woman sleeps with, the first would always be the one she never forgets. And when that man also becomes the father of your child, the combination becomes irreplaceable. She had been so fortunate...whose evil eye had made everything go wrong? Made her lose everything she had ever loved. Why on earth did God take away the people who are so much a part of you, so early? If there is a judgment day for humans, then what about Him? Who is to question His cruelty? What made him snatch away everything that He Himself was supposed to have granted?

She had to do something constructive now to steer her mind away from these thoughts. She ate her lunch in haste and went to the study and turned the computer on. She needed to check if Shahbaz had emailed her. Life was so much easier with email. People complained about the dying art of hand-written letters but she considered it amazing and so convenient. Distances didn't seem frightful anymore.

She signed into her account and her heart leapt when she saw Shahbaz's name pop up in her inbox. Eagerly, she clicked on the message. It took ages to open up, as always happened whenever she was in a hurry! Finally, the page loaded and her eyes eagerly read his letter:

My dear Ammi,

Sorry for the silence! I have been meaning to write to you in detail ever since I reached but I have been so busy. You must have been disappointed to read my rather short, cryptic emails earlier but I honestly had no time! Not because I wasn't thinking of you. I have, I miss you so much. It's strange but when I do things like toss a wet towel on the bed I can actually hear you saying, 'Shah, not there, you lazy boy!' Yesterday we got the results of our first test, I was quite disappointed with my marks and I could hear you say, 'Don't fret, Shah. As long as you did your best it doesn't matter how the others do!'

Peter, my roommate, is a really nice guy. Thankfully we get along well. Last night we got talking and he was telling me about his life. I felt so grateful for having a strong, loving family. For providing me with so much security and above all, normalcy. Ammi, you have no idea what this guy has been through, felt really sad for him. He talks about it like it's some kind of a joke but when life becomes a joke, we all know it's not funny. I'll tell you everything in detail when I come home. There's too much to cram into an email. The weather here is mostly awful! There's usually no sign of the sun. It's going take some getting used to as I miss the heat!

And I miss you and Abba...I guess we realise how much people mean to us only when we're away from them.

Ask Abba to take good care of you. I'm signing off now Ammi.

Keep smiling. When you smile, I can feel its warmth, miles away.

Hugs.

Shah

God, he sounded so mature. He had never 'written' to her before, of course he never had a need to, but she liked the easy way in which he told her about his life. He was growing up. Into a wonderful boy. She was so proud of him. Shehzaadi clicked on 'reply' and started typing...

My darling Shah,

I know that you're far away from me, there in England, miles and miles away, yet I feel your presence all the time. I guess that's because you're such a big part of me. I probably know you better than you know yourself! Wherever you are, whatever you do, one thing will never cease to exist—the bond between you and me.

I'm glad you're settling down although it will take a while to get used to things. Especially the weather! Do keep warm and make sure you eat properly.

It's really important to get along with the person who's your flatmate and if, as you said, he has had a hard life I hope you can be there for him.

Yes, now you have to learn to stand on your own two feet, and my success as a parent comes only when you are able to manage on your own. I feel proud about that.

That's all for now, my sweetie, I miss you terribly. It's a nice kind of missing because I know it's for your growth. And yes, I shall pass on your message to your dad. May Allah grant you everything you need.

Hugs to you too.

Ammi

She pressed the 'send' button. It was comforting to know that he would read it in a while. If only she could send a mail to wherever her daughter was! If only God had a messenger service.

She headed to the bar and reached for the wine bottle—her only ally in solitude and sadness. Only after she emptied the contents did she feel lighter and better...happier.

So far Varsha had known only indifferent men—her father and Som. Both had taken indifference to soaring new heights. One communicated indifferently. The other was indifferent to communication. The former was better, she decided, at least you knew where you stood with them. Now, she added a second category to her classification—men who imagined themselves in love with every woman they got close to. They revelled in giving up—the loser guy. Like Madhav, the Abominable No Man. His negativity about life, people and situations, his delight in wallowing in self-pity and misery was apparent in the standard beginning that he had for every sentence. Whether he meant yes, maybe, anything, very rarely was it 'no' for a no.

She didn't miss having a steady man in her life. Yes, she needed sex. Which was what had resulted in the present situation. But otherwise, she felt no need for them. She appreciated the freedom of being on her own. Free to laugh. Free to cry. Free to speak her mind.

When Varsha told Maya that she'd slept with Madhav, she was aghast.

'What? You're joking! How could you?'

'Yup. I'm telling you. Quite easily.'

Maya remained quiet, trying to digest the information. It was too difficult to swallow.

'You know what, babe. When you're in a desert, chasing mirages is essential. Chances are, you just might find water.'

'In other word, you've got to kiss a lot of toads if you wish to find your prince, is that what you're saying?'

'What toads? What princes? I can only see amoeba. Actually amoebae, to be more precise.

'God, you have always been inimitable. Now you're turning out to be incorrigible.'

And they laughed heartily, a free schoolgirl laugh, a laugh between friends who knew each other too long and loved each other too much to be judgmental. They laughed like they used to whenever they spotted Manjunath Sir's red undie. Scrawny little Manjunath Sir, their math teacher in school, would bend to pick up a fallen piece of chalk, and up went his untucked shirt, down came his trousers and out came his undie. Red. Very bright red. What kind of a man would own a stack of red undies in his cupboard, they used to wonder. Or was it the same one, they would debate and their eyes would widen in disbelief and disgust. And they would double up with laughter. Until their sides ached and tears blurred their visions.

They had come a long way since then but the bonding had only strengthened. They didn't always share the same interests, but they usually found the same people interesting and above all, they could laugh at situations that went unnoticed by most people. Sometimes, shared jokes were far more binding than shared sorrow. In their case, it was a lot of both. Only recently had Varsha acquired a new area of interest—hitherto unexplored by the two of them—men. But that hadn't come in the way of their comradeship. Not yet.

When the laughter subsided, Maya asked, 'But seriously, tell me, Madhav's not your type at all, from what I know of you. So what about him appealed to you?'

'Sweetheart, it's like this. When you're hungry, you don't look for appeal. You just look for food, any type of food that can satisfy your hunger. Haven't you eaten food that you didn't particularly like or care for, only because you were hungry and nothing else was available at the moment? All of us have, I'm sure. At some point of time. It's that simple. Well, it's a different matter that we don't consider hunger for sex and hunger for food the same. I don't see how they're different. Both of them drive the human race. Both of them keep the human race alive. Then why the pretence? We may not be willing to see it but that doesn't mean it's not true. You know something, for the longest time, I pretended too...no...actually I believed that sex wasn't such a vital need. But now, I think otherwise. That's the beauty of life. You grow, you outgrow, you learn by unlearning what you'd learnt all along. Don't you think?'

Maya nodded, unconvinced.

This whole affair, if you could call it that, with Madhav had begun in the most unpredictable manner. One evening when Maya hadn't returned until late, Madhav dropped in. Varsha was happy to see him. She had already begun working herself into a frenzy over the prospect of spending the evening alone. She was dreading what it would be like when she returned to Mumbai when he had made his appearance at the doorstep ringing the doorbell insistently. He'd invited her to his place for a drink. 'Leave a note for Maya. She'll know where to reach you when she gets back,' he suggested. Sounded good enough for her to consider it. So she followed his advice and left with him. Maya was delayed. Varsha returned earlier, but long enough for her to have satisfied her recently acquired appetite for what, she thought, was the only thing men had to offer. Again, like with Rajeev, she realised that her body acted on its own will and when it did, her mind surrendered meekly to its strength.

A few drinks down—her glasses of wine and his whisky on the rocks—and they were entwined in each other's arms, holding on to the other like clinging vines. Contrary to his appearance, Madhav wasn't bad in bed. But a man was just an instrument in the path of her unorchestrated relief.

Some relief was better than none. It hadn't taken long—the whole act—yet it had left her ravenous for food—of the abdominal kind. Madhav had fixed her a sandwich and she had returned filled and fulfilled.

Early next morning, she was woken up by Maya who handed her the phone. Wondering who was calling her there, at that hour, she held it to her ear only to hear Madhav telling her that he was already missing her. Taken aback, she said, 'Hang on. Wait a minute. Let me take a breath. We need to talk.'

'No. Should I come over now?'

'No, no,' she said hurriedly. 'When you get back from work, give me a call.'

'No, I'll come and fetch you.'

She didn't like the authority in his voice. What made a man think that by sharing a woman's body he had some kind of a hold on her? It was time to break the myth before he started believing in it. Before it left behind a trail of disappointment. For him. On her part, she felt nothing towards him. Not even desire at the moment. She didn't know about later. And she didn't care.

When she told him that in the evening, he was crestfallen. 'Oh, I don't wish to impose myself on you but I want you to know that you're the first woman I've fallen for since my divorce.' She consoled him saying that he probably hadn't spent time with many women, the way he'd spent it with her.

'No,' he said, meaning it this time, 'You're wrong. I really like you.' And he kissed her clumsily. She kissed him back. And they had sex. He found that strange, and later he said. 'I can never understand women.'

'Don't even try,' she advised, 'When you think you know them, you don't.'

'No, you mean a lot to me. But I won't follow you because I know you won't like it. I just want you to be happy. Wherever you are. Whatever you do.' His eyes were moist and she felt sorry for him but she thanked him. 'I'm looking for a man to whom I mean the world, not just a lot. And I know that that species is extinct. Or completely non-existent, perhaps.' From the look on his face, she knew he could see that he had lost her. Before he could embark on his 'no' trip again, she upped and left.

'Was there any need to get into all this,' Maya chided her, 'Why can't you just have a peaceful holiday while you're here?'

'I can but I may not want to. And peaceful? What's that?' she remarked.

Maya rolled her eyes and threw up her hands.

The next few days were filled with a whirl of activities. The days quickly changed into evenings which in turn ushered in the nights. Varsha, accompanied by Professor Hai and Maya, toured the city enthusiastically, only to return dead tired.

On one such day, they visited Purani Haveli, the palace where most of the Nizams had been born and lived during their lifetimes. It was closed to the public but Hai was related to the Nizams, which made it possible for them to gain entry. As they navigated through the narrow lanes and alleys of the old city, absorbing its ambience, an ancient yet lively aura, they reached an area called Dabeerpura. The railway gate was closed. They waited at the crossing. Maya looked around her. Suddenly an image flashed before her eyes; a toddler, looking like a younger version of herself, calling out to a woman whose back was towards her. Overpowered by a deep emotion, Maya stifled a sob. It came out in the form of a gasp.

Hai asked, 'Anything wrong?'

She recovered and looked at him blankly. As if she was looking through him. He held her arm and shook it gently, 'Maya, what is it? What's the matter?'

She looked at him, this time gaining recognition in her eyes and said, 'Nothing. I feel like I've been here before. I know this place,' and immediately regretted having said that.

Varsha, who had bent forward in concern said, 'It happens all the time, sweetie. Well maybe not all the time but definitely several times. Some places seem familiar to us. Last year, when I was in Sri Lanka, we visited Jaffna. And while passing by, I had this strong, indescribable feeling that I'd been there, seen that place. I could hear my heart beat in my ears. I felt almost ill. Later when I told a clairvoyant friend of mine, she explained to me that it had to do with my past life. Imagine me! A gun-toting terrorist, combing Jaffna for my operations. What a thought!'

Maya mumbled, 'Guess you're right,' but she knew that her present life also had a past life to it. One lifetime. Two lives. One that she knew. And the other that she didn't. Varsha knew it too but she didn't want to rake up a storm that could throw her friend's emotions into disarray.

Hai knew Maya meant what she had just said and wondered, 'How could a girl who lived all her life in Bangalore find any area remotely familiar in the old city?' He had been to Bangalore several times and not one place seemed anything like this. Not that he knew of anyway.

The train passed by. The gate opened and they crossed the track. The three of them had grown quiet, lost in their own thoughts. All along the stretch that led to the palace, Maya kept looking around closely and curiously at the surroundings but she felt nothing.

The rest of the day was uneventful as far as Maya's déjà vu was concerned but fulfilling in terms of learning and knowledge. 'This is where the famous Hindi movie *Nikaah* was shot,' Hai explained as they explored the resplendent palace. Neither Maya nor Varsha had seen the film but Varsha made appropriate noises like, 'Wow, okay.' Maya stayed quiet preferring to scribble notes in her book. Neatly. Precisely. Hai peered over her shoulder and thought, if you could read human beings from their handwriting; the one in front of him was adorable. Every now and then he looked at her green eyes, now seeking, now seeing. As long as she was around, he felt like he had goose pimples. The sensation was so physical that he had to run one arm over the other to prevent it from being visible. Today when he had touched her arm, though only to shake it gently, a thousand volts had hit him. It was that powerful. Her touch. He had seen it happen in movies and always laughed at it. Now, he couldn't believe it was happening to him. So late in the day. He didn't know how to get close to her. Or if it was right to even try. He forced his mind to stop thinking about her. He looked up and saw that Varsha was watching him closely.

On the following day they visited the Golconda Fort. Legend has it that a shepherd found an idol in the land and the Kakatiya kings built the fort around it in the year 1140. That's how the name came into being, 'Golla' was shepherd in Telugu and 'Konda', hill. Golconda was subsequently expanded by the Qutub Shahi kings into a massive granite fort with walls and ramparts extending to a length of five kilometres in circumference. From this fort they ruled the nearby areas even as their capital was based in Warangal. Even now the fort reflected the power that it had once wielded. Maya tried conjuring visions of how regal this place must have been at that time. Kings, queens, courtesans, chariots, ghazals, mujras, music ...Wow! How resplendent! There was some other-worldly vibe to the whole place. It seemed as though even inanimate monuments had a life span. Once the glorious phase was over, they remained mere graves of their original selves.

'While entering the main gate of the fort, if you clap below the portico, echoes can be heard in a Darbar Hall some hundred and twenty-eight metres away,' explained Hai, 'just imagine the genius of the architects. Can you imagine what kind of planning must have gone in for those kind of acoustics to be executed? Apparently, this was to enable people to get the authorities' attention during troubled times. All they needed to do was come here, clap and promptly the king would send security to summon them in.'

'We're eleven kilometres away from the west of Hyderabad,' Hai continued in a travel-guide tone. 'The fortress city within the walls was famous for the diamond trade. This is where the famous Koh-i-noor diamond belonged. The first three Qutub Shahi kings rebuilt Golconda, hold your breath, over a span of sixty-two years! Does that explain the grandeur?' The two ladies were completely under the professor's spell as he fleshed out the history that surrounded them, almost bringing it alive. Varsha was totally enamoured by him, he was a mine of knowledge. When she told him that, he said, 'Thank you lady but one small correction. Please don't confuse information with knowledge. What I've been giving you all this while is just historical information. I know so much because I've lived in this city all my life.'

'Oh come on Prof. Don't be so modest. Living in a city doesn't in any way ensure that. What do you think? Every Hyderabadi knows all this?'

'I guess you're right. That's one of the reasons Maya is here. The responsibility is on her now to awaken the people to their past.'

'What irony!' muttered Maya to herself, thinking about her own reason for being in the city.

As they drove back along the Himayat Sagar Lake, the professor pointed to a mosque and told them that it was dedicated to a courtesan, Premamati, of the seventh Qutb Shah. 'That's incredible,' said the women almost in chorus.

'Yes, it is,' Hai agreed while bringing the car to a halt, 'It was an era full of paradoxes. On one hand, the rulers fought for land and religion, on the other, there was unparalleled harmony and respect for all professions. Can you see the hillock on the opposite side? Now, there stands a testimony to another accomplished dancer, Taramati. It's called Taramati Biradari. The pavilion is made in a combination of Hindu and Persian Architecture. Both Premamati and Taramati were deeply respected by Qutb Shah. They were both buried in the royal cemetery of the Qutb Shahi kings. Courtesans have a special place in the history of Hyderabad. In fact, Hyderabad used to once be known as Bhagyanagar, named after a courtesan Bhagamati whose love made Quli Qutb Shah cross the Musi-river in the middle of the night just to meet her.'

From there they drove over to Falaknuma Palace. Once a royal guest-house, the palace was now the most popular venue for parties held by Hyderabad's elite. By the time they reached the place, it was twilight and lights were being turned on as they approached. The moment the lights came on, the scene before them transported the visitors to a world that they had never been a part of. The exquisite structure made of Italian marble atop a two thousand feet high hill, gleamed like a mirror. Despite the fact that it was the end of a hectic day, the three of them still went on a walking tour conducted by the caretaker of the palace, listening enthralled as he described every little detail. It was one of the finest palaces in Hyderabad built by Nawab Vikar-ul-Umra, the fifth Paigah Emir. It was later purchased by the sixth Nizam in 1897, who used it as a royal guest-house. Presently it was being run by the Taj Group. The palace was designed by an Italian architect and it took nine years to complete. The palace's lavishly decorated interiors spoke volumes about the wealth of the Nizams.

They were given a quick peek into a large collection of rare treasures collected by the Nizam including paintings, statues, furniture, manuscripts and books. The Jade collection was simply out of this world.

The palace was laid out in the shape of a scorpion, its two stings spread out as wings on the north. In the centre was the main building, the kitchen and harem quarters stretched to the south.

Since the Nawab had been an avid traveller, various influences showed in the palace architecture, Louis XIV-style decor co-existed with a lavish Mughal ambience, Italian marble staircases and ornate fountains. Its stained-glass windows threw a spectrum of colours into the rooms. The library, with a walnut carved roof was apparently a replica of the one at Windsor Castle. Also, it had one of the finest collections of the holy Quran in India.

The three of them travelled back quietly, Hai concentrating on his driving, and the two women too exhausted to speak.

Days quickly passed by and when it was time for Varsha to leave, both Maya and she realised how much solace each had derived from the other's presence. Whoever said that absence makes the heart grow fonder must've been out of their minds, they decided. It was only when two people share the same space does the bond grow stronger. On the drive back from the airport, Hai and Maya didn't exchange a word. Lost in their own worlds. She in hers. He thinking of her.

'There has to be some way to make her a part of my life,' he thought.

'There has to be some way to find out which how this city was part of my life,' she thought.

Chapter 11

RAMZAN DAWNED. A DAY THAT WAS DECLARED BY THE POSITION of the moon. 'Chaand nazar aa gaya,' proclaimed the Imams. The Hyderabadis got ready to welcome the annual event. This year, it had fallen in the winter, and the Muslims were relieved that the fasting ritual would be easier. In the summer months, fasting had the tendency to leave them dehydrated.

Haleem joints sprang up all over overnight. Mosques alerted the namazis with their azaan through loudspeakers five times a day—Sehar, Zohar, Asar, Iftar and Isha—from dawn to night. People discussed which Irani restaurant served the best haleem. For the Hindus, the Ramzan month was like no other. This was the only time in the year when they could taste the divine Haleem—the preparation of lamb and wheat flour, cooked and stirred overnight. Several Irani restaurant owners lived off their earnings during this period for the rest of the year. What they earned serving haleem for one month was almost a hundred times more than what they earned serving chai, samosa, kebabs and biryani during the rest of the year. Such was the craze for the delicacy that had originated from Arabia.

Hyderabad was home to many Iranis and Arabs. The Iranis were spread across the city but the Arabs were mostly confined to an area in the old city called Barkas—a distorted version of the original 'barracks.' The Nizams had housed their army men in this area during their rule. But of late, it had gained notoriety for infamous Arab marriages. That was where most of the Arabs went in search of young, virgin brides.

The Nizami reign ended soon after India's independence but Hyderabad still retained their influence. Hai's father belonged to their clan. Though he had married a Hindu, who subsequently embraced Islam, their children were brought up as Muslims.

Today was the day of his first roza. Hai began with the Sehar namaz at four-thirty in the morning. He intended to say his prayers five times a day at least during this holy month. At lunch, Maya came as usual to the professor's room—she hadn't seen him all morning—she had been busy working on her research notes. From the entrance, she noticed a man with a white crocheted cap, his back towards the door, kneeling on a colourful carpet, and his open palms behind his ears. She couldn't figure out who he was, so she decided to stand and watch. She observed him, kneeling, bending to touch his forehead to the ground, chanting what she thought were Arabic verses. After about ten minutes, he stood up, removed his cap, folded the carpet, and turned around to face her. She was stunned to see that it was Professor Hai. He looked at her and said, 'Oh hello Maya, come in.' She regained her composure and said, 'I thought you were somebody else, sir. I'd never seen you praying in your office, so...'

'True,' he said, 'eleven months a year my faith is restricted to home but during this month, I pray at work too.'

'Yes of course,' she said.

Hai felt she wasn't saying quite all that she was thinking. 'Why? Are you surprised,' he asked.

'No, why should I be?' she said, caught unawares by the forcefulness with which she denied that he was right. She was indeed taken aback. This religious, traditional namazi was not the English-speaking, suspender-sporting professor she knew. Why it should surprise her so much though, she hadn't a clue.

'Do you pray Maya?' he enquired, 'Do you do your puja?'

'Yes, I do, sir,' she replied. Maya was pretty religious. Every morning when she finished bathing, she went to the puja room. There she would light the diya and say a shloka invoking Ganesha, the remover of obstacles. Lighting the agarbatthi she would do the aarthi while ringing the bell and chant more mantras—the Gayatri mantra, Vishnu sahasranama. Then Maya would kneel, fold her hands to do the namaskara with her eyes closed, and touch her knuckles to the temples. She had developed a liking for the ritual when she had observed her mother in the act. She had learnt the shuklambharadaram vishnum in a record twenty minutes when she was four, perfectly intoning and pronouncing the words, a feat that had made Appa an extremely proud father and teacher. Appa was not a great one for rituals. But he knew much more than Amma ever did. Amma's religious knowledge was limited to her belief but Appa's in-depth knowledge of the Gita, the Upanishads, the Vedas and other scriptures had sometimes surprised the pujaris when he pointed out errors in their chanting. He had studied the books as an ardent student and he had a shloka for every occasion—from consummation to separation, from birth to death. He could recite impromptu from the Geeta Govinda, the Ritu Samhara, the Bhagavad gita, Shiva Purana, Ramayana. 'Hinduism is not a religion,' he would say to her, 'it's a way of life.' Maya had grown up to believe that hers was the most liberal, most scientific religion. She had been his most receptive student, Appa had told her so on several occasions.

Professor Hai realised that she was expecting him to join her for lunch, 'Maya, I forgot to tell you that I'm fasting but I'll accompany you to the canteen if you want me to.'

'You're fasting?' she asked.

'Today is my first roza. I'm sure you know what roza means.'

'Of course, I do. Okay, I'll look for Sumathi then. It's not fair on my part to eat while you watch.'

'It's perfectly all right. The whole purpose is defeated if I look at somebody eating and miss it.'

'Perhaps. But in case you do get affected, then I'll be to blame. No sir, I don't want to be the one who leads you into temptation,' she said, laughing and walking out of his room.

Hai was amused. She sounded like Eve tempting Adam to take a bite of the forbidden fruit. In a way it was true. She wasn't the least bit responsible for his desire to taste the apple though. He mused at her usage of such strong words and their connotations.

Maya went around looking for Sumathi who wasn't in her seat. After peeping into a couple of rooms, she found her in the corridor, her hot-case in hand. 'Hey Maya,' she yelled, her voice echoing in the corridor, 'Good to see you. Where have you been? How's your project coming along? How far have you gotten with it? How's your friend, huh, what's her name, Varsha? Is she still here? I wanted to invite her for a meal but you people were so busy going here and there…'

Maya was glad to find her, despite the barrage of uninterrupted questions. The thought of having to eat alone was not an interesting prospect at all. What is it about eating, she wondered, that makes us look for company? After all, eating alone, for most people, is not done out of choice. A meal is a social event, she concluded as they trudged along to the canteen. Maya answered Sumathi's questions one by one, amused at her sustained interest. At the canteen, they ordered two glasses of fresh limewater and ate their lunch between taking gulps of the sweet, refreshing drink; sharing the food in their boxes and the activities of the days when they hadn't met each other. 'You know what happened last week,' said Sumathi, 'Mrs Bedell caught two students necking in the science lab and created a ruckus. She sent a letter to the VC demanding their expulsion. VC called for a meeting of all the HODs and after a long, heated discussion, he let the students go with a warning. Mrs Bedell was most unhappy. She stuck to her stand. For once, I agree with her. Students, these days, I tell you…'

'Oh come off it, Sumathi,' said Maya, 'These things happen all the time in co-ed institutions. After all, this is the age for boys and girls to behave recklessly. Yeah, I do understand that decorum has to be maintained. After all, the university ground is sacred. But I think there's no need for anything drastic. A warning should serve the purpose.'

'Hello. Who's talking about boys and girls?'

'What do you mean?'

'There was no girl. The two people necking were guys. I mean boys. Now tell me, Miss Liberal, what do you think?'

'Well so what? I think it's time we opened our eyes to homosexuality. It's just another choice that people make, like we decide who we love or want to spend time with.'

'Sorry to say this but I'm not as open-minded as you. For me, homosexuality is unnatural, abnormal. I feel very uncomfortable the moment I come to know somebody is gay. Take our boss, for instance, I limit my interaction with him to the absolute minimum.'

'Don't be ridiculous Sumathi,' said Maya in a burst of uncharacteristic indignation. 'How on earth do you know that he is gay?'

'Why? Don't we all?'

'I don't.'

'You don't? You're probably the only one then. Anyway, why are we getting into all this? Tell me about your friend Varsha. I saw her only a couple of times but I think she's very sweet. Just like you.'

Maya was ruffled. But she forced herself to be polite. Inside she was fuming. Not exactly at Sumathi but at people in general, people who knew nothing, who pretended to be broad-minded yet were petty and judgemental. What gave them the right to judge?

Maya stayed in that mood for the rest of the day.

Late in the evening, while she prepared her coffee for the next morning, she mulled over the day's events and analysed that the major part of her irritation came from Sumathi's comment about Hai, which was completely uncalled for. The other reason why she'd felt uncomfortable was the discovery of Hai's religious side. That was what was disconcerting her to a great extent. She had been so surprised to see him like that, knowing him, she thought, as well as she did, she never really gave it a thought that he was a religious person. Maya silently chided herself, saying that she was being untrue to what she believed in, freedom of choice and all that. Perhaps she thought, this feeling stemmed from the fact that she had lost herself and her family in the communal riots...this was something she would need to work on and overcome.

Chapter 12

THE RAMZAN MONTH PROVIDED MANY MORE SOCIALISING opportunities to Hyderabad's elite. If they were not hosting Iftar dinners, they were attending them. Shehzaadi and Anwar decided it was their turn to throw a party after they had attended a few. Anwar was relieved because his wife had stuck to her word. After that night of binging, she hadn't touched a drop of alcohol. As a matter of fact, she had gone to the other extreme of minimising her food intake even during non-fasting hours. Pre-sunrise was hardly an appetising hour but even after sunset, she hardly ate. She broke her fast with fruit juice and dates. Her dinner was frugal too. Though Anwar fasted only on Fridays, he was happily digging into all the season's delicacies. 'You're fasting while I'm feasting. I think you should eat better,' he told her.

'Since you're making up for the both of us, I don't need to eat more.'

The responsibility of getting a guest list together for their Iftar party was on Anwar. He made sure he included all his cousins, friends and associates, Radhakrishna, the CM's PA, Murlidhar, the Director of the Archeaological Society and a few other high level bureaucrats who mattered to him. They added up to more than fifty. At the eleventh hour, Shehzaadi enquired if he had included Amita, Zeba and Hamid. Anwar hadn't and Shehzaadi was most upset. He suggested that they have another party for people they had missed out and apologised earnestly. But Anwar knew the truth—he had deliberately excluded them. He wanted to take no more chances especially while his wife was staying off alcohol. There was no way he would allow them to rock the boat of his domestic life which was just about returning to normal. God, how he detested those women! But he lacked the guts to tell her what he thought of them. Or why he did what he did. What if she turned around and questioned him about the company he kept. She had every right to. Even when she hadn't approved of a couple of his philandering friends, she hadn't been disapproving of him mingling with them. Now, how could he do this to her? He knew that he was being weak, falling below his own standards, but the thought of his wife changing filled him with fear. All he wanted was his Shehzaadi, his wife, to be the way he had always known her, and for his life to stay the way he was used to. Anything precious must be guarded zealously. And for him, there was nothing more precious than his wife. If somebody had pointed out to him that his wife was a living, breathing human being and not an object, it would have peeved him to no end. Unluckily for him, nobody did.

The Iftar party was a huge success. Shehzaadi's choice of cuisine and her mastery over it had people raving for days. 'Anwar Miya, that Iftar dinner at your house was outstanding. When are you inviting us again?' they kept asking. 'Very delicious, very tasty, next year you must invite CM Garu also. I'll make sure he attends,' said Radhakrishna. Anwar beamed with pride. His wife, his jaan, was his perfect woman. A loving partner, an excellent mother and an outstanding cook. He would do anything to keep her with him.

A month of fasting, sehars and iftars later, Eid arrived. Once again the imams proclaimed 'chand nazar aagaya' and the city switched to celebration mode. Frenetic shopping preceded the big day. On Eid, Anwar, like countless other Muslims, dressed in his traditional silk sherwani, pyjama, makhmal topi, went to the Mecca masjid and joined the mass in prayer. Shehzaadi wore her khada dupatta and the Basra pearls her husband had gifted her a while ago and prayed at home, like the other women. At lunch, a whole group of them gathered together and tucked into sheer korma, kacche-gosht-ki-biryani, mirchi-ka-salan, tamatar-ki-chutney, dum-ka-murgh, dalcha and other Eid specialties. The feasting that followed was as faithfully kept as the fasting. All the discipline and self-control during the month made people not only appreciate the importance of eating moderately, but also reminded them of how delicious Hyderabadi food could be! There were those who kept their roza in the true spirit of what it stood for but for the majority, every sunset during the fasting season, ushered in a feast. Having spent the whole day without food or water (even wetting one's lips with saliva is forbidden for a kattar namazi), most of them went berserk at the sight of food. Although with food as delicious who could blame them.

Shehzaadi fasted all of thirty days, barely ate during the non-fasting hours and only a little more on Eid. Anwar fasted on four Fridays, hogged during non-fasting days and on Eid. Shehzaadi lost a few kilos from her average fifty-seven while Anwar added the same to his present hundred.

When Amita and Zeba came to wish them in the evening, they fawned over Shehzaadi. 'My, look at you. You're looking so sexy. You should start wearing clothes like mine. And believe me, you'll beat me hollow. You don't look like the mother of a twenty-year-old. Not from any angle,' raved Amita.

Zeba nodded in agreement.

All three giggled. Anwar had to grit his teeth to conceal his displeasure.

'I hope you're not taking her seriously,' he said to his wife, 'I love the way you are. Elegant and beautiful.'

'Why bhaijaan?' said Amita, mockingly, 'You don't think I wear pretty clothes?'

'Well, not to my liking.'

Shehzaadi objected. But Amita put her hand on hers and said, 'That's okay, darling. I want to hear what your husband says. I want to know what he thinks of me. After all, he's your better half, isn't he? Okay bhaijaan, go on.'

'I believe that women or rather everyone, should dress their age.'

'And what, according to you, should we wear to look our age?'

'I don't know about others but I certainly know that my wife's dress sense is perfect. I wouldn't like anybody to influence it. Not even you,' he said, thinking she looked a tart in her outlandish clothes.

'And if your wife would want to dress differently, then what? Pray, tell me.' She teased.

'I don't think she will. Actually, I know she won't.'

'Really? I like your confidence, bhaijaan, it shows you understand her pretty well. Okay darling,' she said, partly turning to Shehzaadi, her arms outstretched, 'I almost forgot why I'm here. Eid mubarak.' Both the women hugged each other. While Zeba was wishing Shehzaadi, Amita moved close to Anwar who had by now stood up. She put her arms around his neck saying, 'Eid mubarak bhaijaan.' Anwar stood unresponsive, all the while conscious of her nipples beneath the sheer silk kurta brushing against his chest. He mumbled a reciprocal greeting with unconcealed disgust. But Amita mistook it as the 'amita effect' as she called it.

In the confines of their bedroom when Shehzaadi was unfastening her earrings, Anwar protested. 'Let it be, jaan. Let me admire you at leisure. Subhan Allah, you look ravishing. Breathtakingly beautiful. Your friend is right. You don't look like the mother of a twenty-year-old. In fact, you don't look like a mother at all. I must ask Rukhsana to remove nazar tomorrow.'

'Shukriya. Thank you. But I didn't like the way you spoke to Amita.'

'What did I say?'

'It's not what you said but the way you said it. You ridiculed her dress sense.'

'No. I didn't. I admired yours.'

'Oh, really?'

'Yes, honestly.'

'Tell me something. You don't like my friends, right?'

'Right.'

'Why? What's wrong with them? They're just different from us. That's all.'

'Sweety listen to me, I'm not being judgemental. As far as I'm concerned, your friends don't exist. For me, whoever comes between us is wrong. Simple and straight.'

'What makes you think they're coming between us?'

Anwar was tempted to tell his wife of the nature of Amita's hug but restrained himself with great difficulty.

'I don't know. Just a weird feeling.'

'It's just that—weird.'

'Maybe.'

'It's true.'

'Okay. True. Pleased?'

'As punch.'

'I love you.'

'I know that.'

'And you?'

'You know I do.'

'No, I don't.'

'Yes, you do.'

'I do?'

'I do.'

'What a way to renew our wedding vows! You, my dear, are truly one in a million. Rare and precious.'

Both of them laughed. Anwar was ecstatic. His wife had returned to her old self. Shehzaadi looked at him and asked, 'May I change now?'

'No, don't ever change. Just your clothes. Actually, take them off. It's been too long since I saw you naked.'

'Some hope that is after the way you insulted my friends!'

'Where did that plural come from?'

'Well, you've done it to one. You'll do it to the other. Sooner or later. It's just a matter of time.'

'Don't let's go into that now please, my beautiful wife, my precious, my pride. Come into my arms.'

Shehzaadi found his coaxing irresistible and yielded. He laid his hand on her arm, drew her nearer gently; slowly, deliberately, with an intense appreciation of every move, every contact. He circled her waist, encircled her neck, and then holding her to him with all his strength, gazed for an infinite moment into her eyes before he lost himself in the long, sweet pressure of his lips against hers. Only when he lost himself thus did he feel he could find her.

The response of her passion was so like his own that he never doubted its sincerity. And she, who welcomed the certainty of his embrace that comforted her, could never guess that through her response she was helping him experience a deeper rapture—a joy that emanated from a sense of reassurance.

Anwar would never have been so happy in his love for Shehzaadi had it not contained that element of selfishness.

~

Chapter 13

ZEBA WATCHED HAMID AS HE UNDRESSED. HE'S SUPPOSED TO BE a doctor, she thought scornfully, just look at that bulging tummy, hanging under its own weight. His penis was hidden somewhere underneath it. He almost looked sexless. Do eunuchs look like this, she wondered. She felt overcome with revulsion. It made the hair on her arms stand on end. Ugh, how could she have married this man? He ate, drank, walked and even slept noisily. So much for the culture, she had imagined, that came with money. What had she married him for? Security or children? Or the tag of Mrs Hamid. He had given her no pleasure—neither material nor physical. What kind of security was she looking for? She made more money than him, anyway. That left her with the surname. What use had it been to her? Sometimes she envied Amita. Free and carefree and nobody to please. Nobody to tolerate. She could do what she pleased. And Amita did. With as much gay abandon as she could. When she saw Hamid coming towards the bed, she quickly closed her eyes. He lay down next to her. She realised that his face was close to hers when she smelled raw onions and meat on his breath. He had this sickening habit of partially breathing through his mouth. She wanted to pretend to be fast asleep but the hot foul air on her face wouldn't let her. She opened her eyes. His face looked like a frog's from that angle. 'Why don't you go brush your teeth?' she snarled.

'If I brush, will you let me?'

'No, it will just do you a lot of good. You're a doctor. You should know.'

'And you're a wife; you should know that a man needs sex, once in a while, at least.'

'You can go wherever you please, with whomsoever you want. You have my permission. Just leave me alone.'

'Who cares about your permission? I have my reputation to think of. And my family's. Nobody in my family screws around when there's a wife at home.'

That's because no woman would want to sleep with you, whether you have a wife at home or not, she thought. And what reputation was he talking of? At least Hamid had a practice to speak of but his two brothers did absolutely nothing.

They lived off the rent that came from several real estate properties they had inherited. His older brother was an alcoholic. His wife had left him and pushed off to London with their son. The younger brother had married Nafisa, a divorcee with a daughter from her first marriage. She had already seen her daughter go through the trauma of her parents' divorce. Now, she had no alternative but to put up with him because she now had the status of a married woman, Mrs Ahmed. God, what women would do to have the 'status' of a wife. Anybody's wife was better than being single, was that it?

Though mostly quiet and tolerant, Nafisa complained to Zeba only when she was at her wit's end with her husband's frequent vanishing acts. 'Allah miyan only knows what He wants from me. First He gave me a violent husband who never left me alone. Now, He has given me a jobless husband who's so busy that he leaves me alone all the time. I don't know which is worse?' Nafisa was always alone. Tending to the house, cooking, cleaning, gardening, looking after her ailing in-laws, her daughter. 'Why don't you ask him where he goes, what he does? Seriously, tell me what work does he have?' Zeba had said. 'I did everything Aapa. He gets very angry. He tells me that a man has several responsibilities, "Am I not looking after you and your daughter. Am I not providing for you? What else do you want? My blood!" After that I'm scared to say anything to him, Aapa,' she had confided.

Zeba felt terribly sorry for her. At least, she was in a better position, she thanked her lucky stars. She earned her own money, drove her own car, employed her own staff, ran her own office. She was a successful architect and interior designer. She planned other's homes. But when it came to her own, all she had was the façade with nothing concrete in it. Her married life was more or less like Nafisa's. She had no idea why Hamid had married her in the first place. 'Trophy wife, my dear, that's what you are,' Amita ridiculed her when she had expressed her doubts, 'You're young, pretty and successful. A man's social standing goes up if he has a pretty wife to show off.' Hamid's attitude had been pretty much that. He wanted her to accompany him wherever he went. Every party, every social engagement, every wedding, in fact he wouldn't go if she didn't want to or was unable to. 'I'm not one of those men who leaves their wives home and goes alone,' he'd told her when she tried to convince him that she was fine with him going alone, in a bid to break the pact that was tightening around her neck like a noose. She was finding it increasingly difficult to breathe freely when he was around. Just his presence was oppressive. She'd gone through hell during the initial years of their marriage. She was twenty-five, he was forty. He was so set in his ways. If she moved a pen, he would move it back where he had kept it. His obsession for method drove her mad. She was neither careless nor messy but he made her feel inadequate, always telling her what to do and how to do it. There was only one way to do things—his way. 'You're totally wrong. That's not how you trim a plant, place the cushion, cook the dish, switch the TV on, off, eat, sleep, drink, talk on the phone,' he would tell her. For a long time, she thought he did that only with her but gradually she realised that he was like that with everybody. He was basically a pompous, opinionated man, expressing his opinion whether anybody asked for it or not. And to make matters worse, he had an opinion on everything and how each thing had to be kept and how a person should behave. It was a kind of compulsive disorder. He saw no faults in himself. As far as he was concerned, he was perfect. Or the mirror lied. So did everybody who told him to lay off. His know-it-all attitude had left him with very few friends. And those few were hardly whom you could call friends. Basically birds of the same feathers, they were all comfortably off with inherited properties, club memberships and no major cash flow. So they frequented The Nawab's Club where they were still treated like royalty because nobody else went there. Every evening while their wives looked after their children, their parents, their homes, these men drank, played their cards, planned their moves, criticised society and whiled away most of their time. Out of curiosity, Zeba had gone there once and found the whole atmosphere dismal with dull lighting and just as dull men. Barring a couple of women, all the rest were men. She found it most depressing and wondered what they saw in that place to return to evening after evening. At the same time she marvelled at their contentment with such moronic activity and their mechanical lives. If only she could be one of them. Life would have been so much simpler.

Now she was forty, he fifty-five. Life was more or less under her control but his presence was something she now abhorred and didn't know how to deal with. She swung between tension and indifference when he was around and was tense, unsure of what he would say or do. And when he said or did something, she was filled with disgust. What did she expect from him? That he should be grateful to her for having married him. Probably, yes. If not grateful, she expected him to at least realise her worth. To recognise her as a thinking, feeling human being. Not as if she was a piece of furniture. When one became a 'thing' for a person, it was awful.

Is this how all marriages are? She thought of her parents. They had never had more money than absolutely necessary, yet they seemed so much at ease with each other. How do two people reach those comfort levels? But then most couples in her social strata at that time were like that, complementing each other. They were neither highly educated nor wealthy, yet there was a serenity, a kind of peace that came with an acceptance of each other. Their house had been overcrowded. Five rooms and twenty people. At any given time, there were always more than four people in a room. All the women took their clothes with them into the hamam to change after a bath. The men walked out with a towel wrapped around their waist and changed wherever they could. Most of them bathed once a week. But she needed a bath once, sometimes twice, a day. So she cribbed about other people's presence and their lack of space.

Now, she had an abundance of space emptied of people. She remembered Mumtaz Phuppi, her paternal aunt, an ordinary-looking woman, her husband Fazal Phuppa and their five children. Despite the chores, the financial burdens, the responsibilities of rearing their kids, Phuppa was absolutely smitten by his wife. He followed her like a puppy around the house hassling her, at times, with his over attentiveness. 'Chodo miyan,' she had heard Mumtaz Phuppi chiding him many times, 'I've got work to do.' But Phuppa was never put off. He had his usual reply ready, 'You do yours, while I do mine.' 'What'll others think?' she would say. 'I'm following my legally wedded wife not some gair woman. So what's there to think?' He always had the last word but it was Phuppi who seemed victorious. How does it feel, Zeba wondered, to have a man who loved you? She had no inkling. Hamid had never made her feel wanted or needed or in any way, despite the fact that she had been his chosen one from several prospective brides. Even their love-making sessions were most unimaginative. He was a selfish man. After having had what he wanted from her, he would snore without even turning the other way. She could write volumes on his snoring; it drove her insane every night. She barely slept because of the noise and sometimes she observed him for want of anything better to do. His nostrils flared, a deep grunt emanated from the depths of his abdomen that rose and fell rhythmically. Sometimes, he opened his mouth and the notes underwent a drastic change, stretching the decibel levels to the extremes. He was a doctor, he knew that snoring was anything but healthy, that it had to have an underlying cause needing medical intervention but he refused to even acknowledge it. Once, when she joked about it to their friends, he flared up in front of everyone. She was terrified of his temper that turned foul for no obvious reason. His sense of humour was non-existent. No, actually, it bordered on the sadistic. Lampooning was his forte and pontification his strength. He laughed when people fell and hurt themselves or when they said nasty things to each other. He didn't know what a healthy joke was. And a joke on him was nothing short of blasphemy. She had seen him insult a friend of his who had cracked a joke about Hamid's ever-increasing paunch. 'So, how many months?' Hamid was so livid that he launched a tirade against his friend's entire family and the friend had since then vanished. The joke *was* corny but it was innocent enough. Zeba didn't understand Hamid's almost violent reaction to it.

Why, she asked herself, did she continue to live with a man who didn't love her and whom she never had. 'You're chicken,' Amita had told her several times, 'You're scared of people. "What'll people say?" and all that nonsense. These people who talk are like street dogs. They chase you as long as you keep running. If you turn back and face them; they retreat with their tails between their legs. Once I realised that, I said this to them,' Amita stuck out her middle finger. Zeba wished she had the courage to do it. More than that, she lacked the inclination. What would she do being on her own? She had alienated herself from her family. If she told them now they would laugh at her failure because she had ridiculed theirs. Whoever knew her in society, knew her as Mrs Zeba Hamid Hassan. Nobody recognised Zeba Khatoon Ansari. Going back from being Hassan to Ansari didn't have anything worth doing it for. Like a passionate love affair, for instance. Passion, love, children, family...would she ever experience any of those before she died? Or would she die an old, unfulfilled, unhappy, lonely woman? How terrifying!

If only she had not married for social status. Why had she not waited for love? She sometimes wished Hamid was like Shehzaadi's husband. If only she had courage like Amita. Perhaps her life would have been more meaningful if she had had children. She longed to know how it felt when a man held somebody he loved passionately. She didn't even know what it was like to have an orgasm…she had never felt exhausted after making torrid love. Perhaps if Hamid would talk less. Maybe she should try talking to him more. If only somebody was there to listen…she didn't even have family to turn to.

If only.

Zeba's life was full of just that. When a reporter from a local newspaper had asked her if she would have lived any other way for one of those 'one question' columns, she had replied, 'No regrets.'

Chapter 14

AMITA WAS VERY EXCITED. HER DAUGHTER, SITA, WAS DUE TO arrive to spend her winter vacation with her mother. She was driving the entire household—her cook, housekeeper, maali, driver—up the wall to get everything in order. Nobody was complaining, though. The only time they saw their 'madam' genuinely happy was when her daughter visited. Three times a year, every year, for the last ten years. Before that Siddharth Saab had also lived with them. In a different house. They were hardly a happy couple. Always squabbling over the pettiest of issues. And when they fought—they really fought—a fight to finish the opponent. Baring their fangs, hurling abuses, calling names, provoking each other, they had even got physical once after which there were no more fights. Because the warring couple had decided to put an end to the fights by going a different way—their two separate ways.

Everybody knew that the two had a volatile marriage with temperaments to match. They had elephantine memories for each other's minutest mistakes and shortcomings, everything except their love for one another. Nobody who looked at them post-marriage could have guessed that their love story had all the trappings of a fairy tale. Only the end was different—they did not live happily ever after.

It had taken less than a year of married life for a most passionate love affair to turn into a doomed relationship. Maria, their Anglo-Indian housekeeper, had analysed it perfectly in her mind. Both the master and the mistress were spitting images of each other. They were both good-looking, they had similar tastes, they were ambitious, they loved each other, they were crazy about their only child, and their friends, and most of all, about partying. There was only one aspect lacking—respect for each other. So many shared interests and just one problem. But that outweighed all that they had in common, spelling doom with a capital D for their marriage.

If you asked Maria, she would have said that they could have had a happy marriage if they had more respect for each other, a little less fondness for their social life and a control over their inflated egos. But nobody asked Maria. And Maria kept her opinion to herself. If they'd turned to her instead of their lawyers, the disaster could probably have been averted. But an ill-fated plane and an ill-fated marriage carry their passengers to the same irrevocable end. No advice is any good once the plane is mid-air and all you can see are signals of impending doom. You know your doom is in sight, yet you can't get off mid-way.

Maria had a different way of putting it though. Marriage is akin to cooking, she would say. Once you master the art, you can handle it with your eyes closed. But before that, attaining the right balance is the trickiest part. The most trying one too. And excess heat is the most disastrous of ingredients. Even if your recipe is perfect, subjecting it to extreme heat entails not only ruining it but also having a lot to clean up after. That is how the cookie crumbles, she would say to the other relatively newer servants. Excess of anything is disastrous.

In the early days of their marriage, it was all good fun, the newly-weds enthusiastic in their passion for each other, leaving love notes all over the place, partying every night, seven nights a week. And then the lull came. Siddharth was getting busier. As a bright anaesthetist, his work demanded more time and energy from him, leaving him with less to devote to his young wife. On the days when he had the time, he had no energy and therefore no inclination. For Amita, not meeting people meant boredom and stagnation. So she tied up with Hamid and Zeba and continued just like before. The day the first crack appeared began most innocuously. That evening when Siddharth came home early, he found his wife all dressed up to go out. When Amita saw him, she grinned widely, thrilled that they could now go together. 'How nice,' she said happily, jumping up to greet him, 'it's been so long since we went to a party together. They'll be so happy to see you.'

'Who?'

'You forgot? Don't you remember Mina and Mahmud invited us to their anniversary bash at their farmhouse?'

'Mmm... oh yes, I remember. Listen sweetheart, why don't we stay home. It's been ages since we spent some time alone at home.'

'Okay. Let me call and apologise, then,' she said, rushing to the phone. For the next twenty minutes, he heard her conversing and laughing over the telephone. How long does it take to apologise, he thought, irritated at her preoccupation. After she finished she came to him, sat on his lap and teased him, 'Okay, your highness, can I take your order for dinner?' 'Let's have a cozy candle-light dinner,' he replied playing with the fringes of her hair. 'Sounds great but I've invited Anirudh, Ram, Karishma and Dolly home. I thought we'd order in some Chinese. What do you say?'

'Come on Amy, how could you invite them just like that? You didn't even bother to check if it was okay with me. Or if I had other plans. The whole purpose of not going to the party is defeated now.'

'Hey! That's not fair! Remember the time when I had an upset stomach and couldn't accompany you to Vishal's party? What did you do? You went alone. At least I haven't left you alone and gone out. Did you bother to check if it was okay with me, to stay alone when I was sick?'

'Of course, I did. You said you would be all right.'

'Great! So if I'm on my deathbed and tell you I was going to be okay, you'd take my word for it, and go anyway. Is that it? Can't you understand without being told that a sick person needs someone around?'

'But you had Maria around.'

'So, what are you saying now?'

'I'm not in the mood to socialise with other people.'

'They're not people, Siddharth. They're our friends. You like their company.'

'Maybe. But not today.'

'What do you want me to do? Tell them not to come? I can't do that. Besides, they would have left already.'

'So what? They have their mobiles. Pass me the cordless, I'll call them.'

'No, you won't. I'm the one who has invited them and they'll come. If you're not in the mood, you stay upstairs.'

'So, they're more important to you than me? Is that what you're implying?'

'I'm not implying anything. If I want to say something, I say it. If I'd asked you the same question on the night you went to Vishal's party, what would you have said?'

'Okay, fine then. Now, I know where I stand in your list of priorities!'

'Listen Sid, you're blowing this out of proportion.'

Their first of innumerable rows was interrupted by the arrival of their guests. Siddharth retreated to their bedroom like he had threatened.

Anirudh, their friend, asked her, 'Hey, where's Siddharth?'

'Oh, he's sulking.'

'Trouble in paradise, huh?'

'No, no, nothing of that sort. He's just overworked. Needs to rest.'

The rest of the evening was like any other for Amita. Friends, fun, drink, food and fags. Upstairs, Siddharth thought, 'If she comes up and pleads with me, I'll go down.'

She didn't come up. He didn't go down. They stayed stubbornly in their self-accorded positions. Amita partied. Siddharth stayed up watching TV until he dozed off.

The next morning their fight resumed. He didn't say a word. She said many but only to the servants. She told Maria to 'inform sir that breakfast was served.' Siddharth wanted to sulk longer but he was hungry. He ate quietly thinking, 'she didn't even bother to ask me for dinner last night. She doesn't give a damn.'

Amita thought, 'What does he think of himself? Sulking like I've committed a major crime or something. He doesn't care about me one whit.'

A couple of days later, the steam fizzled out, they resumed talking to each other. But the rift had appeared. The tenderness was gone.

A week later when Siddharth invited a few friends over, it was Amita's turn to go on strike. 'Don't be ridiculous,' he said to her, when she said she preferred the company of her book.

'Oh, so when I'm not in the mood, I'm ridiculous. When you're not, you're a man. Is that it? Talk of double standards.'

'Don't do this, Amy, they'll feel bad.'

'Did you care about my friends' feelings when you decided to boycott?'

That's how their friends got divided into his and hers. A pattern was set and followed. She went out when she felt like, so did he. They did go out together but those times were few and far between. The 'can't keep their hands off each other' couple had turned into 'hands off' individuals. She stayed out of his way. He never came in hers. That's when divinity seemed to grant them a chance to mend their relationship, Amita discovered that she was pregnant. But when human egos clash, even opportunities like these are turned into disasters.

Amita was confused. She didn't know if she wanted the child. At this point in time anyway. They'd been married for less than a year. She had plans to start her own boutique. But now if she were to have the baby, she'd have to put her plans on the back-burner. And if the baby came, she would not be able to do anything for a couple more years at least. She just wasn't sure if she wanted to wait that long.

But she obviously couldn't make an independent decision. She had to talk to Siddharth; after all, it was his child too. When she voiced her apprehension to him, he was appalled. 'How could you even think in terms of terminating the pregnancy? You must be out of your mind,' he yelled, flying off the handle.

'It was just a thought,' she said, 'I'm really confused...'

'Instead of rejoicing, you're entertaining criminal thoughts. What kind of a woman are you?'

'There's no need to be so harsh, Siddharth. I was just confiding in you. If you think I'm not happy about my pregnancy, you're mistaken. I'm sorry to say but you're over reacting. I'm the one who's carrying it in my womb. I'm the mother.'

'Well. You're not behaving like one. And I'm not sorry to say that.'

That set a pattern of fights over Sita. Even before she was born. So soon after she was conceived.

Nine months passed like a dream with Siddharth fussing over her like she was the child. On a bright sunny day, in the early hours of the morning, their daughter, an eight-pound baby, was born. The parents were ecstatic. Everything she did was a marvel. They noted down every little detail in a book called 'Sita's Milestones.' Her first haircut, the first nail cutting, every little progress and occurrence complete with photographs. Her name was chosen in the most ingenious way. The first two alphabets of Siddharth and the last two of Amita together constituted Sita. Luckily for them, it also happened to be the name of a Goddess, Lord Rama's wife. Divine coincidence, they thought.

The restlessness set into Amita after Sita's first birthday. The celebrations were spread over a week. It was the parents who enjoyed their daughter's birthday more than the birthday girl who could not understand why she was left alone with the servants all the time. They had so many concerns to make their daughter's birthday a grand success. Unfortunately for Sita, it didn't include her hunger or thirst. Amita had engaged a well-known event manager to handle the occasion. There were clowns, Disney characters, helium balloons that floated around, a music band that played nursery rhymes. The dinner spread had the hundred or more guests admire the lavish buffet spread—every dish was named after Sita—Sita's choice, Sita's favourite, Sita's sweet, Sita's desire, Sita's dream, so on and so forth. Even the instrument that was played during the band's respite was the Sitar. 'I think you're carrying it a little too far, if you ask me,' said Zeba to Amita. 'I'm not asking you, so just shut up,' retorted Amita, 'Moreover, honey, you ain't seen nothing yet. Just wait and watch.' Zeba rolled her eyes partly out of envy and partly out of disdain. Everybody had a blast. Sita cried all evening and slept hungry. Mamma was too busy looking after the guests. Maria had given up all attempts to feed her when the toddler spat out the food consistently. She had tried telling the master and mistress but her voice got lost in the din on the dance floor.

Two days after their excitement settled down, Siddharth was faced with a dilemma. One of the hospitals he was a consultant for, was opening up a branch in Atlanta, USA. They had offered him a good position with fantastic perks that he was finding hard to resist. When he told Amita, she threw a fit. 'When I wanted to delay my pregnancy, you went on a puritanical trip about parenthood blah, blah. Now if you go away, how am I supposed to look after Sita on my own? And why do you need all those perks, aren't we happy with what we have? In any case, I'm planning to start my boutique soon. I'm sure it'll do well. We'll have more money coming in.'

'It's not about money, Amy. It's more about the exposure, the experience, the position, you know. There's no need for you to earn for our survival or luxuries. By the grace of God, we have enough to last us a lifetime, if not our future generations.'

'You're right; it's not about money, at all. It's about putting to use my creativity, my talent and my education. And also upping my declining self-esteem. That's why I *have* to start my venture. I'm sure you understand my need, now.'

Before Siddharth realised how she had turned the tables on him, she was on the phone talking busily to the owner of a vacant store that she had liked. Later that night, he pleaded with her, 'Listen Amy, I think Sita's too young to be left with Maria. Let's make a deal. I won't take up my offer and you postpone your boutique for a while. For the sake of our daughter, please.'

'Listen Sid, life's not about making deals. If you do this, I'll do that…what nonsense! If you wish to take up that offer, do so. By all means. But I'm not going to put off my plans. If I told you to stay home while I go out and pursue my dreams, will you do it? Like you said sometime back, we have enough money to last us a lifetime even if we don't work. So, why don't you take a sabbatical while I go do my own thing? Is it because you're a man? I need to know what makes you talk the way you do so tell me! Just because you have balls, you think you're superior?'

'Hey, calm down Amita. This is not a debate on the equality of the sexes. All I'm interested in is my child's well-being.'

'What makes you think I'm not? She's my child too. I carried her in me for nine months. She breathed the air that I drew in. So don't give me a bhashan on what's right and what's wrong. I know it as well as you do.'

And their argument continued late into the night. In the next room, Maria stayed awake listening quietly, while Sita slept in her lap. Everytime she tried shifting the child to her crib, she would cry. Not wanting to add to the existing confusion, Maria sat up all night.

~

Chapter 15

AMITA WAS DELIGHTED WHEN SHE FOUND THE IDEAL LOCATION for her boutique. In the heart of Banjara Hills surrounded by five star hotels and the city's elite residential areas—her prime target. She named it 'Valmiki'—after the author of the Ramayana. The event manager had roped in a superstar from the Telugu film industry for the inauguration of the boutique. They served hors d'oeuvres and wine later in the evening. Siddharth didn't attend either the inauguration or the function later. Amita didn't invite him. She felt she was better off without Mr Sulk Master creating a scene.

In a short span, Valmiki became a hit with the city's clientele. Amita's designs were original—she used kalamkari, pochampally, venkatgiri and other famous forms of Andhra handlooms and art and created beautiful pieces of clothing and accessories. People started ranking her alongside established fashion designers elsewhere in the country. She expanded her operations to a dyeing and printing unit. Meanwhile, Sita was growing up into an angry child much to her dad's anxiety. The recipient of Sita's heated outbursts was the only person who was with her almost all the time—Maria. She would kick her, hit her, scratch her and even bite her at times, especially when she wanted one of her parents around. Most of the time they weren't. When Maria complained to Amita about her daughter's behaviour, she said, 'Don't be funny, Maria. Look at my daughter.

Look at the way she's smiling right now. She's such an angel. How can she do anything like that? Give her some time. Must be a passing phase.' Sita was, indeed, an angel when her mother was around, delighting in her baby talk and baby steps. Time grows wings when babies are growing up. Sita was growing up. Her parents were growing apart. The husband disapproved of everything the wife did and she didn't give a damn, one way or another. They were indifferent to each other but when it came to their daughter they fell over each other to please her. It had become some kind of a game. A one-upmanship. Who does how much for her? And it was all shown in the form of gifts, chocolates and goodies. 'See, she loves me more,' was all they wanted to prove to each other. Sita, with her little eyes and little knowledge of her world, exploited it to the hilt. She played favourites to her advantage. The only unconditional love she got was from Maria who continued to suffer her kicks and blows in silence while she bathed her, clothed her and fed her.

Before they realised it, Sita was three. Two more birthdays had passed with the same fervour if not more. Now, the time had come to send the little one to nursery school. 'She's too young, I think,' said Amita. And since Siddharth had to counter everything she said, he continued, 'No, this is the right time to begin. All the other kids start at this age. I want my daughter to be normal. She will go this year.'

'Okay, then. *You* find a good school and *you* organise the admission. Because I don't believe in being one of the herd. Everybody is sending their children so we should too... what kind of an argument is that?' criticised Amita.

'What do you think? I can't do it? I can't get her into a good school? I will. I'll get her in with the best of the lot. I'll show you.'

Amita laughed sardonically and walked out of the room. Siddharth felt such a surge of anger that he felt like throttling her. Who the hell does she think she is? Laughing at him. Much to his annoyance, her boutique was flourishing. He didn't know how much money she made, but he had an idea it was a lot. She had stopped asking him for anything. Earlier, it used to give him a sense of pride and control when she asked him for money. 'Sid, will you get me a solitaire for my birthday, please?' or 'Is it okay if I pick up a few more outfits?' It made him feel good. He liked the power it gave him. Nowadays she neither asked him nor told him anything. He'd noticed her, on several occasions, wearing new jewellery and outfits but he pretended he hadn't.

Siddharth had a habit of cribbing about electricity bills. Every evening he would religiously turn off all the lights that he felt were unneeded while telling Amita to take care. Out of habit, he'd done it a month ago and the next morning he found the right amount of cash, down to the last rupee, on his bedside table. He told her later, 'Listen Amy, I didn't mean anything when I cribbed about the bill; you know how I am, don't you?'

'No, I don't,' she replied curtly without looking him in the eye.

How had things come to such a stage, he wondered fleetingly. Was it his fault?

No way! He'd only asked her to wait for a while before starting the boutique. It was from that time that she had started moving away from him, becoming so busy with her work. Exactly as he had predicted. He did feel proud of her when his women friends told him that they were loyal customers of Valmiki because it was in a league of its own. But he never told her that. She already had a swollen head. Besides, when did they talk these days? Every conversation they had led to an argument. He had no energy left, after a hard day's work, to waste over quarrels. He preferred playing with his daughter. At least that made him happy.

Though he had boasted to her, Siddharth realised that school admissions were no child's play. With great difficulty and influence, he managed to secure a seat in Vidyashram School, considered one of the best. He had to as he had claimed he could to Ms Swollen Head. She had seemed pleased with his choice when she came for the interview. He realised that schools interviewed parents first and then the student later. Phew! Life was getting more and more complicated. And all this, just for nursery. He dreaded to think what it would be like later! But that could wait. What needed his attention right now was their marriage which was on the verge of collapse.

To begin with, he had to reopen the lines of communication that had gone completely awry. Did she really not care? Did she hate him now or was it some kind of a built-up anger, resentment that made her retreat into her shell. She was still vivacious, energetic and interesting. But that side was reserved only for her friends. The moment she saw him, the look on her face changed visibly, she clammed up. The other night when he had tried to kiss her, she pushed him away with such force that he was scared for the first time since the rift appeared. Both of them, he analysed, had built barriers around themselves that were turning out to be impenetrable. He was at fault too but then he had sacrificed his job opportunity only because she had asked him to, hadn't he? Didn't she see that? What was she trying to prove? That whatever he did, she could do better? Or did she simply not give a damn about him? Whatever it was, they had to patch up. For the sake of their daughter if not each other. He was aware that it was no easy task. He knew how stubborn she could get when she wanted to. Something between them had cooled off; it was not the same anymore. However, he decided to give it a try. So he suggested to Amita that they take a break. Go on a vacation. Just the three of them. He asked her where she wanted to go. Amita said, 'It doesn't matter where. But we'll take Maria with us.'

'Why? Are you trying to tell me that you can't handle her? Or you don't want to?'

'I'm not trying to tell you, I *am* telling you that it's not easy to handle her. Have you any idea what it takes to handle her on your own? Have you ever done it?'

'No, I haven't. But I'm sure I'll be able to if I try.'

'Yeah? Why don't you try then? Take Sita and go alone. I dare you.'

'Let's not get into this Amy, I want us to go together. Both of us need a break.'

'If you mean it, why do you have objections to Maria coming along? Either we take her with us or we stay here. The choice is yours.'

'Shit! This is going nowhere. You know how to drive me nuts. Tell me in one word—yes or no.'

'Please refer to my earlier option. Because if I repeat it you'll call me a nag.'

'So, it's a no.'

'No, it's not a no. It's a no to your suggestion. We can still go if you listen to me. For the simple reason that it's practical. Don't you see that?'

'No, I honestly don't. You're probably the only sane one around here.'

'I am glad you realise that now.'

'Have it your way. We're NOT going anywhere, okay?'

'When did I say I wanted to? It was your idea, remember?'

'God! I wonder what I ever saw in you.'

'Now that you've seen my true colours, what's stopping you from leaving me? By the way, have you seen yourself in the mirror lately? You've got a perpetual frown on your face. You're not the same guy I used to know.'

'You're the one who's made me this way.'

'Yeah? Thanks for telling me that. That's all I needed to hear.'

Tears streamed down her cheeks. In the next minute she started sobbing uncontrollably. Sita came running from the other room on hearing the commotion. When she found her mother crying, she asked in her baby lisp, 'Whath happen, mamma?'

Amita wiped her tears, shook her head and hugged her daughter close.

'Your tummy aching?' the child persisted.

'No, my baby, my heart is.'

'Papa, we'll go to doctor.'

'No doll. No doctor can cure this.'

'Papa, give medicine to mamma.'

'No baby, if your papa gives me medicine, I might just die. I'll be okay. You stay close to me like this, I'll be okay. See, I'm already feeling better.'

Siddharth was livid.

'There was no need to say such things in front of the child,' he said, raising his voice.

'Sshhh...' Amita said, with a finger on her lips, 'Don't ever raise your voice in front of her. Do you understand?'

And then she carried her daughter and walked out of the room rubbing her nose against Sita's who was now chuckling.

Siddharth sat with a thud on the diwan. He held his head between his hands and pressed the lower half of his palms against his temples. He could feel them throb as if they were ready to burst with the pressure. 'This woman has an amazing knack of giving me a headache,' he murmured to himself. During happier days whenever he complained of a headache, Amita massaged his head with warm oil, teasing him, 'Shows you actually have a head.' He would close his eyes and smile, enjoying the soothing sensation. If she saw him like this now, she would probably derive sadistic pleasure out of it. God! She had changed completely. He didn't know this woman who was his wife. He went to the bedroom and looked for Disprin in the medicine box. He found none. Before she had started this damned boutique of hers, everything used to be in order. He found some balm and applied it. He detested the smell and the strong odour it left on his pillow but he had no choice. He slept without eating his dinner.

Around midnight, he woke up, restless. He was starving. He switched on the bedside lamp. That's when he realised she wasn't in bed. Where could she have gone at this hour? With his heart pounding, he picked up the phone and dialled her cell phone number.

He heard it ringing somewhere around. Before he could hang up, he heard her sleepy voice, 'What is it now? You have a problem even if I sleep with my daughter?'

'I didn't know where you were so I got worried.'

'You can worry as much as you want, now let me sleep.'

He sat staring at the phone for a while and then decided to go look for something to eat. He found some chicken curry and rice and mixed it up before putting it in the microwave oven. Once the food was consumed, he felt better. The headache and hunger had subsided but he was still restless. How could she sleep so peacefully when everything around them was falling to pieces? For the rest of the night, he tossed and turned in bed. Somewhere in the wee hours of the morning, he slipped into a deep, dreamless slumber.

Amita was at her boutique, brimming with happiness as she saw customers thronging to catch a glimpse of her latest collection. She had used a lot of lucknowi chikan work on light mulmul fabric and given a thin lining for the kurtas with high cuts up to the waist and teamed them with lengthy semi-transparent churidaars. They were mostly in pastel colours except for one in lemon yellow and green and the other in bright orange and blue. It was summer and the collection was bound to sell out. 'Nothing can be more delightful than success,' she thought. If she had listened to Siddharth, she wouldn't have tasted it. It was all about being in the right place at the right time. She would have been sitting at home, whiling away her time on telephone conversations and ladies lunches. There's only so much a mother can do. How long could she have stayed cooped up in the house even if it was to look after her child? Moreover, the man himself would have been in the US if she'd not put her foot down. She didn't mind single parenting, she was perfectly capable of managing her child on her own (with a lot of help from Maria) but what use was it having a husband and not having him around when you needed him? Thank god she hadn't paid heed to his selfish advice. God had been kind to her. She had already recovered her investment and her profits had doubled.

She touched the idol of Ganesha in her handbag for good luck. Her grandmother had given it to her when she was alive. Amita's parents were in the US with her brother, his wife and their twins. Her mother had gone visiting when her daughter-in-law was expecting and stayed back when she had given birth to twins. Now, they had got their green card. They'd come to see her when Sita was born but Siddharth found fault with everything his mother-in-law said about caring for the new born. They had left soon after. 'I would rather be with people who trust me,' her mother had said to Siddharth who didn't take it kindly. Now, barring a stray e-mail her brother sent on behalf of their parents, she had no contact with them. Somehow, their strained relationship with her husband had affected hers with them. It was not like he was close to his parents, either. They had no relationship to speak of. It was the same with his three brothers and sister. He was not even on talking terms with the older brother. And the younger two were too scared to get close to him. And he didn't like his sister's husband, so he had snapped all relations with them. She had found it strange initially but when she advised him to let the past be and make an attempt to strengthen his family bonds, he told her very tersely, 'You stay out of this, please. I've lived with them; I know what kind of people they are. Let me handle it my way.' Fine then, Amita had decided, what did it matter to her anyway? But in retrospect, she felt that Siddharth was perhaps a difficult person to know and live with. He was too rigid in his thinking. She had lived with him long enough now to recognise that trait in him. How could she have not seen it when they were going around? She had blinkers on. It was true that he had been an attentive lover but on the other hand, also always a demanding one. She had probably expected him to mellow down after marriage. On the contrary, he had become even more difficult. Last night was probably the first night in the last three months that she had slept peacefully. Any other man in his place would have rejoiced that his wife had made a success of her business. But not Siddharth. He had not visited her boutique once. He's jealous, she thought, jealous of my success. He would have been thrilled if I had failed, probably even consoled me. It was time for a reality check. She had seen the signs for sometime now but last night it was crystal clear that she had to get a grip on her married life if she wanted Sita to be happy.

Chapter 16

AMIDST STONY SILENCE AND STUNTED CONVERSATION, ANOTHER year dragged its feet. Their socialising had reached its peak, not withstanding the fact that they rarely spoke to each other. But they had become adept at keeping up appearances. Both of them were show people. Although there were places that they went to alone, sometimes joint appearances were customary. One such place was that of Hamid and Zeba's. Siddharth had been many years junior to Hamid in medical college but the two had struck up a rapport. Amita had grown pretty close to Zeba, who had not the slightest idea of the state of her friend's married life.

Life carried on the way it had to until it was time for Sita's primary school admission. And the storm that erupted blew away the remaining scraps of their marriage. Amita wanted her daughter to go to Vidyalaya, a famous school on the lines of Rishi Valley. Siddharth would have none of it; his daughter had to go to a public school and nowhere else. It was a question of status. Amita carried on with her plans, irrelevant of what Sid thought and so did he. Sita, the bright little toddler, unaware of the complications she was creating, had secured admission in both. The tug-of-war had begun.

'Siddharth, you have no idea how stressful public school education is. Any mainstream school, for that matter. They are so performance oriented that the child's childhood is lost in academic pursuit. Please listen to me just this once.'

'Do you understand that this once means the next twelve years?' Siddharth said sarcastically, 'Every child needs to get used to the stress and strain of today's life. If Sita doesn't learn to cope with it, she'll reach nowhere. I'm speaking from experience. I'm a public school product. Is there anything wrong with me?'

Amita laughed bitterly and answered, 'Well apart from everything, no. From your attitude towards people to your insensitivity, every aspect of your personality reflects your selfishness. Do you think I am going to let my daughter grow up to be like you? Over my dead body!'

'Yeah? If I have so many faults, how come a smart woman like you has fallen for me?'

'Not has, had. Please understand that subtle difference. Actually, I don't expect you to. Subtlety has never been your forte.'

'You've studied at Rishi Valley right? Tell me what good has it done you?'

'See for yourself. I am a caring human being. And a successful businesswoman. All without anybody's help. I did it all on my own steam.'

'Caring and you? You wanted to abort your own child, kill her even before she was born. If that's caring then all murderers are Mahatmas.'

'Stop it.'

'The truth hurts, right? And all that about being a successful businesswoman...well how did you get there? By staying in my house, eating the food I provided you and maintaining a lavish lifestyle with my money while you set up shop. If you had paid for all that and then established yourself, then *that* would have been some achievement.'

'Hold on a minute. What did you just say? And all this while I thought this was my house too. In that case, what were you doing sleeping with me for free? Did you have to pay for my housekeeping, gardening, for looking after you and your house? And all that sex you had with me, it would have cost you more to keep a whore. So, Siddharth, let's draw a balance sheet. Since I'm an educated, well-bred, well-groomed woman and a virgin when I met you, let's decide on a price for my nocturnal services.'

'Shut up, you uncivilised woman,' he shouted and slapped her on her right cheek.

'How dare you?' she screamed and reached for his face scratching him with her nails.

He howled in pain and felt his face. He was bleeding. 'That's it. I've had enough. I'm not going to live with you for one more minute. You're not a woman, you're a witch. Chi,' he spat, 'you're disgusting.'

'And you? What are you? Men don't hit their wives.'

'Enough is enough,' he yelled at the top of his voice. Sita emerged from her room, hiccoughing, tears streaming down her cheek, the cold worsening her crying. Siddharth picked her up and walked out in a huff.

Amita heard the car engine revving as she sat like she had been struck by lightning. She couldn't believe he had hit her. And that they had said all those nasty things to each other. God! They brought out the worst in each other. They had fought like animals. Now she was certain that their marriage had slipped out of their hands.

She sat there too spent to feel anything, waiting for them to return. They didn't. She called on his cell phone and all he said was, 'It's over Amy.' 'I know. But we have Sita to think of,' she sobbed. 'Sita's my daughter. You don't have to worry about her. As for my coming back, you can forget about it.' Even as she was telling him that Sita was her daughter too and that he had no right...he disconnected. She tried calling him again several times but he had put his phone off. The end was final.

The following months, when they should have been running around for their daughter's school admissions, Amita and Siddharth frequented lawyers, courts and hearings. Both were bent on gaining custody of their daughter. Lawyers extracted as many negative details about their client's opponent as they could. Friends took sides, several of them playing double games. Fuelled by their friends' ill intentions and their lawyers' desire for victory, Amita and Siddharth did their best to paint each other as a devil unfit for parenting. But, with an experienced lawyer on his side, and his accusations that Amita smoked and drank excessively, that she was an irresponsible, career-oriented woman, and had never wanted to carry the child in the first place, Siddharth won the case. Sita, who had no clue what was going on, stayed back with her father. Siddharth offered Amita alimony, which she rejected, and visitation rights as well as fifty percent of their daughter's vacations', which she accepted. 'The couple is incompatible and cannot resolve their differences. They are irreconcilable and simply cannot live together again. The mother is unfit for responsible parenting and therefore, this court has decided to hand over the custody of their minor daughter to the father' was the judge's verdict.

Siddharth moved to Mumbai. Sita joined a new school in a new city.

For a long while after the divorce, Amita shunned all company. She mourned alone. With Maria watching in the background. Maria cared for her like a mother in those dark, depressing days. Their relationship transcended the mistress-servant equation from then on. Maria was heartbroken in her own way. Sita was the only child she had ever looked after in all her lonely life. She had provided the maternal care that the child needed. Friends wanted to reach out to Amita but they didn't know where she was. She had moved out of their old house. Zeba did her best to find out from the neighbours but nobody knew. Just as she was beginning to give up hope, Amita rose like the proverbial phoenix. She bounced back, a new woman with boundless energy and zest for life. She was almost the same old Amita before her marriage except for one new development—her insatiable hunger for men. The change came in one dramatic sweep —from being a committed wife to a coquettish flirt. The new

Amita knew how to get men to do her bidding. She had experienced real life closely enough to not want to go anywhere near it again.

She was no longer turned on by love. She was stimulated by vanity and an unquenchable thirst for admiration. Most of the men she eyed responded willingly. The admiration from men, especially distinguished ones, served as a morale booster and did wonders to her sense of self-esteem.

More than a few men would go to any lengths to win her affection. She now considered men being drawn to her as inevitable; she knew she possessed the looks, body and personality to floor them. Something in her manner, however, held back most of her lovers when it came to staking claims on her. She recognised the unspoken signs of love but never encouraged them to declare it. She often bragged to Zeba, 'Did you notice that Aslam's fallen for me?' When Zeba asked how she could tell, Amita replied, 'The eyes and body language of a man gives his desire away. The one thing I'm sure of in life is that if I should ever want a permanent lover, I'll have no dearth of them. I can pick and choose.'

Amita's qualities justified her pride but they also nourished her vanity. She felt a sense of triumph for surviving in circumstances that other women would perhaps find trying and at times, humiliating. She was proud that she had bravely survived in a world that thrived on double standards and hypocrisies capable of crushing many other women. Despite the triumphs and conquests, however, bitterness lurked beneath her sparkling persona. There also existed a great deal of self-pity. She thought of herself as 'a good soul overwhelmed by the heartless ways of the world.' She spoke to Shehzaadi of the long years of anxiety and suffering after she was separated from her daughter so abruptly, and Shehzaadi couldn't help but feel terribly sorry for her. 'People condemn my behaviour today but they are free to think whatever they want to. I don't give a damn because only I know the turmoil—physical, mental and emotional—that I've been through. But I'm not one to mourn the past and lose sleep over my future. Each for themselves. That's my take on life.' Shehzaadi trusted her version because she didn't know any better. Zeba, on the other hand, had seen the transformation of Amita from a wife into an incorrigible flirt. Though the two sides seemed at odds, she saw a common thread—that Amita had no respect for marriage or commitment. 'Every divorced woman must divide her life into BM and AD.' Amita had said to her once, elaborating that BM meant Before Marriage and AD, After Divorce. Zeba had asked, 'What about married life?' Amita had laughed saying, 'A married life? You don't have a life when you're married, darling. Trust me.'

She entranced men and left them pining for more. 'Serves them right. How dare they screw around when they're committed elsewhere,' she had said to Zeba on several occasions. She derived the highest form of pleasure when she succeeded in ensnaring supposedly 'happily married men'. 'I doubt if such a species exists though,' she said after she had encountered many who were ready to cheat on their wives, pledge undying love to her, do anything just to be around her. 'Borrowed husbands are better than owned husbands because all the harshness is reserved for their wives,' she would say to Zeba who couldn't help but feel an admiration for Amita's skills. 'So far I have succeeded with every man I've wanted. And boy, am I choosy.'

Zeba had, so far, had no objections to her friend's conquests but recently her suspicions were aroused everytime she met or mentioned Anwar Ali Mirza. She was sure she wasn't imagining things. She'd had enough experience with Amita to not over-react in such situations. She knew the kind of men that appealed to her and that Anwar fitted the bill perfectly. But Zeba also didn't know how to warn Shehzaadi. She had to think of a way to intercept Amita's plans—and she was sure she had many—without trampling on anybody's feelings. Much as she was against Amita's indiscretion with married men, she knew that she was trying to fill the all-encompassing vacuum deep within her. Now, she sighed with relief knowing that her friend could pose no immediate peril because Amita was a different person when her daughter was around.

When Sita was around, Amita vanished from the social world. All her energy went into spending as much time as she could with her daughter who had grown up away from her. Sita was fifteen now. She was a bright, level-headed girl, despite her early roller coaster childhood years. Though it was hard to admit, Amita knew that Siddharth had done a good job of bringing her up. But she never told him that. They hardly spoke to each other except to exchange vital information about their daughter's arrivals and departures. But then who could go wrong with a child as good as her daughter, Amita thought, giving more credit to the child than to her father for the way she had turned out. Much as Sita loved her father, it was her mother that she felt sorry for. She made a concerted effort each time she was with her to make her as happy as she could. Her father had remarried and she was fond of her stepmother but Amita was her mother. A week after Sita landed both the mother and daughter went out on a long drive one evening. Amita wanted her daughter to see the Secret Lake. On the way, Sita asked, 'Is it true that you never wanted me?' Amita brought the car to a screeching halt. Luckily for them, the road wasn't crowded and the vehicle behind them was a mile away. 'Who told you that? Oh, look at me asking such a stupid question. Who else could have told you? Obviously, your father. That's not true at all. Did you believe him? Did you believe what he said?' Amita was hysterical. Sita hadn't meant to hurt her, it hardly mattered to her what her mother had thought then, she had casually asked the question out of curiosity. Both her parents clammed up when it came to their divorce. It was an event shrouded in mystery. 'I'm sorry mamma. Please don't cry. I'm really sorry. I didn't think about what I was saying.' Amita spoke between sobs. 'No darling, there's nothing wrong with what you said. Whatever is wrong is with your father.'

On the boat, at the Secret Lake, Amita told her the whole story. 'Now, tell me, do you believe that I didn't want you?'

Sita said, 'Believe me, mamma, I always felt there was something more to it. I understand you perfectly. What I don't understand is the way both you and papa have treated this whole thing. Sometimes mamma, in life, two people don't click as husband and wife. It's no big deal. But how could you and papa completely negate the friendship you shared before you got married? Obviously, you must have liked something in him to get close to him. It could be anything. Why can't you be friends now? That's all I want to know.'

'You must ask your dad that.'

'I did. And he said you hate him so much that he wondered if you would ever be civil to him.'

'Did he actually say that? What about him? He hates me too.'

'No mamma. You're mistaken. He regrets many things and even holds himself responsible for the way things turned out. He says he didn't know which devil had possessed the both of you to behave the way you both did.'

She knew the answer. Maria had told her which devil it was—their inflated sense of pride. They didn't mind being emotionally bruised and battered but they wanted their pride to remain intact. She hadn't agreed with her then but as time passed and wounds healed, she understood the truth in what Maria had said. What was surprising her now was the fact that Siddharth had said what Sita just told her. 'Why didn't he tell me that even once in so many years?' she asked Sita. 'What about you, mamma, did you ever tell him what you thought?' As far as Amita was concerned the question was rhetorical. Wow, she thought, sometimes kids have an amazing capability to make you feel childish. And they had been juvenile. With their whimsical behaviour and no-compromise attitude. During their married life and after it. What purpose had fighting over the child served? What had they given their daughter—a disjointed family? A broken home? It was sheer good fortune that she had grown up into a mature young girl. What if she hadn't? What if she had fallen prey to booze, drugs like many confused kids do? As a matter of fact, her daughter had handled it much better than she herself had. All she had done since her estrangement was devour men. And hurt them to derive sadistic thrill. For the first time in her life, Amita wondered if it had been worth it at all. But it was only she who had chosen to live alone. Siddharth had found Nina. He hadn't called to tell her that he was getting married, though. Typical. She had learnt about it from her daughter. She was tempted to ask him but Zeba advised her to refrain. 'How can my daughter grow up with a stepmother?' she had grieved. 'What are you going to gain from fighting with him now? Sita's been with him all her life. Do you want to uproot her because of your fears, which might be unfounded anyway? She'll be eighteen in a few years. Let her decide for herself.'

'So how do you like Nina? What's she like? Is she happy with your dad?'

'She's a nice person, mamma. She's a lot like you. But she's not you. I like her but she can't replace you. Nobody can. To her credit, she has never tried to. In many ways, she reminds me of you. She reads a lot. She was pretty career-oriented she tells me but she has given up working for now. Says she is tired and needs a break. She smokes too. You must cut down on your smoking, mamma. She must be happy. I never ask. Why?'

'Just wondering. Is she good-looking? How old is she?'

'She's pretty. Not as stunning as you. I think she's as old as you.'

'Oh, and was she married before?'

'Yes, mamma. She was a widow when she met pappa. Her late husband died of some liver disease. Actually, he was a friend of pappa's.'

'And children?'

'No. She says I'm the daughter she had always wanted to have.'

'It's impossible for anybody not to love you, darling. You're made that way. Adorable.'

Sita was happy her mother had resumed control. Amita didn't show it but she was feeling rather anxious. Though Sita had assured her that her position in her life was irreplaceable, something within was niggling her. She didn't know whether it was hurt or envy.

The rest of the holidays, Sita and Amita, spent shopping, visiting friends and partying. Amita's friends who had seen Sita after a long time complimented her for having such a sweet daughter. She also didn't look like the mother of such a grown up child, they said. Amita swelled with pride at both the compliments.

When Sita's holiday ended, Amita cried uncontrollably. Her daughter consoled her, saying she would be back soon. She advised her not to smoke too much, to quit if possible. Amita remembered the time Sita used to cry when she left home for work and how she would console her. When Sita went overboard on chocolates, she would chide her and explain the ill effects. How things change. The role reversal was so apparent.

~

Chapter 17

VARSHA WAS BACK IN MUMBAI. SHE HAD EXPECTED THE BREAK to do her a lot of good. It had, in a way. She had reconnected with her best friend, picking up the threads, like they had never been apart. She had left behind all the pain and worry plaguing her mind. But the trouble was that she didn't feel like getting back to her humdrum existence in Mumbai. All the gnawing anxiety she always felt in the city had returned with a vengeance. The gloom she thought had lifted was back like the wintry polluted fog that appeared every morning outside her window. Was it the city, or its memories, or had she stagnated at work. She couldn't pinpoint what it was that made her feel so restless. Was this how people who survive a separation feel? Was this how Madhav had felt when he resumed his single life? Poor fellow, she thought of him with empathy. In a way he was just like her. Both of them were chasing mirages in the hope of finding an oasis. Little company and physical comfort was all she had given him. In return, he would have given her his all, if she had asked. She hoped he found somebody soon before he turned cynical like her.

It took a great deal of effort to shake off the lethargy and get to work on the morning after her break ended. Her colleagues were more relieved than happy to see her. She had never taken such a long time off with such clear-cut instructions not to disturb her come hell or high water. Soon she was sucked into the whirlpool of pending work. There were campaigns to be approved, bills to be paid, payments to be collected, phone calls to be made, orders to be placed. It was getting late and one by one the staff left. Varsha and Tripti decided to stay back so that they could organise their work.

All of a sudden, in the midst of sorting out stuff, Tripti asked Varsha, 'I don't mean to pry but is everything all right on the home front.' Varsha decided to be candid. She knew that people were talking; at least Tripti's intentions were genuine. She was by no means the office gossip. 'No. We've split. Som and I,' she said trying to keep her voice steady, but she thought she heard her voice quiver.

'Are you planning to get a divorce? Or you already have?' Tripti enquired.

Oh hell, she thought, the separation had done nothing to help her retain her sanity. She hadn't even thought of divorce.

'I guess so,' she said, hesitantly.

'Thank goodness there are no kids involved. It can get quite traumatic otherwise.'

'Yeah. True.'

'My parents got divorced when I was fourteen. Though I was old enough to understand why it happened, it took a lot for me to cope with it.'

The world seemed full of divorced people! Ever since her split with Som, all she had been hearing about were divorces and separations. That's what she said to Tripti who laughed and said, 'You know, Varsha, only when we experience something do we open our eyes to it. Pleasant or not. My mother used to tell me that she named me Tripti because she thought it was an unusual name. But soon after, she would hear it everywhere. I guess she started noticing my name only after she named me. I don't think it had suddenly gained popularity.'

Varsha gave it a thought and realised how true it was. How simply she had put it!

'Do you have a boyfriend, Tripti?'

'Not at the moment. But until a month ago I was seeing this guy who was my college mate.'

'A college romance! That was quite a long relationship, then?'

'Not really. We weren't going out when we were in college. Two years ago we sort of re-met and things happened. Just before we broke up we were contemplating marriage.'

'What went wrong?'

'Nothing went wrong as such. It was just that the moment we began talking in terms of marriage, his attitude towards me suddenly changed. He started behaving like he owned me. The very qualities that he said had attracted him to me were the ones he wanted to change. I was damn perplexed by this behaviour and realised it was not going to work out. So we called it off. If I had agreed to marry him, I would have lost myself. I would have turned into somebody else. Most of us make the mistake of either changing ourselves or trying to change the other person. Personally, I believe that a relationship that doesn't let each other be will not let it grow either; more than change you need compromise. I don't know if I'm right but that's me. I did hurt for a while but along the way I saw that it was nobody's fault. Now, I strongly believe that what we do to ourselves and not what people do to us is what is important. We're responsible for everything we feel. Once we own up to that fact we'll stop blaming others for our problems.' Varsha saw her in a completely new light. This petite little woman was a bundle of conviction and courage.

'You're right. What you did was an act of self-preservation. I'm glad you realised it before getting into marriage. Pity I didn't.'

Varsha derived inspiration from the conversation.

'We're supposed to be here to work. To sort things out. All we've been doing is talk,' said Tripti.

'You have no idea how important that has been to me. I've suffered in silence but I don't want to anymore. So there.'

Agnivesh landed in India with his pretty blond wife, Sylvia. She accompanied him to the office every day but did nothing except watch them work and read a magazine when she got bored. One day Varsha asked her, 'Sylvia, from what I hear, you're really enterprising. Why don't you take an active part in our agency? Actually, take over! I would love to work for a woman boss.'

'No way,' Sylvia replied emphatically, 'I was enterprising but that was before I got married. Now I don't want to have anything to do with work. I like looking after my home, my children and myself. I'm having a good time now. No strain or pressure. You know what I mean?'

Varsha nodded but she didn't know or understand. Well, each to their own she supposed. As far as she was concerned, her work was her life. In fact what did she have besides work? God, that sounded scary. What did she have when Som was still around? Maybe just the feeling of having someone with you was comforting and whether you shared anything together or not didn't really matter. It was all in the way we looked at situations. Life may be the same but our perspectives change. Depending on what phase you're passing through. What you consider reality today might turn out to be a sham tomorrow. The time had come now for her to face reality and accept it. What mattered was how receptive you are to the lessons that life doles out to you. Varsha perked up, resolving to look at the positive side of things.

All her resolve came undone when she got home. Demons of loneliness possessed her and she had no choice but to slay them the only way she knew—by numbing herself with tranquilisers.

Agnivesh returned to Italy satisfied. Varsha and her team had done a remarkable job. Before he left, he offered Varsha a partnership in the agency. He asked her to think it over. She did. A partnership meant she would be tied down just when she was learning to spread her wings. How could she bear to clip them? She wrote a detailed letter to Agni appreciating the gesture and explaining why she couldn't consider it. At least not right away. Maybe later, when she knew what she wanted from life. So far, she had been following whatever life had handed to her. But now, she wanted to take charge and do things that she wanted to.

Later in the month when Agnivesh saw the annual report, he suggested they have a conference in Goa to plan for the year ahead. 'Take the whole team with you,' he instructed her, 'stay wherever you want. Don't think about the costs. All expenses will be on the company. You deserve the best.' Varsha was pleased. She knew it came from his appreciation of her performance. After all, she was helping him make money with minimal involvement. She was glad she hadn't let the trauma of her personal life cast a shadow on her work.

After a brief brainstorming session with Tripti, she drew up an agenda for a six-day conference at a five star hotel in South Goa. Som preferred the northern part because all the action, so to speak, was there. Varsha loved the Benaulim beach that was less crowded and therefore much more fun. She loved the sea food in the shacks—the drool-worthy crabs, prawns, lobsters, calamari fish... just the thought made her mouth water.

'But I must eat less,' she said to Tripti, 'I have a tendency to go overboard at the sight of good food. Stop me, okay. I've put on something like eight kilos in the last year. I'd better lose weight.'

'Okay, fine,' agreed Tripti, 'Let's play diet keepers for each other.'

'What do you need to lose weight for? Just look at that hourglass figure of yours. You look fit.'

'Yeah? You think so?'

'Of course! Don't tell me nobody's told you that before? Not even that guy you were seeing?'

'Well, a few times but I thought he was saying it to please me.'

'What about the mirror? Don't you look at the mirror?'

'I do. But mirrors are sometimes deceptive!'

'You're crazy. That's the problem with women. We're so harsh on ourselves. We take criticism to heart but when it comes to compliments, we think of one hundred reasons to disbelieve them. You're gorgeous. And I'm not a man or a lesbian to flatter you for ulterior motives. So don't you think a simple thank you is in order,' Varsha said, laughing.

'Thank you.'

'That's better. You're welcome.'

Chapter 18

MAYA FINALLY RECEIVED HER PAY-CHEQUE. HER FIRST FOR forty-five days. Since she joined mid-month, due to a university policy, she had been paid her full salary only now. Her first serious earning. She had earned earlier too when she was a student, but that was pocket money to spend on films and fun. This was different. This was earning her living. She felt a sense of accomplishment when she held it in her hand. Now, she was truly standing on her own two feet, so to speak. She was capable of running her house, paying her bills, spending or saving, she could do whatever she wished to with her money. My money, she said aloud, smiling. Once the initial euphoria settled, she wondered where she was headed. After this, what? Was she losing interest in finding her roots? Was she once again falling into the pattern of letting life take her where it wanted?

On the day they passed by Dabeerpura, she knew she had been there before. It was not déjà vu...she was sure. She considered taking Professor Hai into confidence and telling him why she was here. Maybe he would understand. She could expect sympathy, but empathy? Probably not. How many people did she know or meet or had even heard of who were in a situation like hers? She felt lonely and unsure. Like a child that was taking its first step without knowing if it would lead to a fall. Stop it Maya, no negative thinking, she chided herself. She had read enough books on positive thinking, now was the time to put them into action. She didn't really have a choice anyway. Her life would probably be no different if she failed. And what if she did succeed...what if her parents, or at least one of them, had survived? Was she ready to face them, get to know them? God! Why did everything have to be so complicated? Why couldn't her life have been normal like a million others? Before self-pity got the worse of her, Maya shrugged as if to brush off the negativity and stood up. She needed to deposit her cheque in the bank. She phoned Professor Hai on his cellphone and told him she would meet him an hour later.

After she discovered his religious side, Maya made serious efforts to understand her reaction to it. After all, hang-ups are nothing but distorted versions of realities. Wrongful assumptions. Based on the way *we* perceive things.

She was now more comfortable with the Professor, after thinking things through and realising that the person he or anyone else was for that matter, had nothing to do with his religion. The night before Varsha went back, she told Maya that she had caught undisguised admiration in his eyes while he was looking at her. Maya had feigned nonchalance saying, 'Well, I'm like that, you know.' But Varsha had explained that she thought his interest was romantic in nature. 'No way,' Maya had said, 'your imagination's working overtime. He's so much older. In fact, he reminds me of my father.' 'So what if he's much older? You have a father fixation, don't you? Now what is it that they call it, wait a minute, I'll remember the term, got it! Elektra complex, right?' Maya had pummelled her with a pillow and they laughed it off. There was never a dull moment with Varsha. She hadn't called in a long time. Out of sight, out of mind, that's the way that bum is, she thought as she collected the deposit form from the clerk across the counter who was eyeing her curiously. She was used to such glances wherever she went. She always thought it had something to do with the colour of her eyes. She wondered whom she had inherited the colour from. It was not a colour that you saw normally. While filling out the form her mind drifted back to that morning's dilemma.

She decided she would speak to Hai. He wasn't being himself, of late. She had put it down to his fasting. All that starvation was bound to affect one's behaviour! She turned cranky at the slightest hunger pang. She hadn't known it until Appa had pointed it out to her. She'd learnt to manage her hunger and her irritation better now. Every sensation, every emotion is in some way interlinked to other things, Appa told her many times. As always, he understood her more than she herself ever did.

Now that Eid was over, she hoped Hai would return to his normal, light–hearted, funny self.

During lunch-hour, Sumathi came to her room with the intention of sharing her meal with Maya, like they had been doing for sometime. But Maya said, 'Listen, don't feel bad but I need to meet the boss for lunch. Actually, why don't you join us?'

Sumathi asked her to carry on and proceeded to the canteen visibly put off. Maya pretended not to notice. When there's nothing you can do about somebody's negative reaction to an innocent enough request it was better to ignore it. They won't know that you know so the next time you meet them, they won't hold you responsible for what they felt. Because by then, the feeling would have passed. But you can only take that chance with people you don't live with or are not very close to personally. Otherwise, it borders on insensitivity.

Maya was stuck at various points of her project and it had been a long time since she'd had lunch with him. She missed his cheerful banter. He had enquired after her several times when they met in the corridor or when she went to his room to greet him. She had answered that she was doing okay only because she didn't want to burden him during his roza. Now, before he asked to see the report, it was better to brief him about her doubts. When she entered his room she found him reading a book, engrossed. She stood nearby for a while hoping he would notice but when she realised it was hopeless, she dragged the chair to his desk noisily, saying, 'Sorry to interrupt you sir, but it's lunch-time.'

He looked up looking rather lost then smiled when he saw her and said, 'Good to see you Maya. So what have you got in your tosha?'

'Tosha, what's tosha?'

'So you haven't learnt any Hyderabadi Urdu yet? Tosha means tiffin-box in our lingo.'

'Oh. I've picked up a bit of Hyderabadi mainly from Sidhu, the dhobi and Yaqub, our peon. But I guess tosha is of a much higher standard.'

'Nothing of that sort. It's a commonplace word.'

Maya had heard that Dakhni Urdu was as queer as its people. Sumathi had joked the other day, 'Urdu was born in Lucknow, murdered in Hyderabad and buried in Bangalore. Did you know that?' Maya quickly jumped to Bangalore's defense saying it was not so bad. Sumathi had reminded her that since Hyderabad was where she lived now, she better show more loyalty to the city. In Maya's mind, Bangalore was home, though now, there was neither a home nor a reason to visit the city.

The language took some getting used to and she found it quite hilarious, actually. A few days after Ramzan, Maya had asked Karim the date on which Eid fell and he answered, 'Zamana ho gaya, medam.'

'What do you mean, didn't it happen just recently?'

'Wohich bolrun na main bhi.'

And then another time she asked Sidhu, her dhobi, why he had absconded for a week.

'Arri kaisi baat karre medam, parsun ich tho aaya na main?'

'What do you mean parsun? It was a week ago.'

'Wohich bolrun na main bhi.'

She had learnt that while parsun meant day before yesterday for the rest of India, in Hyderabad it could range from day before yesterday to a few years ago.

She narrated both the incidents to Hai and he laughed heartily.

'I know it sounds funny to outsiders but for Hyderabadis, our language is obviously considered the best. Just before you walked in, I was reading a book on the Dakhni lingo—its origins and relevance. Quite interesting. I'll lend it to you once I'm through with it. Now, pass on your tosha. Let me taste the upma.'

After relishing a mouthful, he continued, 'How do you survive on such little food? Take the parathas from my carrier. I asked my cook to make some turai for you. I've given him strict instructions not to pack any non-vegetarian food from today. He was quite surprised—the meat addict making a request of that sort.'

'I eat well sir. What about you all these days? Living on love and fresh air.' No sooner had the words slipped out, than she wondered if Hai would mind her taking such liberties with him. But as her Hindi teacher had taught in school—baat zaban se, teer Kaman se ek baar nikal gaya tho vaapas nahi aate. Now all she could do was watch his reaction.

But the professor seemed unshaken. 'No love, just fresh air and a little food. Listen, I think I'll finish this upma. It's delicious. Did you make it?'

'No, I have a fleet of domestics. My head cook made it especially for you.'

'Hah! Where did you learn to cook? Who taught you?'

'I've started cooking everyday recently. My mother taught me all the basics. She'd sit me down on the kitchen platform while she washed the rice and chopped veggies, and reel off recipes. When I started to cook, I just followed what she did. The food I cook tastes pretty much like hers but I still have a long way to go.'

'You must miss her badly.'

'I do, like crazy. Both of them. But Appa always told me that departed souls hurt if their loved ones grieve on earth. He always said that the soul lives eternally; it's only the cloak that they discard. So I do my best to remember them fondly, lovingly and try not to get too sad.' Suddenly it occurred to her that this was the right time to bring up her past. This was the right opportunity. But she wasn't sure if it was the right place. She said, 'Sir, there's something I need to discuss with you.'

'Shoot.'

'No sir, not now, not here. Actually it's a rather personal matter. If you could come over one of these days to my place before leaving the campus...'

'Let's do it this way. You come over to my house this Saturday. I'll organise for some good vegetarian food. Let's have lunch together. If it's okay with you.'

'Of course, it's fine with me.'

'That's settled then. Saturday lunch, at my place. I'll come and pick you up.'

'No sir, thank you but I'll manage. I need to start moving around on my own. All these days you've been driving me all over the place.'

'There will be plenty of opportunities for you to venture out alone. And correction, I didn't drive you all over the place; we were working on our project. Is that clear? Now, allow me, just this once.'

'Okay. After all, you're the boss. And the boss is always right.'

'That serves my purpose. I'm glad you remember I'm your boss.'

The rest of the day, Hai spent contemplating what she wanted to tell him. He was correcting answer sheets, compiling question papers, referring to books, doing everything he usually did, but a single question was doing endless rounds at the back of his mind—what personal matter does she want to discuss with me? A few guesses floated across but none seemed very likely. Anyway, Saturday, was just two days away.

After having said that to him, Maya debated if she had done the right thing. But she saw no other choice. And no better person to turn to. He would be of great help, she was sure, and she trusted him enough to ask for his help.

Saturday dawned and with it came the unlikeliest of rain showers. The weather was not promising. There was a depression across the Bay of Bengal and at such times, Hyderabad experienced unseasonal showers. Maya awoke earlier than usual; in fact, she had hardly slept the previous night. And when she had fallen asleep, she dreamt that she was caught in a whirlpool, in a large river, and Appa and Amma watched helplessly from the shore, as she drowned. She tried to decipher its meaning. She looked for Carl Jung's *Dreams and Their Codes* on the bookshelf. When she found it, she settled down in the verandah after switching on the light—the day was gloomy. She scanned the book, reading the interpretations of other dreams along the way until she reached page thirty-three. 'Drowning indicates a fear of the unknown. If you are the one drowning, it's a warning. A warning of the way things could turn out in the near future.' She closed the book and looked at the cover. On it was an illustration of a man and a woman against a blue sky. They seemed to be flying but there were no wings. Like her dream, the meaning of the cover picture eluded her. Suddenly she became aware that she was holding her breath. She did that often whenever she was full of trepidation.

She wasn't in a good mood. Maya had never had a great love for the rains. 'How come you like me?' Varsha would ask her. 'What makes you think I do?' she would reply. Heavy rains were still tolerable, it poured and then it stopped. And if sunshine followed, it inevitably led to the appearance of a rainbow. She loved rainbows. Once she and Amma had gone to the terrace after a heavy downpour, and they had seen two of them, criss-crossing the entire length of the sky. Amma had screamed in delight like a little child and had run inside to get the camera to capture it for posterity. The photograph was in one of her albums. Amma leaning against the parapet with two rainbows in the background. But this incessant drizzle got on her nerves. And the day had just begun.

She walked into the kitchen, made herself a steaming mug of coffee, went to her bedroom and opened the cupboard looking for the photo albums. A little coffee spilled on to her fingers, the warmth felt good. She reached for a tissue on the dressing-table, wiped her fingers and placed the mug on another fresh tissue on her bedside table. She stood on tiptoe to reach out for the albums that she had kept in the topmost compartment of her almirah.

She sat on her bed spreading the albums out before her. All of them were marked systematically with a red sketch pen. Maya as a baby, Maya at school, Maya's college days, Maya's friends, Maya's graduation, Maya at university. Each one was named after her, by her parents. It was as if she was holding centre stage while they stood in the wings. How much they had loved her.

Cradling the coffee mug in one hand, she started turning the leaves of her 'Baby Maya' album with the other. There she was in her tunic, she remembered it was on her first day of school—Appa promptly took her picture on this important day. There was Amma beaming, carrying her. Her on Appa's shoulders, one leg on each side, her suspended in mid-air while Appa watched with raised hands to catch her. Amma, Appa with her in front of them, Amma and her-right cheek to left cheek. So many pictures, so many memories. She went through all of them until she found the one she was looking for—Amma and the rainbows. It was almost at the end of the last album, no more photographs after that, yet the memories lingered on. When Appa had seen the rainbow photo, he had said to her, 'You're a genius, Mayu, what a lovely photograph!' Appa was like that—always appreciative of whatever she did.

Once when Amma had a severe headache and was in bed—she never laid down unless it was very bad—Maya had offered to make breakfast. Amma had prepared the batter the previous evening. She walked into the kitchen confidently, lit the stove, put the pan on it, smeared it with oil, just like she had seen her mother do. She filled the ladle with the batter and spread it on the pan. The dosa simply refused to rise. 'The next one will be better,' Appa encouraged. The next one did an encore. And so did the third. She gave up after that. All she had at the end of the whole exercise were lumps, black and brown. She was distressed. It seemed so effortless, so simple when Amma did it. But Appa ate it with great relish dipping it in the chutney, making appreciative noises. She had believed him until she tasted it. It was raw in places, burnt in the others, in one word—inedible. She realised to what lengths her father went to keep her spirits up. 'Why did you have to go, Appa?' she questioned, letting the tears flow, breaking her resolve to not cry at his memory. She had heard that when somebody died an untimely death leaving behind their loved ones, they came back in spirit or conveyed messages in some form or the other to communicate with them. But she had received no indication whatsoever. Didn't they love her enough? Or was it her own love that lacked? Just then a familiar scent reached her nostrils. The distinct smell of Appa's aftershave. Smells were inseparable from their memories. 'Is that you, Appa? Are you around? Have you come back to me?' she said. The smell turned stronger enveloping her.

'Are you expecting somebody?' She turned around and found Hai standing at the doorway.

'Good morning, sir. Please have a seat. I'm sorry I didn't notice you.'

'I'll wait in the living room. You shouldn't leave your door open if you can't hear someone entering. I waited outside for quite some time. I even pulled a chair to make a noise. But you were nowhere in sight so I decided to look in the bedroom. Sorry.'

'No, that's perfectly all right. I'll be ready in a minute. Sorry to keep you waiting.'

'Would you mind if I look at those albums while you get ready?'

She handed them to him and he walked out. From the photographs, Hai gathered that she came from a close-knit family. He felt terrible for her. In a while Maya emerged, dressed in a simple orange kurta with a light green churidar. The colour of her kurta complimented her complexion and her almond-shaped eyes looked striking. She looked even more stunning with her hair loose. She always underplayed her good looks. A contrast to most women he saw, flattering what they had and disguising the rest with make-up. The media bombarded women with images of what beauty was considered to be and a lot of them succumbed. But this girl was different. She did nothing to enhance her beauty. Not that she needed to.

He wanted to compliment her but held back. He had to play the part of the middle-aged, wise man. Half our lives we spend in putting up some act or the other, he thought. To camouflage our true selves. The rest of it we spend in building barriers. To not say what we feel.

He sat in the car and waited while she locked the house. After she rushed into the car to avoid the rain, he noticed that she had tied her hair up. She looked so good with it open. He wanted to tell her that. To let it be. To leave it free. But he wasn't sure how she would interpret it.

As they drove off, Professor Hai asked her, 'Were you expecting somebody this morning when I walked in? A boyfriend tucked away or something? Is that what you want to discuss with me?'

'Nothing so romantic sir, I'll tell you soon, what's the hurry?' Hurry? She had to be kidding. He was bursting with anticipation. All the suspense was killing him. Not letting him sleep, eat or behave normally. And she was asking him casually what the hurry was.

'Whatever it is, Maya, I want you to know that outside work, I'm your friend. Unless you consider yourself superior,' he said chuckling at his own joke, 'but seriously, feel free to tell me anything. I care for you and I'm always there for you, no matter what, ok?'

After he made the declaration he felt better, unburdened. At least she knew now that she was special to him.

'Thank you, sir. Thank you very much. You're the only one I could think of.'

For what? The rest of the drive was quiet except for the continuous drone of the wipers on the windscreen. There was no respite from the drizzle.

They finally reached. Hai honked outside the gate. A man holding an umbrella came running to open it. As they drove in, she noticed that it was an old-fashioned house with a garden and a huge courtyard. He parked the car behind the house. They walked straight into the kitchen. 'This is the back entrance. If we came through the main entrance we would have had to walk around the house and I didn't want us to get drenched. Sometimes, in life, to get ahead you have to get back.'

'What prompted that, sir?'

Hai looked at her and remained quiet.

They walked into a sprawling kitchen the size of which could easily match her living room. The strong spicy aroma wafting from various pots and pans was overpowering, but generating warmth that made Maya feel welcome. She found a man engrossed in stirring something in a pan while a woman chopped coriander and chatted. When they noticed Hai, they did a quick salaam. Hai responded and they walked into the dining room, past the huge dining table with a dozen chairs and into the living room. This was larger than the two rooms put together. The seating arrangements were made on three levels, the leather settee, low diwans and gaddas, with colourful-mirrored bolsters and cushions, on the floor. He asked her where she would be comfortable and she opted for the sofa. 'My favourite place too,' he said as they settled down. She hadn't seen the entire house but she could tell that it was large. From the sofa she was sitting on, she could spot a sit-out and the door of a bedroom. Beyond the dining room was a spiral staircase that led to the first floor. 'Don't you feel lonely in such a huge house?' she asked.

'When all of us lived here, my parents, my three brothers and sister, we fought for space. It was just about enough. This house has only four bedrooms. My parents occupied one and the other was for my sister since she was the only girl in the family. That left us with two bedrooms and four boys. We fought all the time. But now, there are three vacant bedrooms and only one occupied. Life changes so quickly. I guess it's too big for a single person but I can't imagine living elsewhere. Neither can I rent out any portion of it because it's just not built that way. In those days, people built homes for living in; unlike now.'

He paused for a while. 'Sometimes I still hear their voices, my mother calling me. This house has too many memories. You know how it is with a place where you grow up.'

'True. I must tell you what happened this morning before you walked in.'

'What happened?'

'I was looking at the photo albums…one photograph led to the other, one memory to another. Before I realised it I was crying and asking my father why he left me. At that moment, I smelt his aftershave. It got so strong that I was overwhelmed with nostalgia.'

'And then?'

'You walked in.'

'What happened to the fragrance?'

'You were wearing it.'

'Really?'

'Yes. You walked in and I realised that you use the same aftershave. If I had not figured out its source, I would have gotten carried away to the extent of sensing his presence. The tricks our minds play on us.'

'I know.'

'In fact, it was him I was talking about when you asked me if I was expecting someone.'

'I even teased you about having a boyfriend tucked away somewhere!'

'Yeah.'

'Tell me honestly, what's a pretty, young girl like you doing in the university? Away from your hometown. You must have a boyfriend. Every girl your age has one, these days. At least most of them do.'

'I did. But that was years ago. Nothing tragic though. It was good as long as it lasted. He had wanted to get married. I didn't want to rush. So we parted.'

He liked her candour. He had never met a woman who talked so simply and directly about herself. No put-ons, no pretences.

Straight. Saying it like it was. At the same time, she had answered his question leaving a lot unsaid. And that was what was of interest to him.

They had a drink of fresh lime before lunch. The spread on the dining table was lavish. Enough to feed an army she said to him. 'At the risk of sounding immodest, let me tell you, this is not even the normal fare because, of course, you are a vegetarian,' he replied.

There were rotis, dal, varieties of vegetables, raita, chutneys, papad.

'But sir, I've no problem if you eat non-vegetarian food. You're a self-confessed meat addict. You should have got something made for you.'

'The advantage of being a non-vegetarian is that you eat vegetarian food too. There was a time when I used to eat meat at every meal. But I have drastically cut down; I know it's a healthy alternative.'

She ate quietly appreciating the taste of a different cuisine.

'Why are you so quiet? Is the food okay?' he asked.

'Slightly oily for my taste but otherwise delicious. I don't talk normally while I eat. I think it's been ingrained into me by Appa!'

'This is nothing. Jaani Miya, my cook, goes berserk at the sight of oil. His mother was the same. She used to cook for my parents. For them taste is directly proportionate to the amount of oil.'

'If I'm not being too personal, why didn't you get married? You can tell me if you don't want to answer.'

'Not at all. I've told you that I'm your friend. You can ask me whatever you want but I thought you were here to tell me something. Is your question connected to that?' He was letting a glimmer of hope form in his mind.

'No,' she said.

That one word did to Hai what a million spiteful words hadn't done to him in all his life. He felt a bleak, empty ache and then quickly composed himself.

'Can we talk about it when we finish?' she asked bargaining for time. Jaani Miya served dessert—khubani ka meetha—in porcelain plates. Hai scolded him, 'How many times have I told you to serve dessert in dessert bowls?'

Jaani Miya extended his hand to pick up the plates but Hai told him to let it be. 'Madam is coming first time, I'm thinking,' he said scratching his hand.

'How's that connected to this?' Hai asked, exasperated. Jaani Miya returned to the kitchen with a wide grin on his face. Maya liked the fact that Hai was so at ease with the domestic help.

'Somebody told him that he looks like Aamir Khan. Much to my misfortune, he believes it.'

'Actually, he does resemble him a little,' she said.

'Et tu Brutus,' Professor held his chest feigning pain.

She laughed out loud. Hai grinned. He became aware of a sense of great comfort, as if a time of anxious waiting had been followed by relaxation; every nerve was suddenly soothed, he was conscious of pleasure where there had so recently been pain. He sank back and closed his eyes in an expression of contentment. It was nice—this whole thing—sitting with her, at his house, chatting with ease. Sometimes it takes a life-time to reach such comfort levels. If he could make time stop now, he would. And then out of that world of peace within, a sentence evolved itself, slowly taking shape while he waited, without patience or anxiety, for the message it would bring him.

Unaware of his master's mental state, Jaani Miya interrupted to clear the plates and made a quick exit. But not before giving the lady a quick once over. She looked very young. When was the last time saab had brought a woman home? He couldn't remember.

Hai looked at Maya, 'Go ahead. I'm all ears.'

'I don't know how to tell you this.'

'Try English. I might understand. It's okay, Maya, I'll try to understand no matter how delicate the matter is.'

'I need your help.'

'Okay…'

'I need to find my parents.'

'You mean communicate with the dead. I know a friend's mother who's into this. But she lives in Bombay. I toyed with the idea when I lost my mum. But personally speaking, I think you should let the dead rest in peace.'

'No, no. That's not what I mean,' she said, letting her story tumble out. Word after word. Sentence after sentence. Uninterrupted. Her eyes not meeting his.

When she finished and looked up, she saw tears in his eyes.

'I'm sorry,' she said, feeling responsible, 'I narrated my story, what makes you cry?' she said, quoting an Urdu song from an old Hindi movie.

'Don't be. I was just thinking what a self-absorbed world we live in. When we have a problem, we think it's unique. That nobody could possibly have a problem like ours. Until we meet somebody who has this kind of story to relate. Everything else pales. All along, I held it against God for having taken my mother away so early. Such a good soul deserved a longer life. But after listening to you, I feel so small. My problem is so unimportant. I don't know how to say it. Sometimes words are not enough to express what we feel.'

'Do you think you can help me? You belong to this city. You know the people, probably the whole town.'

'In a manner of speaking, yes. I happen to have the privilege of being born into a well-known family. Let's see how we can tackle this. I can think of two ways right now. One is to check with the police records and get the details of the '78 riots and see if any of the details of the Hindu victims or survivors match. The second option is to ask people who witnessed the riots. I have a few cousins who survived. I'll check with them although I don't know how fair it would be to rekindle those memories. That should more or less give us some direction. I think we're on the right track,' he said to encourage her.

She said she was positive that it would work.

'But you must have courage, Maya. Chances are nothing might come out of this and that neither of your parents have survived...

although I have no clue how we're going to identify them as your parents, in the first place. The list of the slain is bound to be longer than the survivors. The best thing for us to do, under the circumstances, would be to check the list of survivors first. The number of Hindus in that will be minuscule. Once we get hold of those details, we can try to track them down. I'm only saying it's possible. I'm not saying it's easy. I hope you understand that.'

'Yes. I do. I'm ready for anything and willing to accept whatever we do manage to find out. What matters to me is that I tried. That's what Krishna said to Arjuna, "Do your duty. Don't be attached to the result".'

'I agree. Let's do it for what it's worth. I am with you.'

He extended his hand; she placed hers in his, he held it a little longer than he thought necessary and withdrew. Earlier, he avoided any form of physical contact with her, afraid of its repercussion but now, he longed for her touch.

~

Chapter 19

EVERYTHING WENT AS PER SCHEDULE IN GOA WITH VARSHA AND her team. They had decided to take a break on the third day and resume their conference the next day. The weather was pleasant, typical of Goa in January. They decided that the ideal activity was to lie on the beach and sunbathe. Off they went with their swimsuits, sarongs and SPFs, excited as hell. It was the second week of the New Year and there was a lull, the festivity season and frenzy having subsided. There were not many tourists. It was quiet with only a few relaxing sunbathers, adventurous wind surfers and para-sailors.

Varsha, in her one-piece swimming suit, was lying on one of the benches, with the book she had intended to read used as a cover to shield the sun from her face, in a state of semi-stupor. She heard a husky, masculine drawl, 'Would you like to order something to drink?' Very reluctantly, annoyed with the interruption, she moved the book slightly and stared into the eyes of the sexiest man she had ever seen. He wasn't exactly handsome, but something in his casual manner and build appealed to her. She stared shamelessly at his sharp features, his golden brown hair, grayish eyes that twinkled. He had a proud nose, tanned skin, a toned body, the upper half of which was bare at the moment and a hairless chest. This is how Adonis must have looked, she thought. Unaffected by her scrutiny he repeated the question. Obviously, he was used to the effect he had on women.

But he didn't seem either put off or spurred on by it. To please him, she asked him to get what he thought was good, wondering who he could be. It was difficult to think of him as a waiter. Even the manner in which he asked her for an order was more that of a host. What, in the name of all things that mattered, was a man like him doing here? He should be out there on a ramp!

Later that evening, when she was lying next to him, she told him about her first impression. 'Seriously, you should consider modelling as a career. What a waste of good looks,' she advised, lamenting. 'No, *signora*. I exercise for health. Good looks are a by-product. I consider my body a private possession. I wouldn't like to put it up for display.' This was the first time she had heard a man talk like that. Quickly she checked herself for being so prejudiced in her thinking—attributing genders with specific behaviour.

Jojo owned the shack he ran. He had inherited it from his father who had made his first million with it. His father was Goan and mother, Italian. God knows in what passion they had made him, for he was passion personified. An expert lover, he knew how to stimulate a woman. For the first time in her life, she had met a man who found his pleasure in pleasuring the other. He taught her how by responding to the other person's moves you could lose your inhibitions. He taught her to ask for what she wanted. He showed her how, by taking the initiative, a woman can enhance her pleasure, dispelling the hang-up she had nurtured all along—that the man did the lovemaking. Now, she had learnt how easy it was to follow her instincts. She told him about the inhibition she had regarding undressing and he prophesied, 'Someday when you meet a man you truly love, you'll forget all your inhibitions. In life, don't ever rush things. But don't stall things either. Whatever is, let it be. Everything is the way it should be.'

Jojo was very attentive too. And not just to her sexual needs. He fed her mouthfuls of her favourite food, served chilled white wine and generally pampered her silly. He massaged her feet, planting kisses all over, turning her on while helping her relax. The whole experience was like a dream, a fantasy that never came true for most women. Varsha was grateful. Yes, indeed one needed luck to encounter such people in life. You need such chances to make your choices. Choices are what define life ultimately. A vicious cycle. Love and life are what you make of those choices. Who says love meant only the meeting of hearts and minds? Love could be in the mating of two persons. At this moment, when Jojo was asking if he was applying the right amount of pressure on her feet while massaging them, she felt a surge of love for him. Like the kind she felt when she saw tears in Madhav's eyes. Such love might not last but that didn't make it any less a love. In fact, it was purer in its form than what she had experienced with her husband. People gave it a name—no strings attached. If left to her, she would call it—no stings attached. As long as they were together, they wanted to be nice to each other, without giving up on their own self. Wasn't this better than living together for years and at the end to feel nothing but the need to hurt, to spite, to resent? But of one thing she was sure of, she would never sleep with a married man.

After her tryst with Jojo, she added another category to her list of the kinds of men she had known—men, who were not in love with the woman they slept with, yet knew how to care for her, how to cherish her.

Chapter 20

ANWAR ALI MIRZA WAS IN A GOOD MOOD. ALMOST EUPHORIC. Last night, after ages, he and his wife had made love. He enjoyed it thoroughly even now at his age. 'What's with me,' he said to Shehzaadi, 'I'm already beginning to think like an old man.'

'*Like* an old man?'

'My turn to ask what you mean?'

'That you *are* an old man.'

'Middle-aged, yes. Old, never. What do you say?'

'I say that it's time for you to get to work.'

'And leave you in peace? Is that what you're suggesting?'

'No, I know that it's what you want.'

'Hmm...true. Work's turning out interesting. Different from what I've done so far. How do you know me so well?'

'I've been living with you for twenty-two years now.'

'Why don't you say married to?'

'What's the difference?'

'Well...'

'Then?'

'You're such a proud woman.'

'Proud of you.'

'Good.'

'You have to have the last word, don't you?'

'So what, you always have the last laugh.'

She laughed.

'I told you so,' he said and went to have his bath.

Why couldn't she bring herself to say 'married for twenty-two years'? Maybe it was because, in her mind, her first marriage was never really over. Cut short but not over. She had never forgiven herself for surviving when her entire family had died. Is that why she felt guilty about living? She sank into a deep depression. Casting its shadow on her thoughts. That sinking feeling was spreading like cancer in her body. Spreading its tentacles into her mind. This was happening to her all too frequently these days. One moment she felt on top of the world, in the next she slipped into the depths of despair. She had to do something about her extreme mood swings. Perhaps, she needed to see her gynaec, perhaps it was menopausal in nature. She hoped it was, though she had her doubts.

When Anwar got out of the bathroom, he found her staring blankly at nothing in particular, her eyes narrowed in worry. He recognised that look of panic. He dreaded it. But she was fine just a while ago. What could have happened in that space of time? What was she going through?

'What's it jaan? What are you thinking? Please talk to me. Tell me. I need to know.'

'I don't know what it is but one moment I feel fine and the next moment I feel down in the dumps. There's this gnawing, sinking feeling that turns into panic and my heart palpitates like it's going to burst. I think it's time for me see the gynaecologist. I could be approaching menopause.'

'But you're only forty-five.'

'That's the age for the onset...I think.'

'I see. Should we go now? Come on, get dressed, we'll see the doctor first and then you can drop me to office. You haven't seen my office yet. We could kill two birds with one stone. How does that sound?'

She said nothing but stood up reluctantly. She changed her clothes and then her mind. 'Let it be, Anwar. The weather's awful. I'll fix an appointment for Saturday. By then the rain should subside.'

'But today is Saturday.'

'I meant the next. Because the weather forecast says the rains will last for a week.'

Anwar knew how stubborn she could be. 'Okay then. You take care till I come back. And do not report anything to my Sahebzaada Shahbaz. I'm terrified of him,' he said pretending to shiver with fright.

Shehzaadi laughed. Just the mention of her son was enough to perk her up. Anwar left, this time not finding anything amiss with her not seeing him till the door. She had told him what the problem could be and that put him more at ease.

After he left, she called Babu Miya and asked him for a cup of tea, instructing him to bring the hot water, tea leaves and milk and sugar separately. She liked making her own tea. She liked hers light. With a hint of milk. Anwar liked it premixed though. She had acquired her taste from Rehaan.

She went up to her bedroom and got under the covers. She detested the cold weather. And the rain. It had been raining for the past few weeks in Hyderabad. She could bear the heights of summer but a slight chill in the air, and her body protested. 'That's because you're a warm person,' Anwar had said once, who loved the cold. 'Does that make you cold-blooded, then?' she had taunted. 'Not as long as you're with me,' he had remarked. If left to him, Anwar would have the air conditioner on in their bedroom, every night, summer or winter. Rehaan was not like that though. He was like her. He liked what she liked. Almost like Siamese twins. Joined in marriage. She had fallen deeply in love with him; it was love at first sight for both of them when they had met at a wedding, her cousin was marrying his uncle. She must have been barely seventeen then. When somebody asked her where they met, she would say, 'At my cousin's wedding.' He would interrupt, 'No, at my uncle's.'

It was a private joke between them. Nobody else understood the nitty-gritties.

And then when Rehaan had confided in his mother about his love for her, she had found out that Shehzaadi was his aunt, as his uncle had married her first cousin, and since his uncle was married to her sister, he was her brother-in-law. Highly convoluted but enough reason for people to raise objections. 'I don't think it's possible, bete,' she said, expressing her fear. Luckily for them she agreed to conspire with them and their nikaah took place at Hotel Banjara, the only star hotel in those days. Her mother-in-law, a widow whose world was her son, had passed away soon after the marriage. It was Karan Mama and Vimla Mami who had become her surrogate in-laws. 'God knows what connection it is from previous birth,' Karan Mama would speak of Rehaan whom he considered his son. Neither she nor Rehaan believed in reincarnation but in this lifetime—their Mama and Mami were Abba and Ammi.

She sipped her tea as memories flooded her and she smiled. How happy they had all been. She thought of their spacious haveli in the quaint Moazamjahi market, Famous Ice Creams down the lane, the fruit and meat market at Mir-alam-mandi...Mir-alam-mandi...Mir-alam-mandi, the name buzzed in her mind like a stuck gramophone record. For so many years she hadn't let herself indulge in the memories of her past. Now they emerged and she feared she would drown under their weight. But, strangely, there were no tears. As if her tears had dried up after all those years. From the time of her daughter's disappearance and finding her husband's lifeless body, she hadn't shed a tear. She had cried on other occasions—happy and sad—even while watching films but never over her loss. She sat dry-eyed but spent, mentally exhausted. Babu Miya was at the door enquiring where she wanted her lunch served. She hadn't realised that she had spent close to three hours reminiscing. Three hours. One lifetime. Like a film. She told Babu Miya that she wasn't hungry yet and when she was, she would go downstairs for lunch.

She picked up the phone to dial Zeba's number. Zeba answered on the first ring. They chatted. Zeba said, 'I didn't like the way Amita picked up an argument with bhaijaan. Sometimes she can get so juvenile.'

'That's all right, Zeba. It was partly Anwar's fault too. Anyway, he hasn't taken any offence. So all's well that ends well.'

'I hope, for our sake, it has ended well. That woman sometimes doesn't know her limits. She doesn't know when to stop. I've told her as much.'

'You needn't have. Anyway, where is she?'

'Probably at the boutique.'

'You haven't spoken to her?'

'No. You know how she is after her daughter's just left. It's better to leave her alone for a couple of weeks. She tends to get very nasty.'

'All the more reason for us to speak to her then. Let's meet this evening. Seven-ish, my place.'

'You call her, then. I'm okay with it.'

'Okay, see you later.' Shehzaadi disconnected the phone with the receiver still in her hand, she dialled Amita's cell phone number. No response. She tried her home number. Maria answered, 'Good afternoon, ma'am. Madam's sleeping.'

'Sleeping? In the afternoon! All well, Maria?' Shehzaadi knew Amita avoided noon siestas. Made her feel sick, she said.

'I don't know ma'am. She looks okay but I really don't know. Should I wake her up?'

'No, don't. Let her sleep. Ask her to give me a buzz when she wakes up, will you?'

'Sure ma'am, I'll do that.'

Just then Maria heard Amita's footsteps. She was still in her housecoat, her hair dishevelled, puffy eyes, looking unkempt. When she wore make-up, she was stunning. Right now, she looked haggard, she looked her age. Maria told her about the call and went to the kitchen, to get lunch organised. Amita ate frugally; she was very particular about her food habits. Soup, vegetable salad, a bowl of curd and baked chicken on the days she was home for lunch. Maria wondered how she never got bored of it. Siddharth sir, on the other hand, was a big food lover. She used to love cooking for him. To Maria's delight, Sita had taken after her father in her eating habits. As long as she was here, Maria exhibited all her culinary skills.

The curd had not set due to the weather. When she went to inform Amita, she found her on the phone, saying, 'Okay then, seven-thirty my place. That husband of yours will pounce on me if he sees me there.' Maria knew the requirements for the evening. She knew exactly what each of her friends liked. Most of her friends envied Amita for having found someone like Maria. Maria was proud of that fact and always made an effort to live up to their expectations. She went back to the kitchen after listening to Amita's instructions about the number of people who would drop in.

Shehzaadi had succeeded in drawing her out of her shell. 'Listen Amita, especially when you're feeling down you need the company of friends. I don't know about you, but, right now, I'm hitting rock bottom.'

'Why? If I had a husband like yours I would be on cloud nine. Seriously, that man is crazy about you. I have seen besotted men, but he takes the cake and the bakery. You're one lucky woman, princess.'

Amita preferred calling her princess, Shehzaadi was a mouthful, she said.

With her evening plans settled, Shehzaadi felt a little better. At least she knew now that there was something to look forward to. Weekends, otherwise, had always been drab. She got by somehow when Shah was around and in Mumbai, Anwar's family was good enough company. But ever since they moved here, she didn't look forward to weekends at all. It was getting better, though, with her friends. Anwar had told her even before they got married that horse-racing was one passion that was very close to his heart. The sport served as a stress buster for him. He owned racehorses and wherever they went, racing remained his only and constant diversion from work. On Saturdays and Sundays, while other husbands spent quality time with their families, he was at the racecourse cheering and punting with his race buddies. Usually the activity started on Friday evening itself when he would work on his predictions. Watching him at it one would think he was working on a serious research project. With his reading glasses on his nose, a register with neatly drawn columns in red ink, the book on participating horses in hand, which by the end of his homework would have his day's favourites highlighted in fluorescent green. Shehzaadi had clicked a photograph of him in that pose to show him how engrossed he seemed and how detached from the world. She was disinterested in his weekend occupation but she feigned an interest. She accompanied him for all the important races—the Invitation Cups, the Derbys and the like—dressed in her chiffons and pearls. It was customary for the wives and families in the racing circuit to attend the big races. It was a 'done' thing. Though she did it year after year in different cities for different races, Shehzaadi remained unsuccessful in cultivating an interest in it. Sometimes, her disinterest showed involuntarily but Anwar never noticed it or pretended not to.

When she met the wives of his racing buddies, they would discuss, dissect and rant over the effects of their husbands' collective passion. What bewildered them was that even during the off-season they went to the racecourse loyally, to watch on closed circuit television the live proceeding of races being held elsewhere in the country. The racing community had a solidarity that was almost sacrosanct. None of the men disclosed any details to their wives about money lost or made; how much they bet and other such things. Of course, if the men wanted to they did. Other men, no matter how close they were to their wives, did not. The rule was unsaid but inviolable.

The more liberal racing enthusiasts encouraged their wives to involve themselves in some activity or the other on weekends, to keep them out of their hair and to feel no guilt for not being there when other families were usually together. Anwar was one of them. He always encouraged Shehzaadi to organise ladies lunches, play cards at the club, meet friends, keep herself busy.

Shehzaadi detested such activity. She wasn't the kitty party type, neither did she like playing cards, she just couldn't figure out the logistics. She preferred staying home, chatting with her son and his friends. But now, finally, when she had actually found friends she liked going out with, no matter how frivolous it seemed to him, he had no right, whatsoever, to object. It's just not fair, she thought.

Anwar had left behind all his concerns about his wife and the worries related to her health, while he cheered and rejoiced at the Malakpet racecourse. Despite his craze for the sport, what the racing regulars admired about him was the fact that he never crossed the limits he set for himself where gambling was concerned. He knew where to draw the line. Several other die-hard punters had laid at stake massive fortunes, losing them as easily as they had been inherited. But not Anwar. For him, the fun was in the sheer vitality of the game. It helped him release pent up tension and forget everything

Nowadays, Shehzaadi looked forward to her husband's absence on the weekends. She had begun to like planning her own outings. Doing her own thing without having to consult or inform him. Each took the other for granted. It had taken her two decades to reach this stage. But she was enjoying it now. More than pleasure it provided her respite from her thoughts.

In the evening, she dressed in a pair of trousers and a long shirt, replaced her gold bangle with a platinum bracelet, while waiting for Zeba who was expected any minute, to come pick her up. She studied her reflection in the mirror and wondered if she should replace her solitaire studs for something trendier. But the only alternatives she had were other designs in diamonds and precious stones. All of them beautiful. None of them trendy. She decided to take Amita's help to spruce up her accessories. Amita had a lovely collection of silver earrings—hoops, danglers and other stylish stuff.

Shehzaadi suddenly remembered her husband's comment about her friend's dress sense.

She heard Zeba honking outside the gate. The whole exercise of opening the gate, driving down the driveway, parking the car, getting out of the car and back in, consumed a considerable amount of time and energy. So Zeba either called her before turning into the lane of her house or honked at the gate when she couldn't get through for some reason. Shehzaadi hurried, calling out to Babu Miya to close the gate, Zeba honked again. Shehzaadi grumbled, 'you impatient woman.'

Zeba said gravely, 'You know how I hate waiting.'

On the way to Amita's house, they picked up a bunch of tulips from the florist down the road and a chocolate cake from the Taj to cheer her up. Amita was thrilled to see them and what they had brought for her. Without bothering with, 'you needn't have,' and other such banalities, she handed the cake to Maria and arranged the tulips in the swarovski flower vase that occupied pride of place in her living room. They hugged each other, cheeks touching, lips smacking the air and sank into the huge sofas. 'These sofas are so comfy, you can sleep in them,' observed Zeba.

'I do that sometimes,' said Amita, 'When it gets too lonely in the bedroom.'

'Don't you ever think of remarrying?' asked Shehzaadi.

'Never. I have no energy for the demands of marriage. Men are good, wonderful in fact, as long as you keep them where they're meant to be. In your arms perhaps but at arm's length. You have no idea, princess, what a man can do to you if you let him.'

'Not all men are the same,' said Shehzaadi.

'You've seen one, you've seen all. I've had enough to last me a lifetime. Affairs yes, but marriage is a big no-no.'

'I think you go overboard sometimes,' said Zeba, 'If I were you, I would leave married men alone.'

'You are not me. And I'm definitely not eyeing Hamid.'

Amita and Zeba shared a strange friendship. An unlikely combination of disrespect and empathy.

'Oh, please,' responded Zeba, 'you can have Hamid. He's yours for all I care. Actually, why don't you have an affair with him? Good enough to put you off everyone else's husbands forever. Seriously, give it a thought.'

'Sorry darling, not interested. What you want to do with him is totally up to you. I wouldn't mind Anwar bhaijaan though.'

'Come off it, you two,' Shehzaadi intervened, 'And you Amita, call my husband bhaijaan, that means brother. You haven't forgotten that, I hope.'

'Hope springs eternal, my dear. I know of a woman who calls her sister's husband bhaijaan and sleeps with him when the sister's not around. And the sister's damn naïve. She can't see what's happening right under her nose. I feel bad for her. Come to think of it, it is impossible to look under your nose. Just try.'

'I feel bad for you. Your perversions are going from bad to worse,' Zeba said.

'Thank you. I take that as a compliment.'

'You're beyond repair,' said Zeba.

'If anybody needs any repair, it's you. And your rotten marriage that's making your sense of humour so stale that it stinks.'

Shehzaadi listened to their conversation and wondered how they could speak to each other like that. She didn't like Amita's comment about Anwar. And Zeba? How could she talk of Hamid like that But they were her friends. Warts and all. When you accept a friend, you accept them as a whole. It's a package deal—the beauty and the beast in them.

They had so much to catch up on that they lost track of time until Shehzaadi's cell phone rang in her handbag. She rummaged through it and by the time she found it, it stopped. She looked at the missed call number and smiled. She pressed the green button. She sensed the impatience in Anwar's voice, 'Where are you jaan?'

'Where do you think?' she asked back.

He sensed from her voice that she was tipsy. 'Anywhere between the club and your favourite pub? Right now my instinct tells me that you're at Amita's. Am I right? Should I come pick you up?' He felt sure of his guess because more often than not, her cell didn't work at pubs and even when it did the music was more audible than her voice. She couldn't be at the club because her friends, one in particular, hated the ambience there. It had to be one of her friends' houses—of the two they preferred Amita's because they had all the privacy they needed.

She screamed, 'How did you guess? Just a minute,' to him and asked Zeba what she should do. He could hear Zeba saying that anything was okay with her. Then he heard her saying, 'Zeba says she'll drop me.'

Anwar was mighty peeved at her half-truth. If she wanted to stay back, she could say so directly, he thought. 'Did you have dinner?' he asked.

'Not yet. Just about to,' she replied.

'Come back soon. I'm missing you.'

'Keep it going. I'll see you in a while.'

Anwar hung up. How naïve he had been to believe that she had given up alcohol. He cursed himself for not having taken her to the doctor. 'First thing, Monday morning,' he decided. But between Saturday and Monday, there always comes a Sunday. And Sundays had never been lucky for Shehzaadi. One Sunday, in the distant past, had altered the course of her future.

~

Chapter 21

VARSHA HATED BEING ALONE IN HER HOUSE. SHE LIKED THE freedom but she didn't like the loneliness. She felt free to be herself but secluded from the rest of the world all at once. The eternal dichotomy of existence. But they were two sides of the same coin. When life doles out heads, you bloody well take the tails as well. Whether you like it or not. Life doesn't care. Every life is a tale of convoluted twists and turns.

Varsha had decided, after her life with Som, that she was destined to be disappointed in love. She planned to keep love out of her way. And destiny? Destiny played no part in her scheme of things.

After the Goa trip, she was back in the same old rut. Surviving. Working. Until one day Tripti requested her to accompany her to a party. At a prospective client's house.

'No Tripti. I can't do that. I'm not invited.'

'You are. This man has asked me to bring someone along if I wanted to.'

'Sorry. I refuse to be that someone.'

'Don't be so egoistic. Sometimes, for professional reasons, you need to do certain things. This client is big. He's into distilleries, frozen foods and what have you. If we get this account, we're made. He has a massive ad budget. His ad spend runs into crores.'

'So you go.'

'You're being difficult. It's a huge party. Hundreds of people. One more won't make a difference. He won't even notice.'

'Exactly my point. Why should I go to a party where I won't even be noticed? One less doesn't make a difference?'

'It does. To me. I'll be more confident if you're with me. Doesn't that mean anything to you?'

Varsha gave in. The things one has to do for friendship, she grumbled. She had grown fond of Tripti. She didn't want to upset her in any way.

Tripti left her car behind because she wasn't comfortable driving late at night. They decided to take a cab.

Varsha felt very under-dressed when she saw Tripti in her elegant black sequined evening gown worn with a Tahiti pearl string around her neck and matching earrings. She looked at her own bottle-green flared pants and sleeveless white top with dark green polka dots. She threw a tantrum. 'You should have given me an idea of what to wear. Now I look so boring and childish next to you.'

'You look great, Varsha. Believe me. There's nothing wrong with what you're wearing.'

'There's nothing right about it either.'

'An eternal grumbler, that's what you are.'

'Maybe. But that's who I am.'

'And I like who you are.'

'Don't try to con me with your words.'

'Learnt it from you, guruji. You're the creative director remember?'

For all that reluctance, Tripti noticed later, Varsha was having a gala time. Stirring trouble, she thought fondly, looking at the way Safdar Ali Mirza, their prospective client, was hanging on her every word. Mirza called out to somebody, and when Tripti set her eyes on him, she saw a dashing, breathtakingly handsome young man. A good-looking guy was rare. She had seen loads of good-looking models but none would hold a candle to her present object of admiration. She hadn't come across anybody who looked like him. Now, he was shaking hands with Varsha. He smiled at something Varsha said and it reached his eyes, captivating her with its shyness. She never knew that 'shy' could be so sexy. She couldn't take her eyes off him. He was now engaged in conversation. Hesitantly, she approached Varsha who looked at her and said, 'Hey Tripti. Come, meet Shahbaz Mirza, Mr Safdar Ali Mirza's nephew who's studying in London. He lives in Hyderabad. And this, Shahbaz, is my colleague Tripti, single and most desirable as you can see.'

Tripti was embarrassed. Varsha went over the top sometimes with her compliments and at the most inappropriate times. She managed an awkward smile. When they shook hands, she found that his was cold. Probably because of the ice in the glass he was holding. The rest of the evening she had eyes only for him. But Shahbaz's were on the older woman. He found her fascinating. There was nothing extraordinary about her appearance; but he was impressed with her ease. She was comfortable in her own skin. So unlike him. Almost everybody complimented him on his good looks but when he looked at himself in the mirror he wondered what made people say that. He was inarticulate and took forever to open up, shy and unsure of himself. Ammi told him several times to be more confident, 'Shah, Allah has blessed you with such good looks; you must learn to appreciate it. Don't be so self-conscious. You have every reason to be confident of yourself.' He agreed with her but there was nothing he could do about it. Yet, he had girls flocking to him. Peter, his roommate, always said, 'Buddy, if I were in your place, I would've grabbed each one of them.' There was this American girl who was so smitten that she had literally thrown herself at him. But it did nothing for him. Not that he disliked them but it was just that he wasn't attracted to them. Peter had laughed his head off, when he learnt that he had never 'made it with a woman', as if it was some kind of joke. He had taken it upon himself, like a mission, giving it a ridiculous title—Making a Man Out of Mirza—hooking him up with girls whenever he could. Peter was exasperated when every attempt would lead to nothing. Thanks to Shahbaz himself. 'Man, are you gay or something? What are you going to do?' Peter would laugh. 'Pull your socks up, kiddo, before you become an old man. Don't tell me I didn't warn you.' Peter's jokes irked him at times but he loved the guy. He laughed his comments off. 'It's not funny, man, it's high time you made some serious moves. Or you'll find yourself unable to get it up anymore.'

Peter was a Canadian. His life story bordered on the bizarre. He was an adopted child. His adoptive parents had divorced and remarried different people when he was eleven. His mother was his legal custodian, so he lived with her and her second husband. His biological mother, who had abandoned him, tracked him down when he was fourteen and wanted him back. She filed a case against his mother and finally at sixteen, he went to live with her and the man she had married, who was not his father. 'Man, it's crazy. Sometimes I would wake up in the morning and feel like I didn't know where I was. Too confusing. Lucky you, man, you Indians have strong family values.' Shahbaz agreed and added, 'We're getting there though. We're sometimes more westernised than the people born and raised in the West. But I've been fortunate. My parents love each other and for my mother, I am the world.' He was longing to see them, now. He would be home in a week anyway. For some reason, Abba had asked him to stay back for a week in Mumbai, to spend time with his relatives. He had landed just that morning when Chacha told him about the party. Until Varsha appeared on the scene some time ago, he had been feeling jet lagged. Now, that had been replaced by an enthusiasm that surprised him.

The party was in full swing. Everybody was getting noisier, drinking copious amounts of alcohol. Shahbaz was not too fond of alcohol. A couple of times Peter had forced a mug or two of beer down his throat and Shahbaz had felt rather ill and nauseous. Peter had declared him alcohol and sex intolerant but never forced him again. Shahbaz noticed that Varsha was happily gulping drink after drink, one cocktail after another. He said to her, 'I don't know much about alcohol but I do know that mixing drinks can give you an unpleasant hangover.' 'You dodo, cocktails are mixed drinks anyway, so there!' she replied.

He didn't know the difference, one way or another, but he saw the logic in what she said. So he nodded like a wise man who had just acquired invaluable knowledge. His mother drank red wine. He thought about her, she had sounded weak when he spoke to her last. He wanted to hear her voice. He decided to call her. He bent forward (she's so petite, so delicate, he thought) to tell her, 'Listen. I'll be back in a minute. Gotta make a call.'

'Is it okay if I come with you?' she asked.

He nodded and she walked into the house with him.

'So, there's a woman in your life, huh?'

'What makes you say so?'

'Who else would a man think of at this hour amidst a happening party?'

'Well, you're right.'

'I'm never wrong.'

'Only, it happens to be my mother.'

'Good boys don't lie, kiddo.'

'I'm not lying. And I'm not a kiddo.'

'If you're a man, I'm ancient.'

'How old does that make you?'

'Twenty-six.'

'I am twenty-two. Four years is not such a big gap. In any case, I believe age is between the ears.'

'All I can see between your ears is your head.'

'Very funny. I'm tickled.'

'But I didn't even touch you. Or is touch in the mind too?'

'That is funnier.'

'I'm impressed with your sense of humour.'

'And I, with your intelligence.'

'Thank you.'

'My pleasure. Now, if you allow me, I need to make a phone call.'

As he talked on the phone, Varsha took in the surroundings. They were in the living room of what seemed to belong to a museum rather than a home. Massive chandeliers scattering light through cut-glass and highlighting the blue Persian carpets—of all sizes—on the floor, dark blue silk curtains with beige double drapes, antique sofas, diwans, chairs, bric-a-brac arranged tastefully on carved wooden tables with glass tops. She whistled through her teeth in admiration and he asked her, 'What happened?' She shook her head and gestured him to carry on. Shahbaz asked again, 'What?' She made a 'v' sign and moved a little ahead to continue her exploration. She picked up an Aladdin-style lamp, rubbed it dramatically, and sang, 'I'm a genie in a bottle baby.' Shahbaz hung up and said, 'God, don't you ever keep quiet?'

'Sorry. Did I disturb you? Didn't mean to, was just so enamored by everything around. How does your uncle live in a house like this?'

'Like all human beings do?'

'I beg to differ, my dear child. Not all humans are so privileged.'

'I don't like this business of calling me a child.'

'I'm into cradle-snatching, sweetheart. If I stop the business, what would happen to you?'

'I'll tell you some other time.'

'How do you know there will be other times?'

'I'm into future predictions, in case I haven't told you.'

'A-ha, so let's start with my future.'

'You're going to meet me every day for the next week.'

'Where?'

'That's up to you. Your place or mine?'

'Hey, kiddo you're flirting!'

'If you don't stop treating me like a kid, I'll be forced to do other things too.'

'Don't forget you're talking to an old woman.'

'Old and you! You could give teenagers a complex.'

'Flattery gets you nowhere. But right now we need to go out. There's an attractive young lady, out there, waiting for you to ask her for a dance.'

'That lady in black?'

'So, you noticed her?'

'Of course. You were the one who introduced her to me.'

'So... would you like to get to know her better?'

'You're sounding just like Peter.'

'Who's Peter?'

'I'll tell you the next time we meet. There're more interesting things to do.'

'Like what?'

'Exotic cocktails at the bar?'

'Hmm... *That* is definitely interesting. You don't drink?'

'I do but not alcohol.'

'Now who's being funny? Well, that's what I meant.'

'I tried beer once but never liked the taste. I threw up.'

'Beer is like that. There are some who swear by it and others who can't stand it. You should try a cocktail. Or red wine. Port is sweet and you'll like it, I think.'

'I will, sometime. If you initiate me...'

She pretended she hadn't heard that because she didn't know how to react. Nobody had come on to her like he was doing. But she was quite flattered by his attention. With his looks and style, he could get any girl at the party. Yet, he had singled her out. What had Som said? That she was boring? Too serious. God! Why did she have to think of him every time she experienced some excitement?

They rejoined the party. Varsha found Tripti talking to Safdar Ali Mirza and a few other men and women who had formed a circle.

Everyone seemed drunk to Shahbaz. When you're not drinking, other people seem more intoxicated than they actually are. It was getting noisier by the minute with over-lapping conversation, blaring music and dancing feet stomping on the dance floor.

Later he asked Varsha for a dance, she was quite tipsy when she joined him. Her dancing was just like her—untamed and uninhibited. She looked at him, admiring his shy yet stylish moves. He had natural grace and rhythm. She imagined writing a book, 'How to read a man from his moves on the dance floor,' and laughed loudly. He thought she was mocking his dancing and said, 'I'm not a good dancer.' She giggled, pointing to a pot-bellied man next to him, doing the bhangra. He laughed too dragging her off the floor before she could embarrass him any further. She said to him between peals of laughter, 'You're a great dancer. Don't believe anybody who tells you otherwise.' He liked the way she had reassured him. He needed that from time to time, especially from somebody he felt close to. He was far too self-conscious most of the time.

Shahbaz was lying in Varsha's bed staring at the woman who had made a man out of him (to quote Peter). She had, in a single glance, given him a hint that she was willing to be approached. At around midnight she thanked the host for a lovely party and announced her intention to leave; making sure Shahbaz was looking at her and was within hearing distance. He got up to see her off. As she walked out, she turned and looked at him, pursing her lips and narrowing her eyes, a look that gave him confidence, to chide him playfully for his absorption in polite conversation when he might have been with her. He wanted to kiss her then and he would have if they were alone. Instead he asked, 'Do you have transport?' She said no. Safdar Chacha had handed over his car keys and said, 'Drop the ladies, Shah. The city is no longer as safe as it used to be.'

He followed her directions in a trance and when they reached her place, Tripti collected her car that she had parked there and left, leaving them alone.

When she asked, 'Would you like to come in?' he said, 'I thought you would never ask.'

Inside, she turned on the music system and Santana crooned, *Black magic woman*. Couldn't have been more apt, he thought. He was unable to take his eyes off her. After a while of heavy silence, she moved closer to him to change the music. He stood up and moved next to her and just as he was debating if it was the right time to kiss her, she put her arms around his neck almost forcing her lips onto his. She kissed him so deeply that he felt she was touching his soul. She probed his mouth seeking his tongue, entwining it with hers. He thought he was going to explode any minute. She drew his mouth to her breasts and he began kissing them. His inexperience vanished as desire blinded him to everything else except her and what she was doing to him. Spent with fulfilment he said to her, 'This was the best ever.'

'How would you know?' she teased playfully.

'You're right. I wouldn't unless I know what it's going to be like the next time.'

Several next times followed until their energy couldn't keep up with their desire. Now, as he looked at her sleeping form, he felt warm and tingly.

When he had phoned Safdar Chacha to inform him that he wouldn't be returning that night, he heard him chuckle, 'Bacchu, I thought you were different. But you are turning out to be just like my brother. Chip of the old block, huh.'

Shah didn't appreciate the remark. He knew about his father's Casanova days. On his sixteenth birthday, his dad had told him everything about the birds and bees. He knew what Chacha had meant. He didn't like it at all. She may have been the first one he had made love to, but he was certain she was the one he loved. From the bottom of his heart. There were no doubts about it in his mind. No dilemmas. Except for one. If it was too early to tell her. If she would mistake it for the flush of first-time sex. All along, she had talked of cradle-snatching, 'This is the second time I've been involved with a younger guy,' she had said. How many times had she done it? With how many men. For the first time in his life he experienced a tug at his heart when she had said that. Jealousy. But he was happy he was feeling that jealousy. Because it was connected to her. He had always associated multiple partners with men. Was he just one of the men for her? He'd never heard a woman talk like that. Frankness was one thing, but to be so casual was so uncommon... most of the women he knew pretended to be virginal.

But there was something he had noticed—there was something in her that told him she was wearing a mask. Most people do that to please others, to pretend to be what they're not, to be how they wish to be seen by others. But her mask seemed to be for herself. As if she didn't want to see her real self. He wanted her to take it off. In front of him, she could be herself. He would love her all the more for it. He was surprised at his own intensity. And a little scared too. What if she didn't reciprocate? She hadn't shown any signs that he was special to her. She had shared his passion, aroused it in him, drowned him in hers with gay abandon but her soul, her spirit, gave out vibes like the touch-me-not sapling that recoils at the slightest human contact. Was she wary of something? God, the feelings she had made him feel—good, bad, awful—but always strong. Damn it—they were strong as hell. But he loved her more for it. She stirred in her sleep, turning her face to him without opening her eyes. A million sparks went off in him.

She was the first one to get out of bed. He watched her as she came out freshly bathed, her wet locks framing her face. She looked so innocent. So vulnerable. At the same time devastatingly sexy. She was a child-woman. *His* child-woman. With the right proportions of innocence and seduction.

'You know what,' she said looking into the mirror, wearing her earrings, 'This is the first time there's a man in my bed in this house.'

'Boy am I glad,' he said, 'At least in some department I happen to be the first. Anything else I'm the first in?'

'I would not care to answer that question. Do you want some coffee?'

'Yes, please. The hotter, the better. But I have no toothbrush.'

'I don't share mine but I can offer you a new one.'

'An offer that's irresistible. Just like you.'

When he brushed and got out, she was already in the kitchen. He sat on the counter and watched while she poured warm milk on a heap of coffee powder into huge mugs and stirred. He saw the liquid turning mildly brown and then deliciously coffee-coloured. She extended the sugar container to him while sipping hers without it.

'Are you diabetic by any chance?' he asked.

'Thanks for the concern but no. Just watching my calories. Need to lose weight.'

'Please don't. You're just right. Perfect. Seductive. Sexy. Don't tell me all those men you keep bragging about never told you that?'

'No. Nobody did. I don't have a man in my life right now anyway.'

'What does that make me then? Don't I look like a man to you?'

'You're just a kid.'

'So what's a woman like you doing with this kid?'

'Passing time.'

'You could pass a lifetime too. If not a lifetime, a few more hours at least. When are we meeting this evening?'

'I don't think about the future. I live in the moment, for the moment.'

'Very philosophical, I must admit. I'm asking you about today, in case it's missed your fleeting attention. And today is part of the present.'

'I've got work to do.'

'I'm talking about later. When you finish work. Okay let's do it this way. You give me a buzz as soon as you're ready to leave and give me fifteen minutes to reach your office.'

'But you don't know where my office is.'

'I'll find out now, when I drop you.'

'I like walking. That's the only exercise I get.'

'You've had enough exercise last night and this morning. The credit goes to me. So I should have the privilege of dropping you now.'

'I don't know your number.'

'I know yours.'

'I don't entertain personal calls at work.'

He reached out for her mobile phone that was lying next to her and punched in his number and saved it. 'There you are. Now you have my number and you don't have an excuse. I will be waiting.'

She looked at her watch and let out a cry, 'Gosh, I'm already late.' She got into the car cribbing that all men were the same. Stubborn and stuck-up.

'Thanks for thinking of me as a man. You made my day.'

'Shut up, you nut!'

'I'll wait for your call,' he yelled as she walked into office. Tripti commented as soon as she saw her that she was looking different.

'Good or ugly,' she asked.

'Refreshingly fresh.'

She wondered how that could be possible considering the fact that she had hardly slept. Although she had slept really soundly. For a self-proclaimed first-timer he was terrific. God knows if it was because it was his first experience or his energy levels, but he was like a hurricane that just wouldn't subside. Showering her with his attention and love. As if he couldn't get enough of her. As if he wanted more and more. It felt good. She felt strangely energised in spite of herself. Her thoughts were interrupted by the buzz of the intercom.

'Somebody has sent you flowers.' the receptionist informed her.

'Who?'

'Haven't a clue. The florist delivered it. There's a small white box too.'

She had it sent in. It was a lovely bunch of double coloured roses—a combination of orange and red. She read the little card attached to it—*from one hungry soul to another.... S.* She smiled and opened the box that contained delicious looking sandwiches. She bit into one of them. It was soft, fresh and yummy. She was touched by his thoughtfulness.

She was distracted. Her mind wasn't on what she was doing. Much against her 'hard to please' image she was approving whatever was brought to her without so much as a protest. For once it didn't matter to her. For once, her colleagues were finding the day lighter and their tasks easier. Around lunchtime, when the phone rang, she answered it without looking at the number. Before she could say anything beyond a hello, Shahbaz butted in, 'Listen I know you don't take personal calls but just called to check what you were doing for lunch. If you're free I can take you out. If you're not I can have it sent to your office. Don't worry I won't grace you with my presently shabby appearance; I can have it delivered to you. You know, one of those dial-a-meal things.'

She declined but she was moved. Never before had anybody, not even her parents, shown such concern for her . At around six o' clock she decided she would pack up for the day. Most of her colleagues had either left or were leaving anyway.

When she reached home she debated on whether she should phone him after all. But something about his fervour was unnerving her. His confidence levels matched his energy. He hadn't let her think for herself as long as he was around. She had seen men—lived with one—but just one night with him and all those memories seemed distant. She wasn't sure if meeting him would mean leading him on. He was young and she had no right to do something that might complicate his life. Last night she had overheard bits and pieces of his conversation with his mother; his voice was gentle and caring. Maya always said that you could judge a man's character from his behaviour towards his mother. Varsha had countered that mama's boys would always remain mama's boys. Tied to apron strings. That had put Maya off and she had said, 'You always go to the extremes. What I meant was that when a man is close to his mother he is more compassionate to other women. You and your compartmentalisation. Sometimes I wonder if your brain has several compartments. Like a train. So and so in this bogey and such and such in the other. Uff.'

In a way, Maya was right. She had become a little like that. She wasn't before. In her early days with Som, she prided herself for being unbiased and non-judgmental. But nowadays, that was all she had. And it suited her. Look where being unbiased and accepting had landed her. Rejected by the only man she had loved. She knew she was destined to be disappointed in love. But the question was—would she recognise the love she had been longing for all her life, when it came her way or would she be blinded by her own plans and refuse to see it? If she decided to choose the latter, destiny wouldn't give her another chance. Missed chances are not destiny's fault.

Shahbaz was bewildered. He didn't know what had come over him. He had suddenly become confident enough to pursue a woman and a reluctant one at that. That too after he had had his 'fun', as Peter would put it. At the risk of being called a pest, he was willing to chase her. He was making himself vulnerable, laying himself open to hurt. He knew he was doing that. But he could think of no other way. He knew nothing else. He had known nothing like this and nothing like her. It was as if by a single swish of her wand, she had swept him off the ground. Now he was walking on air prompting Safdar Chacha to remark, 'At the risk of sounding clichéd I need to remind you that fools rush in where angels fear to tread, my dear boy.' He knew that too, that he was rushing. But there was nothing he could do about his own feelings. His mind had a will of its own. Even he didn't know how it would react anymore.

The whole day went by with him looking at his watch and cellphone, rejecting every call that came in, when he realised it was not from her. He felt no desire for conversation—polite or private—if it was not with her. Her name rattled around his head like a trapped bee. He felt it had a nice ring to it. He said it in a hundred different ways, then he would get an urge to say it aloud. He had said it loudly once in his room and the servant who was swabbing was startled. When she enquired if he wanted something, he said, 'No, you can't get me what I want.' She looked at him like he had gone out of his mind and walked out, scared to be alone with a madman.

After waiting until seven and when her call didn't come, he decided to phone her. He wouldn't get offended by anything she said or did. He could tell that she loved her space and independence. He would trample on neither; he had to assure her of that if he wanted her to see him. But the rate at which he was going, he feared he would do just the contrary. Go slow. Go easy. Slow. Easy. He repeated to himself like it was a mantra while dialling. 'Oh hi,' she said and her voice sounded pretty down. He asked her if she was feeling all right and when she said 'comme ci, comme ça,' he ran to her side without being asked. She had thought she would turn him away if he visited her, but when he did, she invited him in. She felt better almost instantly. Once again he called Chacha saying he wouldn't be coming home. And after an encore of the previous night's performance, Shahbaz said, 'The best just got better.' Those were the last words she heard before she dozed off.

The next morning, Shahbaz told her, 'Look at it this way, Varsh, both of us are having a good time. We like each other's company, being with each other, it's not everyday that you come across someone and the next thing you know, you're best buddies. Don't screw it up with your why and what for. I'm here for a short while; you know that, so let's just let things be. I'll see you in the evening.'

She realied the truth in what he said and agreed. That morning when he dropped her at the office, Tripti saw him and asked later, 'So what's cooking with Mirza junior?' Varsha said, 'Nothing at all. He's leaving shortly for Hyderabad and then to England.' Tripti made a mental note of his date of departure and decided she would act quickly. He had caught her fancy. Good-looking guys who can hold a conversation were so rare these days. Later during lunch, she called his house. Safdar Mirza answered and called out to his nephew. He watched from the background as his nephew politely told her that he was too busy. Obviously, he was making excuses not to meet her. Busy? All he did was sit and stare at his cell phone. Safdar wondered why. He knew this girl who had just called and she was pretty. God knows what boys look for in girls these days, he wondered. If he had been younger…but strange are the ways of modern men, he sighed pretending to examine some object on the table nearby when Shahbaz looked at him.

Shahbaz and Varsha continued to meet day after day, night after night, always eager for, never tiring of, each other.

~

Chapter 22

REVATI RAO WAS GETTING IMPATIENT. VARSHA HAD AGREED TO visit her but there had been no sign so far. She felt a surge of sadness for her daughter. She should be out there, laughing, partying, shopping, spending her mother's money and ringing up to ask for more. Not fending for herself in some strange city. But Varsha had always been like that. She had never had any use for her mother's money. She lifted the phone on an impulse and called her. Varsha said she was in a meeting and would call back later. Now, all she could do was wait. She was getting tenser by the minute and kept thinking, what if she didn't visit her and something went wrong, what would she do? She thought of her—Varsha being fed as a baby, Varsha with braces on her teeth, Varsha in her school uniform, Varsha as an adolescent with a huge appetite, Varsha the rebel always fighting for some imaginary cause. A terrorist, my daughter, she thought fondly, always bullying people. She was ashamed to admit it but it hurt her to think that her only child was living on her own. She had even offered her financial help but Varsha's response had been, 'Oh, come off it, mommy. Don't be absurd and sentimental. I love what I'm doing and I'm happy. You don't have to be so melodramatic about it, like I am suffering or something. My pain has nothing to do with money or the lack of it.'

The way Varsha addressed her mother changed from mood to mood. On normal days it was mommy or mom, when she was feeling a little soft towards her it would be mama and when she felt a lot of love, it was ma. So far she had called her mommy most of the time, mama on a few occasions and ma only once, when she had run home crying after having cut her knee with a glass shard that was lying on the ground, tears in her eyes saying, 'Ma, I thought I wouldn't find you home.' The tears that came to Revati's eyes were more for her daughter's pain than her own. The images she saw were like scenes from a film. How innocent. How beautiful. She hadn't appreciated either at that time. She was blinded by ambition—ambition for power, for money, now she had both in abundance. At what cost?

When Shahbaz hugged his mother she cried silently like a child who was hurt deeply. She looked pale but he knew what his absence had done to her. He held her, consoling her like she used to comfort him when he didn't want to attend school. The whole house reverberated with activity. As if it had come to life after a lull.

Shehzaadi liked his quiet presence. It had a healing effect on her. She looked at him eating, sleeping shaving, over and over again. She missed him so much. But she knew that the time had come to let go. Soon he would go away. To resume his studies. Later he would build his own life. With his wife and their children. He was the same calm, quiet young man in command of himself. But something was bothering him. Once he settled down she would ask.

After eight months of absence, he should be glad to be home. Everything was just the way he had left it, except himself. He did everything to cheer up his mother, his father, and the rest of the household; he tried to stay cheerful in spite of himself. But he felt a void, one that he tried hard to fill and not think about but it kept coming back leaving a dull ache behind. Something strange was happening to him. Love was doing incredible things. He felt he could almost sense things better. His feelings had all become crystal clear. And so intense. At the same time he felt gentle, soft warmth when he thought of her. He had come to understand that deep inside her was a vacuum despite the *joie-de-vivre*. There was a cold place in her heart. He wanted to get there. And ignite it. He longed for her and what a longing it was. When he thought of her and how she looked stretched out naked in bed, it was as though if he couldn't get to her fast enough, he would just break up into pieces. Yet, he knew his love was stronger than the lust he felt. Loving her just made the lust stronger. It wasn't just the sex. It was an alive, living feeling; breathing and throbbing. When he looked around at other people on the street, he could see a certain deadness in them. He knew for sure that he never wanted to join them—the mechanised robotic species. He wouldn't reduce himself to that while he waited to have her with him. Not after he had experienced those heavenly feelings with her. Even though she wasn't with him, he could see her. But when he realised she wasn't there, physically with him, he touched new depths of depression. His heart felt so heavy as though he would sink into the ground. No, he wasn't depressed. He just felt weighed down, heavy, hopeless. How crazy to feel something for someone and to be scared to tell them!

She was like a whiff of fresh air. There was nothing 'smart-alecky' about her, no put-ons. She played it cool sometimes but not hard to get. How he loved her candour. How direct she was! Much too direct and logical sometimes. Coming right out with what she thought. Even if it hurt him or put him in his place.

When he pictured her, bright and alive, his mood lifted, he felt clear-headed like he had in London when the fog cleared. He could see everything clearly. He wanted so much for her to be happy with him. He wanted to put his arms around her, hug her, kiss her, rub his cheek against hers, put his head on her bosom, plead and tell her that he loved her. She was his life-giver, in a sense, because if not for her and the feelings she evoked in him, he would have been a part of the automated race.

His preoccupation didn't escape his mother's keen eye. Somehow, she knew, she always knew. She asked him one day directly, 'Baba, are you in love?'

If he had time to prepare himself, he would probably have practised lying. But now, when caught off guard, he admitted, 'Yes, Ammi, how did you guess?'

'I didn't guess, sweetheart. I just knew. You're a part of me, baba. I can feel what you're feeling. Is it the same girl who was with you at Safdar's party?'

Another accurate guess.

Anwar, who was present, hooted like he did at the racecourse whenever his favourite horse won. 'Good show, sonny boy, good show! But how do you know you're in love? How are you sure? Experience more of life and then settle for love.'

'You're making love sound like something you have to settle for! God knows what you mean by that,' Shehzaadi admonished her husband.

'I know Abba. I can feel it in my bones. I have no desire for any other women.'

'You should have brought her with you,' said Shehzaadi.

'I would have loved to Ammi, but she doesn't even know. I'm scared to tell her.'

Shehzaadi's heart went out to her son. 'She should consider herself blessed to find a man like you. What makes you think any woman can reject you?'

'I don't know Ammi.'

'Listen to your heart, darling, do what it says. Everything will fall into place. Any which way, you're going to be a winner. I know it. In life and love, the secret of success is in not giving up. May Allah grant you all your heart's desires,' she said ruffling his hair. Varsha was in Bangalore now and she had given him strict orders not to phone her. If only he could hear her voice, once, he sighed wistfully.

Revati had done everything to ensure that her daughter felt welcome. She gave up her work, rescheduled her meetings and speeches to be with her. She told her, 'If your marriage didn't work out, it wasn't meant to. Some things are best left at that. Don't try to analyse it and make yourself miserable. You're young, you're talented; you have your whole life ahead of you. You even have the qualities to make a good politician. And you don't even have to start from scratch like I had to. There's a lot you can do for people, Varsha, I'm not talking about power at all. I know that doesn't appeal to you. Give it a thought. Think about it at leisure. Whatever your decision is, it's perfectly fine with me. No pressure.'

She spent a blissful week with her mother for the first time. She even felt sorry for her occasionally. She wanted to tell her about Shahbaz but she was not sure. He was doing things to her that no one else had done. He could talk for hours. Sometimes he even ordered her around. The cheek of him, she thought affectionately and felt physical warmth spread through her. She ached with longing. She knew that for her, it was just that. It was good, it was wonderful. But it wouldn't last. If it lasted it wouldn't be good anymore. God alone knew what was in store for her. This fellow had no qualms about expressing anything that he felt and thought. Sometimes it seemed almost like he didn't care about what she would say and later he usually convinced her and made her understand what he meant. His maturity in his handling of her, the way he behaved, everything about him belied his age. She had another day before she left for Mumbai. Let's see how things would have changed for him, she thought, almost as a challenge.

The next day when she was getting ready to leave for the airport, he called. She couldn't help saying, 'Where were you, you swine? Not a call. Out of sight, out of mind, huh?'

'Of course not! You were the one who forbade me from calling. I thought you were serious about it. Had I known you weren't, I would have made your life miserable with my phone calls—morning, noon and night.'

'Oh I did? I don't remember. I'm glad I did though. At least I had a peaceful holiday. How was yours?'

'I'll tell you when we meet.'

She told him her flight was due in an hour and she was leaving home just then.

When she reached Mumbai airport, she found him waiting at the entrance. He was looking cool and casual, dressed in dark blue denims, a white t-shirt with a black jacket on his arm. He had a stubble on his face that added to his charm. She liked the way he rubbed his right hand on his beard.

'You look great. What's with the stubble?' she said to him.

'Thanks. I had become a Devdas, you know, what with your ban and all. You turned me into this.'

'Suits you though. Makes you look grown up.'

'Thank you once again.'

'Girls love this slightly careless look, did you know that? Bad girls like rugged men, remember that.'

'Thanks for parting with such valuable information. Though I'm sure I have no use for it. Come. Let's go,' he said waving to a cab.

When he slid onto the seat after she got in, she sensed his intentions and said, 'Listen. I have lots of work to catch up on.'

'You go work; I'll wait at our love nest like a dutiful lover boy.'

'No way. I'll have none of that. And what's with the love nest, lover boy thing?'

'Let's not get into this right now, Varsh, please. It's okay if you don't want me to stop by. I won't. Now just relax and enjoy the drive. And let me too.'

'So how was it getting back home?'

'It was wonderful. I told my mom about you.'

'You did?'

'You want to ask her?' he said, fishing out his mobile from his shirt pocket.

'Why not?' she said absolutely certain that he hadn't. She smiled at him dialling a number and saying, 'Ammi, just called to tell you I reached in one piece. Somebody here wants to say hi,' he said, handing the phone to her. Absolutely sure he was feigning the conversation, she jokingly said, 'Hello, this is Varsha.' She was so stunned when she heard a cultured woman's voice saying, 'How are you? How was your Bangalore trip? Shahbaz has told me so much about you.' She managed to hold her own for another ten seconds before giving the phone back to him. He took it and laughed, 'Oh thanks Ammi. You take care of yourself. I want colour back on your face the next time I see you.' He hung up and said, 'You didn't believe me, right?' She confessed thinking that he had played the fool.

'I don't say what I don't mean. Remember that or else,' he said pretending to hold her at gunpoint.

'But what did you tell her?'

'That I'm in love with you.'

'How could you? You told her before even I knew?'

'You mean to say you didn't? Okay, have it your way. *I love you.* Have I made myself clear now?'

'Listen Shah, you're young. You're handsome. You're going to meet other women, believe me, many more women, attractive, interesting. What makes you think this is the real thing?'

'My mom always said when in doubt, follow your heart. Not that I was ever in any doubt. With you, I'm cocksure,' he said tongue firmly in cheek.

'Well, I can see that. On a serious note, this is hardly an age to get stuck with anyone.'

'Stuck with you? Happy to be stuck with you,' he hummed a made-up tune.

'Have you considered our religious differences?'

'There are only two religions—men and women.'

'Even that theory makes us belong to different religions.'

'Okay, you're original. A one-piece wonder, I got to admit.'

The nearer they got to her house, the quieter he became. He couldn't tell if it was the emotion of seeing her after a gap or if he was speechless because he didn't know how to tell her that he had no life without her. When they reached her home, he followed her in like a puppy. The moment he closed the main door and turned to her disarmingly, all her protests vanished into thin air. In its place came desire. It was as if they were picking up from where they had left off. Later, she knew, in her heart of hearts that there was no looking back. This had transgressed all the limitations she had imposed on herself. But she was not about to confess this to him—it could just be a passing phase. At his age, guys fall in and out of love every other day. He just might wake up tomorrow morning feeling different.

He left reluctantly when his uncle phoned enquiring about him. 'These mobile phones are the bane of our existence. Luckily we can still lie conveniently about our whereabouts. Soon somebody will invent some stupid gadget and the caller will be able to see the receiver. Until such time, we can take recourse in little half-truths. What say you?' he said, winking at her. She had barely entered the bathroom when his number flashed on her cell. 'Now, what?' she asked, trying to sound irritated while being secretly thrilled.

'I was just wondering what makes you avoid me like an over-used cliché. Tell me why? I'm sure you enjoy my company as much as I enjoy yours, maybe a little less but you do, don't you? Actually I don't mind being your object of amusement, putty in your hands, a play-thing, whatever, as long as I am with you. How's that for an idea?'

'I'll toy with it. But I don't agree with your love thing.'

'Can we discuss this over a drink tonight? Remember you promised to teach me the art of wine drinking.'

'I said nothing of that sort. But we can meet for a drink.'

'I'll pick you up then, nine-ish, okay with you?'

'I'll take a cab, Shah.'

'You don't want to give me an excuse to stay back with you?'

'You can drop me back for that.'

'You be ready and wait for me like a sweet little girl for a change. You're so argumentative, goodness gracious me, wonder how I'm gonna survive.'

'Yeah, right, that's why I'm asking you to double check on what you say about loving me.'

'Okay, so let's resume the argument tonight. See you. Love you.'

How long had it been since she first met him? How had he become such a big part of her life? For the last one-month, barring the time they were away, they had spent every free moment with each other. Something she had not done even with Som. Even when they had decided to get married, she was the one who had initiated the proceedings by speaking to her mother first. And Shahbaz had already spoken to his mother about her! What had he told her? Probably that she was a good friend. Couldn't be more than that. But then he did mean what he said. His relationship with his parents was so easy, as she could see.

Som, on the other hand, had seemed to feel nothing for his parents. His parents, as far as Varsha knew, were perfectly nice people. They were charming, affectionate and caring but for some reason Som had never been able to feel he was one of them. He had never been close to them, though they had given him every possible advantage. His mother had told her soon after they had expressed their desire to get married that he had always been a reserved child who needed time to express himself and that she had never had any. She was a popular TV host; she was on committees, always surrounded by a hundred people with a hundred things to do. And his father was busy touring most of the time. Som was usually busy with school and his friends. The house was always full of people—relatives, guests—there was never a time when they were alone together, as a family, with nothing to do except talk. 'I'm relying on you, to help him establish a proper relationship with the world, with you, your children when you have them, to create a real family life,' her mother-in-law had told her in those heady days when everything held promise. It was too late by the time she had realised that his emotional growth had been stunted and had made him incapable of being a husband or a father.

Why did she have to think of him now? The phone rang and she answered it almost sure of the caller. But it turned out to be her mother. She felt slightly disappointed and in retrospect guilty for feeling so. After enquiring after her, Revati Rao wanted to know if she had thought about her suggestion.

'I have Ma. But the more I think of politics as a career option I know it's not something I want to get into. I don't know how to put it into words but the more I consider it, the worse it gets. I've tried, believe me, I have but I just can't seem to get over the aversion.' As promised her mother said she understood but assured her once again that she always had her to fall back on. Poor thing, thought Varsha, the trouble she was going through to make amends.

She took extra care dressing up that night to make sure she looked her best. She still hated the fat she thought she had but he said it suited her.

He honked while sitting in the car and she said angrily, 'Why are you behaving like a stranger? Couldn't you come in?'

'You know what could and would happen if I walk in and see you like this. All the pains you took over your appearance would be null and void.'

She tried to hide a small pleased smile.

He took her to a restaurant that served Mediterranean cuisine. The setting was romantic with the typical candle and red rose on every table. With soft, soulful music providing the perfect background, they spoke quietly revelling in the newfound lover's status. She had been married, had been in and out of flings, yet this was her first romance in the real sense of the term. For him, of course, this was the only romance he had ever known. The dreamy evening with their passions running underneath ended rather quickly. They drove back home. This time she didn't argue. She was getting her due share of happiness, even if short-lived.

The next morning while they were having coffee, he tried his best to keep the conversation at a safe, sombre level, to ensure that he sounded serious enough for her to take him seriously. They were sitting at the opposite sides of the dining table and as he talked, he kept looking away from her, concentrating on what he was saying, as if he was addressing an audience. He got so carried away in the process that he momentarily forgot his premise for detachment and then remembering his purpose, looked at her directly. He was met by a precise repetition of her now familiar, now intimate little grimace. It seemed that by the naughty pursing of her lips and the mischief in her smiling eyes, she took their affair for granted, assumed that they had always been lovers.

'Oh Varsha, don't,' the words tumbled out as if they were at the tip of his tongue waiting to spill out.

'Don't what?' she replied, her smile still in place.

'Don't let it come out like this,' he didn't say much but she knew what he meant. But she said nothing.

'Okay fine,' he resumed after a contemplative pause, 'Would you ever love me the way I love you?'

'I don't know Shah, I really don't know what it means to be in love, at least not in your sense. I don't think I'll ever know. For years what I believed was love turned me into a robot. Then, as if to balance it, I behaved like an abandoned woman, letting my physical desires drive my behaviour. Though it started like that with you, it's turned out to be different. It's grown into something more complete. I love being with you. I miss you when you're not with me. I ache with desire sometimes just thinking about you. But I don't know if it's love. If this is what love is. I sometimes feel like I'm always running away, escaping from myself.'

'I understand. You see, Varsh, I want you to know this. If I don't tell you now, I may never get the opportunity to. I don't mean to rush you. I just need you to know that you're not just another woman for me. Not that I've had any women in my life. You're the first. I want you to be the last too. For me, you'll always mean the same even if you decide to marry someone else. No one can ever really take you away from me. I'll go on dreaming about you and you'll have to meet me in my dreams, belong to me in a way you would never belong to anyone. You must've sensed it by now, my attachment to you. I'm sure you have your own reasons to stick to your stand but I just had to tell you this. I couldn't wait any longer.'

She bent her head and looked at her nails. He waited for a while for her to say something and then said, 'I want you and me to understand each other in such a way that we must be absolutely sure that we want to marry each other, even if there are the most frightful difficulties in our path. Until you're as sure of me as I am of you, I'm willing to wait. You can decide on how long. I leave it to you. Three, four, ten years, as you please.'

Not only her eyes but her face was also hidden. Her hands folded together in her lap as if she was imposing a restraint on herself. Shahbaz bent a little towards her, trying to look at her eyes but all he saw were tears that fell from them. 'Varsh!' he said, almost crying in pain, 'What have I said?'

She made an effort, lifted her head and without looking at him stared out of the window, with her back facing him. After a moment's hesitation he followed her, but before he was next to her, she turned back and held his hands at an arm's length, as if she wanted to prevent him from coming any closer.

'Varsh,' he said her name again, hopelessly puzzled.

She faced him now, staring straight back into his eyes and said, 'I've got to tell you something, a few things. No, in fact a whole story before you make any more grandiose statements.'

She sighed. He followed suit.

Hers was heavy with memories and his with impatient anticipation.

'So long as there's something in your life that I don't know about or can't share, I'll have no peace. I want to understand everything, to know your mind and soul. You've got to trust me. They're not grandiose statements. They're grand truths. Truth can't get grander than this.'

'Well,' she said and stopped.

'What's stopping you?'

'Have you ever wondered how most of our responses to situations in life are rooted either in love or fear? The largest part of my life so far has been driven by a fear of not finding love. Love, the way I look at it.'

Little by little, word by word, she gave him a full and honest account of everything that had transpired in her life until she met him.

'So you see; I'm technically a married woman. Somebody else's legal wife. Now, you know my fear.'

He listened to every word, digesting every emotion, coming to terms with her situation.

'Marriage is here,' he said tapping his right forefinger on the left side of his chest 'and divorce here,' he said pointing to the mind. 'It doesn't make any difference to me. Though, I'm afraid, at some point you'll need to talk to Som about your divorce. If you're interested in the both of us being together.'

'Love's a very strange emotion Shah. It makes us happy, miserable, sometimes complete, at times it leaves a vacuum, as long as it lasts.'

'I'm sure that my love will not fade. It will endure as long as we do.'

'I don't agree that love is a reason to marry. In fact it is a reason not to marry if you want it to last. Or endure like you're saying. Also, as I told you mine is more sexual in nature.'

'Never mind. Sometimes sexual love is far more binding than an asexual one.'

She knew it was true. Who could know it better than her?

'You don't know what marriage is, Shah. I've seen it very closely. Marriage kills people slowly. I know of people who believe in dying that way, they accept it like how terminal patients accept euthanasia. Even beg for it. I know I sound cynical almost cold-hearted but I need to tell you where I stand. I've decided that I want to live alone. I might, just might, love you forever, but as far as living goes, I'd like to do that on my own.'

'Did you know that loneliness increases the likelihood of disease and premature death?'

'That's better than having a diseased mind and deceased emotions.'

'What do you want to be alone for?'

'To discover myself if you must know.'

'You can never discover yourself by being alone. You need to be a lover, a wife, a daughter, a mother, to have an identity, my dear.'

'And what happens to you, you as a person, as an entity. Won't you get lost in the process of being all these?

'What you are vis-a-vis each of these relationships is what you truly are. How you behave in each relationship, what you learn from every experience is the basis of self-discovery. The relationship of the self with the world is what helps its evolution. That's how you find yourself.'

'I don't agree with you.'

'You don't have to. Take me for example. Who am I? I am called Shahbaz Mirza. Who gave me that identity? My parents. If I feel that I'm losing my identity by being their son, I'm losing myself. I'm depriving myself of all the emotions—positive and negative—that are a part and parcel of the relationship. Even if you believe in living only for yourself, you need relationships to sustain you. Think about it!'

She lapsed into contemplative silence until he sat next to her. She snuggled close to him, resting her head on his shoulder to get a grip on her emotions.

~

Chapter 23

SUNDAY DAWNED AND ANWAR LEFT HOME IN THE AFTERNOON for his weekend gambling ritual. Shahbaz had returned to Mumbai enroute to England. He soon forgot all his worries as he hooted, punted, cheered and generally went crazy at the Malakpet racecourse. When he returned home to share his excitement of his horse's victory at a race, he didn't find Shehzaadi home. He called her cell and after several attempts she answered. The music was deafening and her voice was barely audible. He lost his cool and asked her to return at once. Apparently, the three of them had decided last minute, like they were prone to doing in recent times, to visit the city's only nightclub. Once she got there she had lost all track of time. After he barked orders at her, Shehzaadi hurried her friends and Amita said, 'Angry husbands are quite troublesome, darling. They can prove to be quite a handful. Play it cool.' When she returned home, she found him sleeping with a book on his chest. She tiptoed carefully to not disturb him and went into the bathroom. Anwar was aware of what she was doing. When she didn't come out after twenty minutes, he knocked on the door and pushed it open on not getting a response. He saw her lying in a pool of blood oozing from her head. His hands began to tremble. He was struck by panic like never before. With Babu Miya and Rukhsana's help, he shifted her to the car and rushed her to hospital. She was immediately admitted into ICU. While waiting, Anwar cursed himself for postponing the gynaecologist's appointment. How could he have taken her condition so lightly? What use was his horse winning at the races if he lost the one he loved?

Fortunately, there was no internal injury and she was transferred to a private deluxe room. As she recovered, they spoke a little every day. She told him how lonely and left out she felt on weekends, 'Honestly, it was okay while Shah was around but after he left, you didn't care. You could have seen it if you wanted to but you preferred not to. I did mention my swinging moods, you made appropriate noises, expressed concern and all that but what did you do—nothing. You went away in the morning promptly. What do you expect me to do? Sit at home and cool my heels or paint my nails?'

He apologised profusely to her, she could see how sorry he was and how bad he was feeling. They resolved to reach a compromise on the matter. 'Should I give up going to the races?' he asked her.

'I never said that. At least when I'm not well, I need you around.'

After she recuperated and was fit enough they visited Dr Pratima Devi, her gynaecologist. She conducted tests and declared that it wasn't premenopausal after all. 'The symptoms seem more psychological than somatic,' she said to both of them and insisted they see her colleague, Dr Bhargav Mitra, a renowned psychotherapist. When they seemed hesitant she said, 'Look Mr Mirza, our mindset is truly unfathomable. We have no problems; in fact we overdo it, to see a physician when we have physical problems. But the moment we say mind, mental trouble, we cower. We try to cover it up. I can't figure out how even educated people like you behave so irrationally.'

He assured her that he wasn't reluctant at all and she immediately fixed up an appointment for the next day. Dr Bhargav examined her. After a detailed one on one with her, he told Anwar that she was suffering from chronic depression. 'I'm not one of those to prescribe tranquilisers, mood elevators and be done with it. If I have to treat it, I need to find the root cause. Treating symptoms never cures a disease. You must understand the underlying cause. In order to do that I will need to see her for a few sessions. If you're okay with it, you could give me a call and we'll take it from there.'

Anwar was shocked. The words 'chronic depression' had dealt him a blow that no loss at the race course ever did. He couldn't come to terms with it. What was the point in anything if his wife, his anchor who held his life together, suffered? He should have seen it coming. He should have read the signs. He had always admired her tranquility. He did not know that underneath it lay such turmoil. But what was worrying her? Why was she depressed? He wanted to ask her several questions but said nothing because he didn't want to aggravate her delicate condition.

It was akin to the way you feel when your car gets stranded on a highway and you know that help is at hand, at the mechanic. You're hopeful but you have no idea how long the journey would take. The prospect of walking all the way until you find him is what is daunting. In a way, shrinks are like mechanics, mind mechanics. Fixing the problems of the body's engine.

He felt dejected. He'd had a full, happy, successful life until now. He'd married the woman he loved. Their union had become stronger with the arrival of their son. Perfect in all senses. And now this. What was depressing her? Could it be her past? But that was so long ago.

Hai telephoned the police commissioner first thing the next morning. Indrasena Reddy, had been his schoolmate and a good friend for years. It was not like they stayed in touch, but they were always there for each other. He was put through to him after what seemed like ages. In the meantime he listened to a plethora of patriotic songs. When the commissioner came on line announcing himself, Hai said, 'Mama, it's me.'

Hyderabadis had this strange habit, amongst many others, of addressing close friends as 'Mama', which in Urdu as well as Telugu meant uncle. Somehow it had crept in to become an integral part of their lingo. Reddy abused him affectionately and then asked, 'Where have you been?' But Hai belonged to a class where expletives were never the norm. So he reciprocated the affection minus the abuse and came straight to the point. 'Reddy, I need a favour.' Reddy's trademark laugh echoed as he thundered, 'Hukum karo sarkar.' Hai explained to him that he needed the records of the '78 riots for research purposes. Reddy said, 'Arre yaar, why don't you let the dead rest in peace. Why do you want to dig graveyards now? After all these years. I have survived in my position for so long because of my non-controversial reputation. Now if the Press gets a whiff of this, I'll lose my job. It's a question of my kursi, why do you want to mess with it?' Hai assured him that it was purely for research purpose, and the Press would not get to know, and he didn't need statistics of the dead, he was only interested in the survivors. Reddy agreed for old time's sake but extracted a promise that the media wouldn't get to know. 'These newspaper reporters are like vultures constantly hunting for their prey. If they go and do some first person account of the survivors, I've had it. All they're interested in is sensationalising everything. Human beings can go to hell for all they care.' Hai reassured him again and he put him through to the officer who was in charge of the records division in the municipal office. As luck would have it, the municipal commissioner happened to be Reddy's wife. His added clout worked to Hai's advantage.

Later, when he called Maya to inform her about the morning's development she said, 'You're amazing, sir.'

'As long as I'm not amusing that's fine by me. That's the beauty of English language. A little juggling of alphabets is all you need to turn the profound into profane. I'm allowed to speak a sentence but I don't have the authority to pronounce it. Which other language can give me such freedom of expression? Tell me.'

She appreciated his digression. She wouldn't have known how to thank him otherwise.

When they met later at the University, he made no mention of it. He had always been like that from the time they had met. Matters outside work didn't matter to him at work. He had gone through her synopsis of the Purani Haveli project and was very impressed. She had divided it into three sections. In the first she had reconstructed history, in the second the current state of affairs and the need for its upkeep and the third was recommendations for reform. She had recaptured the glory and splendour of the palace as if she had lived in that era.

Without going overboard with his appreciation, he pointed out what she had missed, verification of facts and figures and then instructed her to do the needful. They discussed it in detail and she returned to her room. For some reason she was distracted. She decided to meditate. Appa had taught her the technique when once she had reached the examination hall and forgotten everything she had toiled over. Since then she tried to do it at least once everyday for twenty minutes but at times like this when concentration eluded her, she did it at any time. 'Calm your mind. Let thoughts pass. Don't suppress them. If you do they'll return. After a while your mind tires itself out, that's when you'll experience tranquility. The key is in disciplining your mind and regulating your breath.'

Energised and soothed she returned to work. At around five in the evening Sumathi came to her room and asked if she was interested in catching a film. Their favourite hero's movie was running in a theatre close by but if they had to see it they would have to rush. Maya thought for a while, she was not in a frame of mind to stay home alone, so she agreed. She turned the key in her cupboard and they rushed out to get an auto. Distances in Hyderabad were nothing compared to other metros. If you had to spend more than half an hour commuting it was considered a long distance. But the place they were going to—RTC X road—was a different ball game altogether. In less than a kilometre's stretch there were half a dozen film theatres situated. So, either the road got jammed with the people who were coming out of a theatre or going into one. They were lucky to have reached on time.

When Hai came out of his room and walked along the corridor, he expected to bump into Maya. When he didn't find her he walked towards her room visualising how she might look, her head buried deep in work. But he was greeted by an empty table. All the signs were that of her having wound up for the day. The table was clean, there were no keys dangling from the cupboard like she left them when she went just round the corner. His heart sank with disappointment. He was planning to spend the evening with her at her house talking of this and that. Talking to her was a pleasure. They could spend hours talking on any subject—from the mundane to the mind boggling. Where did she go? It was not like her to walk off without informing him? She must have had some urgent personal work. What could it be? No, everybody is entitled to their privacy. Had she met somebody interesting? Oh god, that shouldn't even be his concern. What a tragedy that he should meet someone he was looking for all his life now.

Amma always told him that everything had to be done at the right time. But what could he have done. If he was younger he didn't know if she would have agreed to marry him but at least he would have had the conviction to express his feelings to her. Now if he did, it would seem ridiculous, even to him. What a pity that he was just not destined to get the right chance at the right time. Or was he?

The next morning when she walked into his room to greet him Hai did his best to seem uninterested in her previous evening's disappearance. It was better to be guarded than caught. Just as well that she offered an explanation, before he was at his wits end. 'I'm sorry sir, for pushing off without letting you know. It was just that we decided in the eleventh hour to see a film, we had not much time left and so we had to rush.'

'Good, I'm glad you did.' Who was the other person? His pause did not go unnoticed by her.

'Are you upset with me?'

That's the confidence youth gives you. You can say what comes to your mind without worrying how the other person would take it. But when you are over the hill, so to speak, even to express the simplest of feelings is such a difficult task because you fear it could be misconstrued. God is partial to young people.

'No Maya, why should I be? I know you're a conscientious worker. What you do outside work is strictly your business. So how was the film'?

'Nothing out of the ordinary but I cried buckets.'

'That's something I can never understand. When you know that it's all make believe, the emotions are part of acting, how do you cry?'

'Remember what Shakespeare said about the world being a stage. Aren't we all play-acting in life? Putting on an act. Preferring to believe in myths while ignoring reality. Yet we cry, we laugh, we mourn, we celebrate. It's all in the way you look at it.'

'I'm impressed. Your take on life is most unusual.'

'Well my father taught me not to take myself too seriously. You're just a speck in the universe. What you feel is terrible at this moment might seem comical a few years later.'

'Your father was a great man, wasn't he? You're lucky to have been brought up by him.'

'Yes that's true.'

'You called him Appa, did you?'

'Hmm...and you?'

'Abba.'

'Appa and Abba. So similar. And to think that one word originated from Sanskrit and the other from Arabic, incredible.'

'Seriously, and look at us fighting over religion, culture, language and what have you?'

'There's a saying in Sanskrit—Vasudhaika kutumbam—it means, all the world is one family.'

'There's one in Arabic too—All creatures belong to one family—the family of God.'

'Ultimately all religions say the same thing.'

'True. Tell me something. Would you ever consider marrying outside your religion?'

'Marriage. I haven't even given it a thought.'

'Give it some now.'

'Mmm...well that is difficult. But I don't think I would.'

'Why not? You just agreed that all religions are the same.'

'Yes, I did. But on a practical note I don't think it would work. For example, I'm a pure vegetarian. I don't even eat eggs. When I was a kid, the doctor advised my mother to include eggs in my diet. I hated the smell but my mother forced it down my throat anyway and I broke into a rash—an allergic reaction. So it's neither acquired nor cultivated, I'm born a vegetarian. I dress in a particular way. I love my bindis. In this day and age, when marriages are collapsing like a house of cards, I don't think I would like to take on such a big risk. I haven't thought of marriage so far but when I do, it will be for keeps. I don't believe in breaking up unless it's an extremely drastic situation.'

'I see.'

'Why? Don't you agree with me?'

'Not really. It's true that marriages are collapsing but that's not because of the individuals themselves. I think that there's something fundamentally wrong with the institution, the way we have established it. In marriage, like in life, there are no guarantees but if two people care for each other, nothing is insurmountable.'

'It's all well in theory.'

'Why do you say that? Take the case of my parents. My mother was a Hindu. She cooked excellent non-veg but she remained a vegetarian till the day she died. It's not like they didn't argue, they did, but they never fought bitterly. They had a basic respect for each other's values, beliefs, character, integrity. That's what is needed to keep a relationship in good stead, not religion.'

'My parents were like that too. I never saw them bickering. Even their so-called fights were most comical. They would talk to each other through me, passing me around like a bouncing ball.'

'That reminds me we need to go to the MCH later in the day. Now let's get to work.'

'We've wasted enough time talking about everything except work.'

'Actually it all began with you talking about my work and then we meandered.'

'Conversations follow their own course, no sir?'

'Now, don't start another conversation on conversations. You seem to be in a chatty mood. Reserve some of that enthusiasm for later.'

When she left he marvelled at her maturity. In her mind, she was far older. Which twenty-five year old did he know, or had met, who spoke or thought like her? None. Where was the age difference? Life with her would be like a gentle, cool breeze on a summer night.

Chapter 24

SHEHZAADI AND ANWAR REACHED DR BHARGAV'S CLINIC AT THE scheduled time. Anwar had phoned him the previous night to express their consent. He had asked Shehzaadi before if she wanted to go ahead. She was scared. 'Do you think I'm going mad?' she asked him. He had cocooned her in his arms and said, 'Between the two of us, I'm the mad one. Mad about you.' She had slept fitfully. He stayed awake.

At the clinic, Dr Bhargav asked him to leave since the session would take almost three hours. He could collect her for lunch. Anwar left in an anxious mood.

Dr Bhargav relaxed her by talking of various unconnected things. While they talked about the weather he said, 'Winston Churchill once said that everybody talks about the weather but nobody does anything about it! According to me, people who have nothing to talk about discuss the weather. But you and I have a lot to talk about. Tell me anything, whatever you feel like. Pleasant or not. About your childhood, your college, your dreams, just anything that comes to mind. Don't worry about the order.'

She liked him and his gentle, easy-going manner. She began talking randomly as if he were an acquaintance who was interested in knowing about her. He served some excellent lime tea, telling her how much and when to squeeze the lime.

Dr Bhargav spoke about himself as well. He had lost his wife to cancer a few years ago. From then on, he had been a single parent to his daughters. 'Ironically I, whose profession is to alleviate pain, failed when it came to my wife. She suffered from a nagging cough for years. I watched like a silent spectator as she popped a pill or drank a mixture whenever she had those bouts. I didn't make much of it until it was too late. The worst thing about life is you take the best part of it for granted. We always postpone things we want to do with or say to our loved ones. We think life is eternal. We feel we have all the time in the world. Until life and time show their control over us.'

'You must have experienced a lot of pain.'

'Pain is inevitable Mrs Mirza but the suffering is up to us. And when you have young mouths to feed and minds to nurture, your pain seems less compared to theirs. The theory of relativity.'

'Did you ever think of remarrying?'

'Never. I didn't want to dilute the intensity of my feelings for Monica, my wife. She was my best friend. And the best mother any child could have. Sometimes I feel people who live to the fullest every single day are the ones who go away early. Unlike the ones who complain, argue, demand more from life. She was always happy with whatever life offered. She never struggled against a moment or an occurrence. Also, it's not fair to get involved with somebody else while you have several other responsibilities that need not necessarily involve them. My daughters are my life. I don't think I could subject them to getting used to a new person now.'

Shehzaadi wondered how her life would have been if Sameera had been alive after she lost Rehaan. Would she have felt the need to marry Anwar?

'Is there something I ought to know? Do you want to tell me?'

She lied as easily as she breathed.

'Take your time and let me know. That reminds me of a joke. Apparently, the son of one of our ex-ministers who's famous for procrastination went up to his father when he turned twenty-five to enquire if it was the right time for him to get married. And our minister said that he would think and let him know. The son is forty now and still unmarried. I hope you won't do to me what the minister did to his son, Mrs Mirza.'

They laughed like old friends. Later when Anwar picked her up for lunch, he heard his wife inviting the doctor home for a meal. He was surprised because she rarely did that with strangers. Dr Bhargav raised his eyebrows and blinked looking at Anwar. Anwar knew that his wife was in safe hands.

On the drive back he asked her, 'So how did your session go?'

'Oh, you can hardly call it that. We just talked. Did you know that doc is a widower? Apparently they loved each other a lot. I was quite surprised when he told me that. It doesn't show on his face. He's always so cheerful. I feel so sad for him. He's such a nice person.'

'You know what jaan, when life throws out one of its nasty bumps it doesn't differentiate between people. All of us have a cross to bear.'

'Luckily, you don't have one.'

'I know. I should count my blessings.'

'We have so many things to be thankful for. By the way, I forgot to tell you I spoke to Shah's girl before he left.'

'Hey, you didn't tell me that.'

'I'm telling you now.'

'What did she say?'

'Nothing in particular. He just called and passed the phone to her.'

'I think he's too young to get involved. He needs to meet more women. How can he be so sure he loves her and that she's the one for him?'

'You just know. Like I did.'

'Your case is different. Women respond differently.'

'Why does everybody say this? How is it any different for women?'

'Let's not argue now. Tell me, when did you realise you were in love with me? You've never told me your side of our story.'

'What makes you think I'm in love with you?'

'You're not?'

'Maybe I am. Maybe I'm not.'

'Come on. Tell me.'

'Keep guessing.'

They laughed and he thought, that's what I have been doing, ever since we got married.

The next day, Shehzaadi arrived at the clinic earlier than her appointed time. Dr Bhargav called her in anyway. They got talking and she asked him when he would visit.

'Let's finish with your therapy first. Then we'll pop a bottle of champagne at your place.'

'Sure, though I don't like the taste.'

'Try mixing it with orange juice. It's called Mimosa. That's what it used to be called earlier anyway, these days they've invented all kinds of outlandish names for cocktails. What's your favourite drink?'

'I love red wine. Though, of late I've been drinking vodka too. Bloody Mary, actually.'

'Did you know that the barman, Harry Mclehone, who first made the cocktail named it after Queen Mary. The story has it that he was reminded of the bloodshed that led to the queen's death when he saw the colour of the drink. Gory stuff don't you think? How often do you drink?'

'I started out as a social drinker but now I drink pretty regularly.'

'How much do you drink at one sitting?'

'A bottle of red wine easily.'

'What does it do to you? How do you feel?'

'It's a nice feeling. More than anything it helps me sleep. I have a sleeping problem. And it's killing me. Everybody else is fast asleep and I'm wide awake. It's torturous.'

'I can imagine. How long have you had this problem?'

She thought for a while and said, 'Since I lost my daughter?'

'I didn't know you had a daughter.'

'I did. From my first marriage.'

'Go ahead. Forget that I'm here. Just keep talking.'

For the next one hour she spoke about Rehaan, their marriage, the riots, her life that had ended. And then she wept. He let her cry without uttering a word. When she finally regained composure she said, 'I'm sorry, I just lost control.'

'Don't be sorry. It does a lot of good to lose control when the going gets tough. We lead all our lives as control freaks, controlling others, controlling ourselves. Our bodies and minds are closely linked. Our moods and emotions are translated into physical ailments. If suppressed, emotions can lead to life-threatening diseases. A good cry cleanses the mind. Your problem has been just that. You have never given yourself time to grieve. It's good to speak, even to scream and shout but keeping your emotions bottled up is damaging. Say what you feel like, cry when you want. Aren't you feeling lighter now?'

'So light that I'm sleepy.'

'Good. Don't control it. Sleep deprivation can be seriously damaging. There are cases when it has led to accidents, unrest, depression, high levels of irritability and low levels of energy.'

He directed her to the couch and she dozed off the moment her head touched the cushion. When she woke up, it was almost sunset. She straightened her hair and clothes and walked up to his desk. He offered her a cup of lime tea and while sipping it, she asked, 'So when do we pop the champagne? I feel perfectly normal now.'

'I have a confession to make. I don't drink. All that information I gave you about champagne, orange juice, mimosa was all concocted. Right here in this clinic. But the Bloody Mary stuff is true. I just needed an account of your drinking habit. I know I lied. But Mrs Mirza, I strongly believe that ends sometimes justify the means. Let me tell you something. Everything is fine in moderation. In fact, you'll relish it more that way. Compulsive drinking works against the human body. In fact, it obstructs sleep. Your body might rest for a while but your mind's unrest multiplies with alcohol-induced sleep.'

She nodded quietly.

Anwar had come and gone. Dr Bhargav called him saying that his patient was no longer a patient. He reached the clinic in five minutes. As he explained to him, he said, 'She's just one step away from total recovery.'

'What's that?' she asked.

'This is going to be difficult, almost traumatic but you have to do it. You have to go back to the place you lived, to your old house, the area where the riots happened, everything connected with the tragedy.'

'But why?' Anwar protested, 'Why rake up the past?'

'It's necessary Mr Mirza. Your wife has never allowed herself to grieve. In order to live up to her image of being in control and holding it all together even while she was shattered within, she had gone to pieces. She's suffered long enough; you have no idea how much she has. Now there's no choice for you but to accompany her, letting her express whatever comes to her mind, offering her support when she needs it, watching like a detached observer at others. The sooner she purges all those pent up emotions, the better for her. Choked emotions are like clogged drains forcing the dirt to spill back where it came from. You must deal with your past to move on. That doesn't mean you live in the past, hang on to it. That again is harmful. We need to reach a stage where we can think about the past without being disturbed by it.'

~

Chapter 25

MAYA AND PROFESSOR HAI HAD BEEN IN THE MCH OFFICE FOR the last six hours. Raghunath the clerk was entrusted to assist them and he was very helpful. After all, they were the friends of his boss. He had located two registers on the survivors. The reason they were not looking at the records of the slain was because she didn't remember anything, any name or face. With the survivors, it was different; they were alive to tell the tale. After noting down the addresses of the survivors, they looked at the children's section. There was just one survivor. Her picture under the classification—unidentified. She had been the only child who had survived. For the next week they went around looking up the survivors at the addressees. It was tragic as each person they spoke to recounted their gruesome story. Besides the sadness they felt for them, Maya felt sorry for herself at the end of the whole exercise because not one of them had had a child at that time—dead or lost. After going around in circles, they were back to the square one. She wept uncontrollably all the way. Hai asked her to stay at his house but she refused saying that she had to learn to deal with it alone. Though all along she had reassured him that she was prepared for any outcome, when it really had yielded nothing, she couldn't deal with it. But by now she was used to be being left to her own devices to hold her own. A trait of hers that came to her aid in situations like this.

He dropped her home and insisted she eat something. He watched her as she forced morsel after morsel of her otherwise favourite food—bisibele huli anna. Before he left he asked her, 'You don't remember anything Maya, anything at all.'

'I wish I did sir. But I was only two.'

'My friend Dr Bhargav had once told me that people have memories when they're in the foetal stage. There is a term for it, in-utero, or some such thing.'

'Really? How is that possible?'

'He had given me a book to read written by Dr Brian Weiss whose method he follows to treat his patients through hypnosis. Hmm…that gives me an idea. Why don't you see him? As a last resort.'

She looked at him incredulously.

'Why didn't you think of this earlier? As a matter of fact it's not only the last resort but the only one too.'

'I'll fix up an appointment with him. Cheer up now. There's some hope.'

She admitted to feeling a little better. After he left, she went to the verandah behind the house. She sat on the chair and looked at the barbed wire fence. Sleep eluded her. She looked at the twists, crosses and knots on the wire. But her mind was blank. Meditative.

When the first rays of the sun announced daybreak, she saw a butterfly fluttering over the colourful winter flowers in her little garden. After a while, it tried flying over the barbed wire. It got stuck on one of the knots and fell, lifelessly. She walked up to it, picked it up gently and placed it on her palm. There was a perforation on one of its wings. She uttered a shloka softly over it and let it slide carefully onto one of the flowers. The colours merged. You couldn't tell where the flower began and the butterfly ended.

Shehzaadi and Anwar woke up early the next morning and left home. It was a clear day. The rains had abated but the clouds hung heavily still. As they drove to the old city, they reached Famous Ice Creams and she asked him to stop the car. 'You must eat the handmade mango ice cream here. It's out of this world. I don't think anybody can make it as good as they do.' She spoke animatedly as they walked in and took their seats. 'We used to sit outside you know, Rehaan, me, Sameera, Karan Mama, Mami, almost every evening and have bowl after bowl. It wasn't as crowded or polluted as it is now. Sameera was addicted to it. Sometimes Rehaan would have to bring her here in his nightclothes because she would refuse to sleep unless she had the ice cream. Only from here.'

How much she had held from him! He hadn't an inkling about her life before him. He cursed himself for not having gained her confidence. If he had, she would have spoken to him earlier. He watched her placing their orders without consulting him as if he was a tourist and she belonged here. She had never shown such interest in anything before. He agreed that the ice cream was indeed divine.

As they were about to leave, an aged man rubbing his glasses approached them. He wore them and looked at Shehzaadi hesitantly. She studied his face for a while and said, 'Irfan Chacha, I don't believe it's you.' She bent to put her head in his stomach, a typical Hyderabadi gesture done by youngsters (described in dakhni as pet-mein-mundi) who wish to show their respect to elders. Both of them let tears flow unashamedly. 'Allah Maalik only saved me,' the old man said, referring to the riots. 'I had gone to Lucknow to attend my niece's wedding.' He didn't ask her any questions about herself either because of Anwar's presence or his own failing memory. She told him later that the old man had been an employee there.

Things seemed more or less under control, her pointing to some place or the other and narrating incidents related to them, until they reached the fruit market. They had passed by the haveli because the gate was covered by a series of fruit stalls. After enquiring they located it. The fruitwallah outside said, 'Nobody lives there Saab. It has been locked for ages. Just the other day the MCH people came and broke open the lock. And what a lock saab! Even after so many years it was still sturdy. Dead weight. They have moved away the furniture too.' Anwar explained that she was the owner of the house and the guy looked at her as if he was seeing a ghost. The huge iron gate was latched. When they tried opening it, it made a loud creaking noise because of the rust that had set in. Finally after a great deal of effort they pushed it open. There it was, a ruined replica of the original structure covered with a soot-like substance. But spectacular nonetheless. Apparently, somebody had just cleared up the cobwebs or it would have looked even more lifeless. The main doors were bolted with a newspaper stuck into the latch. She ran in and removed the paper. Once it swung open, she roamed around like a haunted spirit. Running from one room to another, going back to where she came from, Anwar wondered if he had done the right thing by following the doctor's advice. He had seen mansions but this was like a palace. How could people live in a house like this?

He felt overwhelming sympathy for her but he remembered that he had been asked to observe. He followed her until she reached a bedroom where the furniture was intact, probably because the sheer weight of the bed and the other furniture made them immovable. He watched her reaching for a solid wooden cradle that was next to the bed. She swung it and he felt she had lost it. That look was back. She swung it a few more times and moved to the bed, sitting on it regardless of the layers of dust. And then the downpour started. She completely broke down and wept. He couldn't hold himself back anymore and he rushed to her side and held her. She didn't lean against him. Instead her body was stiff as though rigor mortis had set in. She could have been a dead body but for her wracking sobs. He was told by the doctor to not stop her crying. So he let her, for forty-five minutes. And then she looked at him and said between sobs, 'We were so happy, Anwar. When I realised that I had survived, I didn't know whether my life had begun once again or ended.' Tears came to his eyes now. He wouldn't have been able to live with such pain the way she had. He was much weaker. He looked at her in awe as well as empathy.

She held his hand and took him outside, almost dragging him in the process. In the right-hand corner stood another smaller house within the same compound. She said, 'This is where Mama and Mami lived. They were like my own parents. Rehaan had grown up with them. Sameera's haqeeqa was held here, in this room. This is where we used to sit and eat. Every Sunday they would come over to ours, Mama was crazy about my cooking, we used to eat on a dastarkhan, the dining table was meant only for guests and huge gatherings, it was really huge, it could seat twenty people at a time.' He listened to her trying his best to visualise whatever she was describing. After what seemed an eternity, they left.

They still had the Mandi to visit. When they reached there, after a little looking around she said, 'Nothing much has changed. I think, I'm not too sure that this store was where I was standing when Sameera slipped out. Sometimes I feel she deliberately strayed to save my life. If I had stayed back with Rehaan in the queue I would probably have been killed too. You know, if I knew that that was the last time I would see them, I would have hung on to them for dear life. After that I have never ever taken anybody for granted. I don't think you'll ever be able to feel my pain. Abba did manage to get hold of Rehaan's body for the last rites but Sameera's couldn't be identified. There were too many children's bodies that had been mutilated beyond recognition. Also, I was not in any state to be put through the identification process.'

'I know your pain is much larger than mine. But even watching you is painful. I admire your strength. I don't think I would have been able to cope with it, like you have. But I want you to know that if you want to keep their memory alive by observing their anniversaries, let's do it,' he said carefully avoiding the word 'death'.

When they returned home, mid-day had given way to evening. The clouds had cleared. They walked in, his hand around her shoulder with the intimacy that only a life that had weathered a storm could bring. For once, Shehzaadi didn't reprimand Babu Miyan who greeted them with duster in his hand. She didn't even notice him.

Maya entered Dr Bhargav's clinic. Nothing about the ambience was clinical. The reception area was sprawling with elaborate seating arrangements. Plush sofas, potted plants, rich double-layered satin drapes, coordinated upholstery, rosewood cabinets, cupboards, a spiral wrought iron staircase in the centre that led to the first floor, strains of *Fur-e-lise* in the air, everything bordered on the opulent. She approached the receptionist who was dressed in a maroon business suit and asked for Dr Bhargav. When she heard her name, she pointed up saying, 'Second room, first floor.'

He was sitting in a revolving chair. In front of him was a sleek L-shaped rosewood table on the left of which was a computer. Behind him was a huge bookshelf, made of an aluminium filing cabinet that was sticking out like a sore thumb. The room was large enough to house a reclining couch at the other extreme where the lighting was dim, a few comfortable easy chairs and sofas were at a little distance from him probably for people who accompanied the patient. Prof Hai had told her that his clientele were the 'who's who' of the city as if mental afflictions were directly proportionate to wealth and fame. She wondered if she could afford him.

'I know what you're thinking,' he said without a prelude, 'have a seat. Then we can talk about my fee. Don't worry.'

God! Are shrinks mind-readers too?

'As a matter of fact, I am worried doctor,' she said frankly.

'I'm not very expensive.'

'It's all relative when it comes to money.'

'You mean like Marie Antoinette's famous line—if there's no bread, let them have cake instead.'

'I don't believe she could have said that. Women are never insensitive to the lesser fortunate. And I would like to know how expensive is not very expensive. I should know if I can afford it at all.'

'Look, it's like this. There's no fixed fee, which is why it's not collected at the reception like it is in most clinics. It differs from case to case. The preliminary discussion in which I gather the case details is free for everybody. Though not free for all. Unless you tell me what is it that you've come here for, I won't be able to give you even a ballpark figure.'

'Actually, I forgot to tell you doctor, Professor Hai conveys his wishes to you.'

'How's the old chap? His manners are diminishing with his age, huh. The least he could have done is introduce you to me personally. You're his assistant, he told me. What do you do?'

'I'm a researcher, doctor.'

'So am I.'

'Sorry?'

'Don't sound so puzzled. I do the same thing with people. Tell me, how can I help you?'

'I don't know where to begin.'

'From the beginning because if you tell me the end it'll kill the suspense, what do you say?'

She laughed.

'My problem is a weird one, doctor, possibly one of its kind.'

'All of us think like that. When it comes to our own problems we're very possessive, almost protective. This can happen only to me. Why me? Look Maya, I would like you to stop being hesitant. Go on. I'm all ears.'

'I was two years old when I got separated from my parents. I was adopted. I don't remember anything about my biological parents.'

She went on with her story, trying to keep it as brief and objective as possible, finally ending with, 'Is it possible for me to remember through hypnosis?'

'Yes, it is. I've regressed people to their past births to overcome their phobias and illnesses. So this is not so difficult. But you need to cooperate. Several people resist it because their minds wander.'

She told him about her meditation.

'Good, that helps. Come over tomorrow at nine in the morning. Tonight make sure you sleep well.'

'Your fee?'

'A nice meal at your parent's house after you're reunited with them. Something tells me you'll find them and soon. My intuition has never failed me.'

'Touch wood,' she said knocking on his table.

Professor Hai was waiting to hear from her. He wished she would carry a mobile phone. He should tell her to. How does one get in touch with people when they're on the move? Why wasn't she calling? When she did, he blurted, 'What did he say?' She narrated their conversation.

'Do you want me to accompany you?'

She turned it down but appreciated the gesture. Really, he had been her anchor ever since she had landed in this city. But for him, God knows, what would have happened. Not only had he helped her learn a great deal professionally but had also been there for her whenever she needed company. The best part about him was his understanding of a woman's need for respect. She had heard stories from Varsha about her dad and Som, about their awful behaviour. Thank God she had found him. He never let her give up. He was always ready to help. God knows why he did so much for her. Her mind went back to what Varsha had said to her. Could it be true?

Whatever his reasons were, for her, he had appeared as a godsend. Appa had recited a shloka once from the second Tantra, 'When a calamity befalls any creature, no one but a true friend will assist them even without exchanging words. When such a friend appears, welcome him like God's own gift.' He had also said to her, 'Don't ever give up, no matter what you do. When one window closes, it does so so that you take notice of several doors that are open. Believe in your guardian angel. All of us have one.' Appa was her guardian angel and the Professor was the friend, god's gift to her. She was indeed blessed.

Chapter 26

DR. BHARGAV WAS HAVING A SHOWER AND THINKING FURIOUSLY. His mind worked better here. The bathroom was his sanctuary, in a sense. He had read somewhere that several scientists had even thought of formulae here. In that sense the place was sacred to him. There was a little plastic stand with books that he read while he was there, a notepad and pen, just in case. He was thinking about his conversation with Maya that afternoon. Something about this girl was very familiar. His memory, however, was definitely not the same anymore. He tried to figure out if he had seen her before. And her story? Of course! He had heard that story just a few days ago. What a strange coincidence. Or divine intervention. When he established the connection he wanted to scream 'Eureka' just for the drama of it but didn't wish to disturb his daughter who was sleeping peacefully in the adjoining bedroom. He hatched a master-plan with a little bit of spice thrown in. Just the way he liked it. 'Yes, that's the way to do it.'

Early the next morning, Shehzaadi rang him up. He didn't bar his patients from reaching him at home. He didn't believe that the office and home should be kept independent of each other. In his line of work anyway. For him, they were a part of his life and at times he did his personal work at his clinic, he even took his daughters there once in a while. Shehzaadi thanked him again for all his help and said that she would be happy if he would accept her invitation for dinner that night. 'Please bring your daughters too,' she said. 'I'm glad to accept it. But I'm afraid my daughters are in the midst of their exams. If it's okay with you I would like to bring a young lady with me,' he said.

She laughed, sounding happy and said that he was most welcome and that she would wait for him around seven-thirty. 'Not my daughters Mrs Mirza but yours,' he chuckled to himself.

When Maya was just about to leave her house for the clinic, there was a phone call from Dr Bhargav's clinic to inform her that her appointment was postponed to seven in the evening. Upset, she phoned Hai. Since she had applied for leave anyway, she decided to visit the library and check if there were any books on hypnosis. She found a few and read up. She was mentally prepared by the evening.

After meditating for twenty minutes at twilight, she dressed simply, stuck on her bindi, and left. When she was paying the auto-driver, she saw the doctor leaning on a car, presumably his, watching her. She felt slightly disappointed thinking that he would postpone it further. She was relieved when he said, 'I need to collect a fee. Would you mind coming with me for a while? They're very nice people. You will be glad I introduced you to them.' She wasn't sure if she had heard him right but she got into the seat next to him anyway. As they drove along, she looked outside admiring the beauty of the area and comparing its disparity with other parts of the city. At one point, he nodded towards a well-guarded house and said, 'That is where the CM lives.'

No wonder everything was so impeccable. She said that to him and he asked, 'Would you like to live here? In one of these houses?'

'It's not a question of whether I would like to, it's a question of if I ever can.'

'Don't underestimate life, my dear lady, when it springs surprises on you, you will forget that you ever doubted its power.'

'Unless I win a lottery of several millions I don't see such a possibility, doctor.'

'Probably you are about to. Who knows?'

She smiled, a little bewildered. In a couple of minutes he stopped at a gate, looking at the piece of paper in his hand and said, 'Here we are. I'll be back in a minute.' She sat looking at the mansions around her; the one opposite even had an elevator in it. What kind of people lived in these homes, she wondered. Most of them were manned by security personnel at the entrance but looked deserted from the outside. She compared them to apartments, noisy and filled with activity, where nobody really felt lonely with comfort in the knowledge that in times of need you had somebody to turn to. Were the residents of these homes lonely? What did they do with so much space? She remembered their two-bedroom house in Bangalore. For some reason, she felt sure that these wealthy people must be really sad people. How she arrived at such a conclusion, she had no idea, but she was sure. She wished desperately for the doctor to return and wondered what was taking him so long.

Dr Bhargav walked in and found Shehzaadi and Anwar waiting to receive him at the door. In an uncharacteristic blunt manner, he asked her, 'How would it be if you discovered that your daughter's alive?'

Both of them were stunned. Anwar recovered and said, 'Don't be cruel doctor. She might have a relapse. She's just about recovering.'

'Sometimes in life you have to be cruel to be kind, Mr Mirza. Is it okay if I park my car inside?'

Anwar said, 'Please do,' more than a little annoyed. What kind of a psychologist was he? He glanced at his wife—her face had gone pale— and both of them looked at the car that stopped in the porch. Dr Bhargav got out, walked to the other side and opened the door for the young lady. Maya walked out, Anwar looked at her closely, and then the relevance of the doctor's lines hit him like a thunderbolt. The shock was so profound that he could feel no other emotion. It took a while before Maya and Shehzaadi took in each other's appearance. The mother recognised her. And the daughter walked with hesitant, baby steps. Unsure. Unsteady.

Anwar ushered them in. Shehzaadi hugged Maya crying, 'Sameera, my baby, it's a miracle.' Maya was moved too but somewhere inside her she was feeling uncomfortable. She sat awkwardly at the edge of the sofa and Shehzaadi said, 'Be comfortable, sweetheart, this is your house.' She tried but the awkwardness clung to her. This manicured, perfectly groomed, fashionable woman was far from the mental image Maya had of her. Mother, for her, was a cotton-sareed, simple, loving woman. Amma with her trademark red vermilion and glass bangles. She hid her nails with chipped nail polish on them between her legs. And her old watch became more obvious. Where would she hide that now? But why should she hide herself anyway? She was what she was. Who cares about the external adornments? She looked sideways at Shehzaadi's platinum bracelet and designer watch. She asked her, 'Sameera, are you hungry? Would you like to eat?' Maya didn't respond. She repeated the question, that's when Maya realised that Sameera was her. 'Please call me Maya, if you don't mind,' she said.

'To me you'll remain Sameera, my doll. I picked the name after going through thousands. Maya doesn't mean anything to me.'

She wanted to scream, 'But it does, to me.'

She wanted to get it over with so she agreed to have dinner. At the dining table, there was not a single dish she could eat; everything had meat in it. Though Shehzaadi tried to organise for some vegetarian food quickly, she refused saying that she wasn't really hungry. They forced her to eat two helpings of cheesecake, which she was not in the mood for. She had to take great pains to keep from throwing up.

When Shehzaadi asked her to stay back, she said she had a project to complete and would come back later. Understanding her condition, Dr Bhargav insisted on dropping her home.

When they reached her house, before she got out of his car, he said, 'Thank you for my fee.'

She didn't know if she welcomed that. She stared blankly at him until he started his car. Her presence of mind had deserted her. Courtesy was the last thing she could think of.

Dr Bhargav called Hai the next day to narrate what had happened. He said he had never seen anything like this before. 'Human beings' machinations pale when destiny's designs unfold,' he philosophised, 'don't let her know you already know about what happened, tell me how she feels about it. If you succeed in getting her to confide in you.'

After the phone call, Hai went straight to her quarters. She opened the door and he saw that her eyes were blood-shot. 'Are you running a temperature?' he enquired and asked her where she kept the thermometer.

'No, I'm fine. I wept so much …last night, the way I did when I had lost my parents.'

'What happened?' he pretended, remembering what the doctor had said about putting on an act.

She told him the whole story. 'I can't tell you how depressed I'm feeling,' she said on a final note.

'But why? You should be ecstatic. You found your parents.'

'Not my parents. Only my mother.'

'That's reason enough, isn't it? Isn't that why you came here?'

'Yeah, I did. But in retrospect, I feel I was better off before.'

'Oh Maya, I can't understand your reaction.'

'Do you know she refused to call me Maya? And I'll never be able to eat the food they serve.'

'Those things will settle with time, as both of you get to know each other.'

'That's the whole point, the relationship that is the most natural one, has to be laboured for. Any mother is believed to understand her children instinctively and here, we'll have to get to know each other. I think I can do without that. That's not what I wanted.'

'What you want may not necessarily be what you need, Maya. You need to be with your mother. That's your home.'

'How can you say that? He's not my father. I even saw their son's photograph. They seem so happy. I have no business to intrude. I feel sorry for her, there she was, all settled and happy, nice husband, wonderful son and I pop up like a skeleton from her cupboard. You should have seen her anguish when I told her I was a vegetarian. Poor thing.'

'I'm sure everything will work out. Give it some time. Give her some time. Have you thought about what she must be feeling? It's as much a shock for her as it is for you. Imagine how long she must have taken to get over your presumed death. Now, when she found you at last, all you have are fears about her. Did you feel nothing when she hugged you?'

'Nothing at all. I wanted to respond desperately, I tried. I hope I didn't give out any negative vibes.'

'Even if you did, she will understand, I'm sure. Call her now; she must be expecting you to.'

After much cajoling, she reached for the phone. Just then it rang. Even before responding she knew it would be her. She couldn't even bring herself to think of her as mother, mummy, Mama. When she did answer it, and Hai realised who it was, he walked out to give her privacy.

'Hello, my doll,' Shehzaadi said, 'how did you sleep last night? Listen darling, my baby, I've organised a little get-together tonight. Is it okay with you? I'll send the driver to have you picked up, okay. Wear something nice. I want to show you off to my friends. What a beautiful daughter I have.'

Maya said hesitantly, 'Okay, what time?' though she wanted to say no, I don't like being shown off. She had always underplayed her beauty. Papa had always said to her that the true beauty is that of the soul. Moreover, her upbringing and her values had had no place or the budget for vanity. She hated herself for not having been assertive and saying yes to her.

Hai walked in after some time and she told him what her mother had said.

'Good, I'm glad you agreed to go.'

'But she asked me to wear something nice. What, according to her, is nice? I don't even know.' She burst out crying.

He put his arms around her, lifting her head and said, 'Do you even have any idea how beautiful you are? What you wear hardly matters.'

In spite of herself she felt secure in his arms. She leaned against his chest and cried, mumbling, 'I can't believe I'm behaving like such a cry baby.'

'It's only me. You can do whatever you want in front of me. I will love you all the more for it.'

He didn't intend for it to come out this way. He looked at her sheepishly, almost boyishly to her teary eyes. But she was grateful for his support. She decided to deal with the confession later. Right now, it was enough that she had him to lean on.

'Will you come with me?' she asked.

'I can't do that Mayu.'

'That woman, you know how she addresses me, my baby, my doll, it's so artificial.'

'What's in a name? Look at mine. All my friends would tease me in college—"Hi Hai" that's the way Hyderabadis lament, eunuchs tease and curse passersby, did you know that? Don't be so prejudiced Maya. I've felt like calling you a doll several times because you do look like one. Now, forget about coming to work. Just relax. Sleep well. Before that eat something. I've got some food from home for you. All vegetarian. There is even some upma for breakfast.' 'You're so considerate,' she said and started crying all over again this time alternating it with laughter as if she found her own emotions silly.

'You know how you look when you laugh and cry at the same time. Like sunshine that appears in a downpour. Soon there will be a rainbow on your face.'

She smiled self-consciously and he said, 'Look, I can see all the colours of a rainbow on your cheeks. Keep smiling Mayu. It makes me happy.'

When she reached there dressed in a white and black salwar kameez, her mother said, 'At your age you should be wearing bright colours. Come with me,' she said leading her to a cupboard and continued, 'I'm sure my clothes will fit you. I'm a little plump but I'm sure you'll find something you like.'

She wanted to say 'No, I don't want to change', but she didn't and instead wore a red and lime-green mini kurta and red parallels that her mother gave her. It did fit her perfectly, accentuating her figure like none of her other clothes did. Shehzaadi then strung a delicate choker with a diamond and ruby pendant around her neck, matching danglers on her ears and then said, 'Just one thing missing' giving her a red lipstick. Maya protested, thinking the colour was outrageously bright, she couldn't wear that! Shehzaadi, after dabbing a little on her lips, didn't push her further.

The party began and nothing could have prepared Maya for it. People drove in in their luxury limousines, all heavily made up and dressed in expensive outfits. They proudly displayed their dazzling diamonds and designer watches. Maya was dumbstruck. She had never seen such opulence and extravagance in all her life. Shehzaadi introduced her to nearly everyone who walked through the door. They gave her 'air' kisses and gushed over how pretty she was. With all the introductions done, all Maya wanted was to escape. She didn't belong here. Yes, everybody was being very nice to her and saying they were so happy for them but she couldn't help but feel uncomfortable, completely out of place. She had been to a few parties at Varsha's but those were nothing compared to this. As the evening wore on she saw that everyone was drinking and looked like they were having a good time, except for her. Most people were gathered around the bar and quite a few were on the dance floor. The few she spoke to or tried to have a conversation with were not doing anything particular with their lives, 'probably living from one party to another' thought Maya in barely concealed disgust. Shehzaadi stuck to her side all evening, smiling widely and looking flushed with happiness while her husband looked on from a distance affectionately. He had been very cordial towards her earlier when they met. He seemed to be a caring man. With a stab of regret Maya asked herself if she had done the right thing. Maybe she needn't have come into their lives at all. They seemed to have done alright without her all this while. And she had survived too. She felt like she was on the set of an extravagant movie, like an alien who had walked into a strange land. She was lost amidst the celebrating crowd. After ages, dinner was finally served. Her mother had been considerate enough to make a few vegetarian snacks which had been passed around earlier during the party but she hadn't felt like eating.

Anwar politely offered her a plate but nothing in the buffet appealed to her. It was an exorbitant spread of Japanese food. Shehzaadi led her down the white-clothed table explaining what the various dishes were: delicate morsels of sushi, beautifully wrapped and presented, minty green wasabi set nearby, large bowls of udon and ramen swimming in clear soup garnished with finely chopped spring onions, yakitori dripping in soya sauce, plates of rare sashimi (that made Maya feel rather ill). By the time they had done a round she had lost her appetite. She had never heard of these dishes and she didn't even feel up for savouring an exotic cuisine. Right now what she felt she needed was comfort food, something familiar and homely like hot steaming huggi, bisibele, rice, sambar. She could feel pangs of hunger but had no appetite for the food on offer.

The party wound up early in the morning, 'late night' as they called it, three a.m. to be precise. She wanted to return home, curl up and sleep and have a steaming mug of coffee when she woke up. But when they pleaded with her to stay back, she did. She dreamt of nothing those two pre-dawn hours because she got no sleep. She was too overwhelmed with fatigue and hunger. Maya finally drifted into a restless, uncomfortable slumber. When she awoke and came out of her room at seven in the morning, the house was dead. There was silence. Not a soul to be seen. She walked softly as if her footsteps would disturb the silence, hoping she would find at least a servant and she could get some coffee. She found her way to the kitchen, it was empty.

In Bangalore, by this time, her parents would have bathed and she would be ready to go for hers. The thought of coffee made her craving even more intense. She decided to get away after leaving a note.

When Anwar woke up around midnoon he found his wife crying silently into her pillow. He had expected to find her content like she had been all of last night. He put his arm on her back and she turned to show him a piece of paper that had been crumpled in her grip. It was a note from Sameera saying she was leaving because she had work to do.

'That's all. You had me worried. Try and understand that she's a working girl. She can't just drop everything and run to us. Give her time.'

'No, that's not all. I phoned her and she said she wouldn't like to live with us. She says she has become too used to her own space. Tell me, would we have hindered her in any way? There's enough space in this house for a dozen people.'

Anwar consoled her saying that all kids grow up and go away. 'Look at our son,' he said.

'I had lost her once when she didn't know what she was doing. Now I have lost her again, but this time she knows exactly what she's doing.'

'But you have me. And I have you. All parents with grown-up children have to go through this at some point. Even if she had come to live with us, she would have gotten married and gone away, sooner or later.'

'That's different.'

'It's the same Jaan. Just look at it that way.'

Hai didn't know what to say when she confessed to him what she had done.

'Why did you have to do it this way? You could have waited till they woke up.'

'I know myself. I would never have been able to do it if they pleaded with me. I'm a sucker for emotion. I can't live there.'

'How do you know? You stayed for one night.'

'You don't have to check the whole container to see if the rice is cooked.'

'As you like it, doll.'

'Don't call me that.'

'Okay. Mayu.'

'That's better.'

~

Epilogue

AMITA HAD SOBERED DOWN AFTER HER DAUGHTER'S REVELATION about Sid's guilt towards their failed marriage. Something, though she didn't know what, had changed in her. She was sure of one thing now—that she no longer craved to hurt a man. She even felt remorseful for briefly coveting her friend's husband. At long last her conscience was beginning to show signs of revival. She no longer felt the need to shatter myths about happily married men.

Zeba, who remained privy to this subtle yet unmistakable change in her friend, was relieved. She no longer had the daunting task of guarding somebody while trying to prevent the other from letting her guard down.

Shehzaadi's attachment to her friends had weakened as much as Anwar's to his horses, after he confided in her about the hug from Amita. The proprietorial feeling had awoken in her. There was no way she would let anybody tread on her ground. She had confided in Zeba who confirmed Anwar's suspicion. Whatever it was, Shehzaadi had outgrown her compulsive need for company and Amita had transcended her compulsion to constantly keep proving her desirability to herself. And that had changed the whole equation.

Shahbaz had left but not before insisting on meeting Varsha's mother. With a background like hers, he was surprised to see her so unaffected. As if it had nothing to do with her at all. As he sat on the large sofa in their living room, which was grandly furnished like the rest of the house but stylish, nevertheless, he marvelled at her down-to-earth nature. The expression on her mother's face had been more formidable than friendly. He was quite impressed with the dignified looking Revati Rao, well-dressed in a resplendent silk sari and pearls. She had been cordial enough to him. They had flown in, in the morning and left the same evening.

'What purpose did it serve?' Varsha asked him, though pleased that he had made the effort.

'A great one. My respect for you has grown enormously. I've seen many people drunk on money and power; your parents have both and yet you're here doing your own thing when you could have lived in their glory. You, truly, are the most genuine person I've ever met in my life. I'm so glad I'm in such scintillatingly original company as yours.'

'But I'm still an older woman.'

'It's better to be an old woman's sweetheart than a young woman's slave,' he quipped.

She smiled at the memory of that conversation in the midst of compiling a report at work.

He had succeeded where other men had failed. He had helped her get rid of her phobia about undressing. She didn't feel in the least bit inhibited lying next to him with not a stitch on her. Something she had done with no other man. The truth was, she had never been as comfortable with anyone else either. Every single time they had met, they had made glorious love, often more than once. And each time it had been different but the ecstasy seemed to last for an eternity. They were so easy with each other. When it came to slotting him, it was her turn to get stumped.

She never knew before that a satisfying love life could be so fulfilling. He was miles away yet she was secure in the knowledge of his love. Unlike Som, despite living together for years, she had never experienced security. She still had the divorce to deal with and she wished Shah were around to make it more tolerable. She knew he would drop everything and be with her even if she gave him a hint. And *that* was enough for her.

Varsha and Maya spoke on the phone for more than an hour. So much had happened in the last month. Maya narrated her story and said, 'It's so shocking that after all that curiosity about my mother, when I really did meet her, all I could think of was Amma. You know what Varsha, motherhood it not about being in the womb; it's about the rearing after you're out of it. *That* defines your personality.'

'Guess you're right. Look at my relationship with my mother. At twenty-six, I'm getting to know her. I didn't even know until she told me recently that I was born on a rainy night and that's why she had named me Varsha. Just imagine. Listen, I need to tell you something. I have a Hyderabad connection now.'

'And what it is being?' Maya asked lapsing into Pidgin English, the way they used to when they were in college.

'Mmm...okay, here goes I'm in love with this Hyderabadi fellow.'

'Ah-ha. Now we're talking. Does the fellow have a name?'

'Yep, Shahbaz. Shahbaz Mirza. He says his name begins where mine ends. A very adorable guy.'

There was stunned silence for a while. Varsha thought they had been disconnected. Then Maya piped up, squealing in excitement, 'Girl, I can't believe this. The world's really, really small.'

'Sweetie, I'm a bad one for riddles.'

'I know your boyfriend.'

'You do? But when I spoke to him about you he mentioned nothing.'

'Well, he doesn't know me. As a matter of fact, I haven't met him either. Okay, let me explain. He happens to be my half-brother.

I've seen his photographs, though. Handsome guy, huh. So what have you decided'?

'Well, no hard and fast decisions but worst-case scenario, I'll be your sis-in-law. If I let him have his way, that is.'

'Wowee! That's great news. I'll put ghee and sugar in your mouth if it happens,' Maya said, translating a Hindi adage.

'Oh, no! I'm on a diet.'

'Why do you need to do that? Just throw your weight around, like you normally do and that should do the trick.'

'He says he likes me this way, though.'

'Hey babe, do you know how you're sounding? Like a woman in love.'

'Yeah? I am, I guess. And what about you? What's happening on the professor front?'

'It's going on. After I found my mother, all my pre-conceived notions about religious differences seem to have lost all relevance. We haven't spoken on those lines. And it's definitely not overwhelmingly physical for me. I think it's more a comfort thing. Though he says I'm his perfect woman.'

'That makes us women in love, huh? D H Lawrence would have been proud of us, had he been around.

'Well said.'

'Well done.'

It was six months since the episode of Maya fleeing her mother's house. She now met them on the weekends. It was a slow, hesitant road they had to walk, getting to know each other a little more everytime. It would take a lot of effort on both sides to sustain and develop the relationship but they knew there was no other way.

All of Hai's turmoil about his age and confusion about the expression of his love for her had vanished into thin air. They didn't even need to talk about it. They had just grown close. There was nothing physical yet but it was enough for him. They didn't even discuss their relationship. But it was there. She still lived in her quarters and visited his house on weekends after she saw her mother.

The first phase of their project was completed. They had managed to start saving several monuments—mosques, temples, graves, several architectural wonders. They had a long way to go but Hai was happy with the way things were taking shape.

One evening after they had submitted their project, Maya and Hai sat in the verandah behind her house. She watched a butterfly trying to manoeuvre past a barbed wire knot. She watched it anxiously and stood up wanting to protect it, but it managed to dodge it successfully, flying away with its wings outstretched, ready to explore a new horizon. 'What are human beings if not butterflies and their complexes, if not barbed wires,' she said aloud. Hai smiled and stood up dangling his glasses ready to deliver a lecture to his most private audience.